Bryce Martin wasn't exactly what she'd call a confidant

But in the dark shadows of the night, when Tasiya felt vulnerable and alone, when she ached for a kind word—for hope—he noticed. He hadn't said much, but the depth of his voice had resonated every shattered nerve, calming her, grounding her. He seemed solid as a mountain to cling to, yet just as forbidding.

There was a kindness to his perceptive gray eyes that had washed over her like a gentle spring shower. A sadness, too, as though the ugly marks on his body were etched more deeply inside.

He called himself a monster at their first meeting, and she believed him. But last night she saw a glimpse of the heart within the beast. And that paradox gave her the strength to survive one more day....

FORBIDDEN CAPTOR

JULIE MILLER

HARLEQUIN®

TORONTO • NEW YORK • LONDON
AMSTERDAM • PARIS • SYDNEY • HAMBURG
STOCKHOLM • ATHENS • TOKYO • MILAN • MADRID
PRAGUE • WARSAW • BUDAPEST • AUCKLAND

Special thanks and acknowledgment are given
to Julie Miller for her contribution to the
BIG SKY BOUNTY HUNTERS series.

ISBN 0-373-88654-3

FORBIDDEN CAPTOR

ABOUT THE AUTHOR

Julie Miller attributes her passion for writing romance to all those fairy tales she read growing up, and shyness. Encouragement from her family to write down all those feelings she couldn't express became a love for the written word. She gets continued support from her fellow members of the Prairieland Romance Writers, where she serves as the resident "grammar goddess." This award-winning author and teacher has published several paranormal romances. Inspired by the likes of Agatha Christie and Encyclopedia Brown, Ms. Miller believes the only thing better than a good mystery is a good romance.

Born and raised in Missouri, she now lives in Nebraska with her husband, son and smiling guard dog, Maxie. Write to Julie at P.O. Box 5162, Grand Island, NE 68802-5162.

Books by Julie Miller

HARLEQUIN INTRIGUE
588—ONE GOOD MAN*
619—SUDDEN ENGAGEMENT*
642—SECRET AGENT HEIRESS
651—IN THE BLINK OF AN EYE*
666—THE DUKE'S COVERT MISSION
699—THE ROOKIE*
719—KANSAS CITY'S BRAVEST*
748—UNSANCTIONED MEMORIES*
779—LAST MAN STANDING*
819—PARTNER-PROTECTOR†
841—POLICE BUSINESS†
880—FORBIDDEN CAPTOR

*The Taylor Clan
†The Precinct

CAST OF CHARACTERS

Anastasiya (Tasiya) Belov—Her father's been kidnapped by the terrorists he dared to betray. The ransom? Cook and clean for—and spy on—an American militia who would gladly kill any traitor in their midst. The price of failure? Losing everything she loves. Including the man who would save her.

Bryce Martin—A battle-scarred warrior inside and out. He'll do whatever it takes to escape from prison and save his Big Sky comrades—and the one woman who might learn to love this beast of a man.

Boone Fowler—Leader of the Montana Militia for a Free America. An escaped convict who has no love for foreigners. But he loves their money. And if their "gift" will help him take revenge on Big Sky Bounty Hunters...

Marcus Smith—Big as an ox, with the charm to match. He wants Tasiya Belov to be his reward for his service to the militia.

Dimitri Mostek—Lukinburg's Minister of Finance. He has no patience for men who embezzle money from him. But he answers to a higher power.

Anton Belov—He was only trying to make a little extra money for bills and food. Now his extravagance might cost his daughter her life.

Prologue

The chocolate-caramel torte was a delicious success. And an incredible mess.

But Anastasiya Belov didn't mind being elbow-deep in suds and dishwater, scraping the sticky topping from the pan. Not when her latest recipe had brought such a delighted smile to her father's face and earned her a hug even before she'd served him coffee.

Lukinburg, an eastern-European monarchy reformed after the disbandment of the Soviet Union, was a country beset by hard times. Even with her job cooking and cleaning for the minister of finance, Dimitri Mostek, she and her father, Anton, barely made ends meet.

But Anton, one of the senior accountants working for the ministry, had earned a bonus in his November paycheck. To celebrate his success, Tasiya had been extravagant with her market shopping and had prepared her father a feast far grander than anything she was allowed to fix for the Mosteks. Her father's smile had been worth the extra pound of butter and brown sugar.

"You look so like your mother when I see you in the kitchen like this."

Tasiya smiled and turned at the sound of her father's musical accent. His rolling *r*s and guttural consonants echoed in her own voice. "You mean hot and perspiring, even though there's snow on the ground outside?"

He brushed aside a strand of curly black hair that clung to her damp cheek. "I mean beautiful. Strong in spirit and body."

"I love you, Papa."

He leaned in and pressed a kiss to her forehead. "I love you, Tasiya. Now—" he stood straight and tall and clapped his hands "—is there more of that chocolate cake?"

Tasiya laughed. "It's a torte, Papa." She reached for a towel and dried her hands, then gave him a nudge back to the living room where he'd been reading the paper. "You go. Relax. I will bring you another slice and a fresh cup of coffee."

"You spoil me, daughter."

"You're the only one who'll let me. Now go."

As her father disappeared around the corner, Tasiya went to work. She twisted her long tresses into a bun and secured them with her metal hair clip. Then she set the coffeepot back on the stove to reheat while she prepared a second helping of dessert.

She was glad to do this for him, glad to bring a little happiness into their humdrum lives. There'd been far too little rejoicing in recent years. Not since King Aleksandr had ascended the throne. His solution to creating order and reviving a badly wounded economy had been to rule with a tight, cruel fist. Inflation was out of control. And while the royal family lived in a palace that showcased the elegance and wealth of the Lukinburg of old, basic supplies such as food and fuel couldn't be guaranteed to its citizens. Financial aid from foreign countries had been rejected time and again, and those who protested the king's strict policies and isolationist philosophy were often imprisoned, or else they mysteriously disappeared.

So Tasiya took joy in her father's success. She celebrated it as her own success because it was the only type of achievement she would ever be allowed.

After setting her mother's silver tray with a plate, fork and napkin, Tasiya reached for the coffeepot and—

Gunshots exploded in the living room. "Papa!"

"Tasiya!"

She ran to her father as the front door splintered and cracked around the lock and swung open. Four or five men dressed in black from head to toe stormed in, along with rifles and curses and a blast of snow and frigid air.

"What are you— Papa!"

She never reached him. One of the men grabbed her around the neck and shoved her back into the kitchen. "Stay back!"

Tasiya twisted to see around the man blocking the archway with his gun. Though her father struggled, Anton was no match for the three men who dragged him outside into the snow. "Papa!"

Not waiting to ask questions, Tasiya pulled the lid from the coffeepot, grabbed the handle and whirled around to sling the steaming liquid into the man's face. Even with a stocking mask on, the scalding coffee did the trick. He screamed in pain, lifted his hands to his face.

She scooted past him and dashed out the door in her slippered feet. "Where are you taking him? Papa!"

She leaped down the front steps and saw to her horror they weren't taking Anton anywhere. Instead, two of the men pushed her father down onto his knees in the middle of the street. The third man pulled a gun from his belt and placed the barrel against her father's forehead.

"No! Don't!"

Tasiya ran straight into the nightmarish scene. Snowflakes bit into her cheeks, and cold soaked into her feet. She shoved the gun aside and hugged her father's head to her breast.

"Don't hurt him!"

"Tasiya, no—"

"What do they want?"

"Isn't this a pretty picture?"

Tasiya recognized that voice. Smooth and arrogant, used to having its own way. She spun around as the fifth man approached, not dressed in black like the others, but wearing a finely cut suit and expensive wool coat. Keeping her hands on her father's shoulders, she stared at the familiar face in shock. But she didn't for one minute think this man would help.

"Minister Mostek." Her employer. Her father's supervisor. The man with the beautiful wife and three children and roving eye. "Why are you doing this?" she demanded. "What do you want?"

"Justice." He trailed the tip of one leather-gloved finger along her jaw and Tasiya flinched. His smile never reached those cold, beady eyes. "Your father has stolen from me."

"It was so little," Anton protested. "I only took enough—"

With a nod from Mostek, one of the so-called soldiers of the kingdom rammed the butt of his gun into her father's temple. Tasiya sank to her knees as he fell, cradling his bleeding head in her arms.

"Your bonus," she murmured. Not a reward for a job well done. But funds stolen from the coffers of men who would terrorize their own country in the name of order and line their own pockets while citizens starved. "Let him go," Tasiya pleaded, looking up at Mostek. "He's an old man. He's no threat to you. He was only trying to keep a roof over our heads and food on the table. You cannot punish a man for trying to survive."

Dimitri Mostek cared so little for her father's plight that he'd pulled a tiny cell phone from his pocket and placed a call. "We have him," he reported, his greedy eyes dropping to the beaded tips of her breasts, made rigid by the wintry air seeping through her blouse. "We will execute him and set an example for others like him who would put themselves before our cause."

Execute?

"No!" Tasiya bolted to her feet, not knowing where to place herself with three guns all aimed at her father. "Minister…Dimitri…please."

His black eyes glistened as she used his given name. He'd asked her to do that before. In the pantry one morning where he'd trapped her unloading groceries. In his son's bedroom when she'd been changing the sheets. One time he'd held on to her paycheck until she'd said his name. Each time she'd reminded him she was there to work, to perform menial tasks for his family, nothing more. But to save her father…

"Take me instead." Bold words for a woman of no value.

"Tasiya, no." Her father's weak voice whispered from the ground at her feet.

Mostek held up his hand. The guns lowered. "You would be killed in your father's place?"

The man she'd burned inside the apartment came charging down the steps. "You bitch!"

Tasiya whirled around and gasped at the raised hand swinging toward her face.

"No!" Mostek grabbed the man by the collar and shoved him into a snowbank. "Stand down."

"But she—"

"I said no." Mostek's deep, articulate order silenced the man. "No one touches her but me."

The man in the snow, nursing his scalded cheek and humilated pride, had shed his stocking cap. But it wasn't enough damage to keep Tasiya from recognizing the chief of security in Mostek's office. Her heart raced at the discovery. She glanced all around her. Did she know all these masked men?

Dimitri shrugged, straightened his coat and faced her with a smile that oozed a repugnant brand of charm. "So, Anastasiya. You would sacrifice yourself for your father?"

He seemed to doubt her loyalty to the only family she'd ever known, the only person she'd ever loved. "If it will spare his life."

Tasiya's deep breaths clouded the air around her as she waited for a response. She lowered her eyes, sensing Mostek's traditional beliefs that a woman shouldn't be allowed to address anyone, especially a man, above her station.

"Such a waste of beauty." She detected the same lustful hunger that had repulsed her when he'd offered to set her up as his mistress that day in the pantry.

"Yes. I'm here." Mostek's voice sharpened. He was talking into the phone now, though she could feel his gaze on her. "Anton's daughter has offered herself to me as a gift in exchange for his life. I would like to accept."

"No." Anton tugged at her skirt. He wavered as he pulled himself to a sitting position and clung to her arm. "She cooks and cleans for you, but she will not be your whore."

Mostek flicked his hand and the guns went up again. "Then you will die."

"Papa…"

Mostek spun away, arguing with the man on the phone. "I have been your loyal servant, carried out every secret…"

"These are very dangerous people, Tasiya." Anton reached for her hand. "I knew the risks when I embezzled their money."

She knelt beside him. "But the punishment does not fit the crime."

"These are terrorists, my love. They do not care who they hurt, only that their cause endures and is triumphant."

"And what is their cause?" A long-suppressed

anger blended with her fear. "Who benefits from their so-called patriotism?"

"Do not question them."

Tasiya cupped her father's swollen face between her hands. She unbuttoned the cuff of her white cotton blouse and dabbed at the blood collecting in his eye. "You are a good man who has been loyal to king and country as long as I have known you. And how do they repay you? With threats and violence." She blinked back the tears that stung her own eyes. "You are all I have in this world. I will not let them hurt you."

"Tasiya—"

"It is done." Mostek stuffed his phone into his pocket as he hooked his hand beneath her elbow and pulled her to her feet. Away from her father. "The arrangements have been made."

"What arrangements?"

Mostek nodded to the others. "Take him away."

"No—" Tasiya lunged for her father as two of the men grabbed him beneath his arms and dragged him toward a long black limousine adorned with two flags bearing the Lukinburg coat of arms.

Mostek jerked her arm in its socket, drawing her up against his chest. He moved his thin, shapeless lips against her ear. "In exchange for allowing your father to live, you are going to take a small journey for me."

Tasiya swallowed hard to keep the bile from scorching her throat. "Where am I going?"

"To America."

"America?" So big. So far away. The country that had given Crown Prince Nikolai asylum after speaking out against King Aleksandr at the United Nations. America—the country Aleksandr had called an empire-building bully. The country that would join the international movement to overthrow the Lukinburg government.

"My superior…" He seemed to find the word distasteful. Any man Dimitri Mostek feared and reviled must be very dangerous and powerful, indeed. "…believes you can be useful to our cause."

"I don't believe in your cause. There has to be a better way to find peace and prosperity for our people."

He smiled. She hated that loathsome sneer. "Your beliefs are irrelevant. I'm putting you on a plane to America where you will be delivered as a gift to some friends." Tasiya shriveled inside at the implication. "They will be warned not to touch you. *That*—" he kissed her temple, making her skin crawl "—will be *my* reward."

Tasiya pulled back as far as his unrelenting grip allowed. What else did she have of value, if not her body? "Then what am I to do in America?"

"What you do so well. Cook. Clean. Serve my friends as you have served me." He reached into his pocket and pulled out a squarish device that looked like a miniature version of his own phone. He pressed the ultramodern gadget into her palm and curled her fingers around it. "And call me every day on this secure line to let me know exactly what they're doing."

"You're asking me to spy on the Americans?"

"I'm telling you what you must do to save your father's life."

Chapter One

Devil's Fork Island, U.S.A., November 7
12:00 a.m.

"Alpha-Bravo-Tango—Abort! Abort! Abort!"
   "Negative!"
   Sergeant Bryce Martin defied the command crackling over his vest radio and slipped a large safety pin into the land-mine housing, holding it in place while he dismantled the trigger assembly. The charge was still there, but it could no longer be detonated by simple pressure.
   Taking deep, steady breaths to counteract the racing fury of his pulse, he spared a moment to glance up at the women, children and old men huddled like live bait in the center of the rows of cultivated coca plants turned minefield.
   Only three more to go and they could lead the hostages out through a safe zone. He had the mechanics down now. Though the jungle of San Ysidro was

laced with these deadly contraptions, their design wasn't any more complicated than a hand grenade. After diagnosing and learning the procedure on the first one, he could neutralize each mine in just over a minute. He'd come this far, he'd finish the job. "I need three minutes, sir."

"I don't have three minutes to give you, Sarge." Colonel Murphy's signal was breaking up. His soldiers were on the move. "The damn setup's an ambush. You gave it your best shot, but you need to get the hell out of there. Cordero's men are lining up mortars. They're going to blow your position. I order you to abort. Powell's hijacked an evac chopper. We're buggin' out. Now!"

Bryce moved on to the next mine and dropped to his knees, his big hands surprisingly agile as he opened the trigger housing and slipped in another safety pin. He couldn't leave these innocent people behind at the mercy of a greedy dictator and his drug-funded army.

Not when he'd been so close to finding something meaningful in his life. Not when he'd been so close to caring.

He jimmied the housing apart and snipped the wire before risking a glance up at Maria. Some of the men in his Special Forces unit saw her as the village madam—older, plumper, past her prime. But he saw her as something special. A kind soul who looked beyond his scarred-up face and truck-size body to offer him comfort and friendship in a decidedly unfriendly country.

Her world-weary eyes had tears in them now as she shook her head.

Two minutes.

"Dammit, Martin—get your ass out of there. You've got incoming."

Bryce averted his ears to the telltale thump of mortar fire. Their fiery trails lit up the sky.

He couldn't tell the civilians to run.

He gripped his assault rifle and rose to his feet.

He couldn't save them. He couldn't save Maria.

"I'm sorry." He barely mouthed the words. He was already backing up.

"Sarge!"

He shouldn't have cared. Dammit. Why the hell did he have to care?

"Gracias." She blew him a kiss. "Be happy."

Bryce turned, ran. The mortars hit. The mines exploded. Smoke billowed in the air behind him and rushed upon his heels.

White-hot pain ripped through his legs and back, cutting through scars and skin and muscle and bone.

He flew through the air, knowing he'd been toasted long before he hit the ground.

Campbell and Blackhaw charged from their cover. He felt their hands on him, dragging him out of the fire and smoke and death.

Bryce twisted in his scratchy, lumpy bed, reliving the torturous pain, inside and out. Replaying the months of recovery that had tested even his considerable patience, unable to find a comfortable position that didn't make something itch or burn or ache.

A gunshot cracked through the night air. The sound jerked through him before Bryce went still. His eyes snapped open to hazy darkness. Not a remembered firefight. The real thing.

Dread made his body rigid, suffused him in sweat. God, no. He swung his legs off the cot and ran barefoot across the slimy cold stones of his cell. Over the rattle of his chains, he heard the hoots of laughter and triumph from outside in the courtyard.

Grasping the vertical bars of his cage, he hoisted himself up to look out. "Son of a bitch."

He dropped to his feet, turned his back to the wall and sank down on his haunches. He knew the wall was as cold and damp from the night air as the floor beneath his feet. But he barely felt it. He couldn't feel much of anything beyond rage at his captors.

This was worse than his nightmares.

The bastards had just executed an innocent man.

Devil's Fork Island, U.S.A., November 8
2:13 a.m.

Bryce stared at the soldier's bloody chest. "Kid?" God, had he ever been that young?

Cruel hands dragged him away from the dead

man he'd scrambled into the slick underbrush with. Despite a flying tackle, he'd been too late to save him. Hell. He and his comrades from Big Sky Bounty Hunters had unknowingly brought the enemy with them in the first place.

Tailed. Like a bunch of amateurs. When they'd been trying to help. To warn their old unit of a terrorist attack.

Only, these were no terrorists. Not the foreign kind, at any rate.

The fight was on.

"Grab the big guy! Take him down!"

How many times had he heard that kind of threat?

Three men piled on, forcing him to the ground. He got his hands around the throat of a black-haired man, butted him in the head, kneed him where it counted and shoved him out of the way. Down to two. More wrestling than punching. Idiots. With all the mud and water they couldn't get a grip. His meaty fists were far more effective.

"Martin!" He heard Jacob Powell's voice, shouting his name. "Money's on you, big guy! Take 'em—"

A deep grunt silenced his cheering section. They were outnumbered. Taken by surprise. Going down or neutralized one by one.

Bryce felt the bonds going around his wrists as they finally wised up and started beating on him. He pitched, kicked, pounded—and with a mighty effort, he lurched to his feet, hauling the two men up with him.

The tattoo of an upside-down burning flag swam across his vision before a new fist connected with his jaw, driving him back to his knees in the muddy marsh of North Carolina's Swamp Lejeune. But it was the telltale click of a military-issue Colt sliding a bullet into the firing chamber that finally stilled the fight in him. "Let me just shoot him like I did the other one."

The man with the curly black hair and the gun, the only man here who could match Bryce in stature, waited for the okay.

"No, Marcus! The ones out of uniform are not to be killed. You've enjoyed enough target practice for one day." Even with the steel barrel of the Colt pressing into the back of his skull, Bryce turned to get a good look at the scraggly beard and brown ponytail of the tall, well-armed man approaching him.

"Boone Fowler."

"I see my reputation precedes me."

Like a rat spreading the plague.

The weasly son of a bitch headed up the Montana Militia for a Free America. Fowler was the fanatic who'd broken out of prison four months ago with his loyal minions, regrouped his own private army and waged a personal vendetta against the men of Big Sky who had imprisoned him in the first place. He didn't care who he hurt or how he hurt them—only that he got his way.

Bryce breathed hard, tasting the blood in his

mouth and ignoring pain in his side, keeping his enemy in sight.

Fowler doffed a distinctly unmilitary salute. "I want them alive. But I don't necessarily need them in one piece."

The man named Marcus needed no urging. He rammed the butt of his gun into Bryce's head, swirling pain around inside his skull.

Bryce struggled against the beating hands that bound his wrists and ankles and inflicted what damage they could.

He was still swinging until the moment his world went black.

Bryce swung at his attackers in his sleep, rattling iron chains, pinching his wrists and startling himself awake.

He sat bolt upright in the bed, orienting himself to surroundings illuminated only by the cold threads of moonlight shining in through the open grating at the small, high window.

Sweat trickled along his cheek and dripped onto the deep rise and fall of his naked chest. It pooled at the small of his back and soaked into the waistband of his jeans. With each breath, he inhaled the stale smells of mold and damp, the pungent odor of the straw ticking in the mattress beneath him, and the cool, salty tang of an ocean breeze. They were familiar smells by now, though not necessarily welcome ones.

Two dead now. Boone Fowler had promised to

kill one man every day until he got what he wanted. Whatever the hell that was. They had to get out of this hell-hole.

As Bryce's eyes and mind adjusted to the here and now, he took note of the stone block walls. The surfaces had been worn smooth, the edges eroded unevenly by centuries of use. He noted the new steel bars and massive lock that kept him from leaving his six-by-eight cell.

His ankles chafed and the chain between them rattled as he swung his legs off the side of the iron cot and flattened his bare feet against the cold stone floor. This fortress was solid as a tomb and sported all the archaic comforts of a medieval dungeon.

Ignoring the scars of his life and the bruises from his capture, he jerked his wrists out to the side, stretching his arms as wide as the eighteen or so inches of chain connecting them allowed. He squeezed his hands into fists, swelling his mighty forearms and biceps until every muscle shook with the effort to rip the restraints apart. Though rust from age and the damp sea air colored the chain and cuffs, each link held fast.

Releasing his breath after the feverish exertion, he dropped his hands to his knees and watched a mouse scurry from its cubbyhole in the corner up to the window and disappear outside.

Lucky bastard.

Bryce was hungry and sore, isolated and trapped

like a caged bear on some uninhabited island he didn't recognize. His injuries were minimal—a puffy right eye, a cut lip, bruised ribs and a gash on his right cheek that would need stitches to heal pretty. Not that one pretty scar would make much difference amongst the marks left by the fiery car wreck that had killed his parents, and the shrapnel wounds from that San Ysidran minefield that had ended his official military career. But his injuries would never heal if the beating and pointless questions he'd endured that afternoon were going to become a daily ritual.

His three comrades from Big Sky Bounty Hunters, as well as the thirteen Special Forces soldiers who'd survived the ambush at the Marine Corps training base nicknamed Swamp Lejeune, could be dead now or imprisoned in another barred room inside this ancient prison. And from where he sat, he couldn't do a damn thing to help them.

Like he hadn't been able to help that kid last night.

"Hell," was all he said. The word echoed in the darkness.

Waking up hadn't made the nightmares go away.

"A GIFT FOR A JOB well-done, huh?"

"Yes, sir."

The man named Boone Fowler read the letter from the sealed envelope Tasiya had delivered from Dimitri Mostek. Though the two men had little in common in the looks department beyond their forty-something age, she sensed they'd been cut from the same arrogant, power-hungry cloth. Mr. Fowler was a good four or five inches taller than Dimitri's stocky build. His hair was a faded brown, long and pulled back into a ponytail. While Dimitri's short, black hair framed a pampered face, Fowler's face was marred by acne scars, outdoor living and a thin beard.

It was the calculating black eyes that made her think of the man who held her father prisoner. Like Mostek, Fowler's eyes were cold and hard. Full of suspicion. Quick to show blame and temper. Unused to reflecting patience or compassion.

Tasiya stood in the middle of Fowler's stucco-walled office, still clutching the carry-on bag she'd brought with her on the flight to New York and a place called Wilmington, North Carolina. The same bag she'd held on the long truck ride to a white, sandy coastline and the remote ferry that had brought her to this place.

Devil's Fork Island, the man had called it. He mentioned something about a conquistador stronghold, a sailor's prison and pirate hideaway.

But Tasiya hadn't been interested in the history of the place. She'd been thinking of that last glimpse of her injured father being dragged away from her and driven off to who knew where. She'd been thinking about how quickly Dimitri Mostek had put together a passport and traveling papers for her. Where he'd gotten the secure, high-tech phone that had been designed to dial only one number. His.

She'd been thinking that her father had taken money from some very dangerous people, and that it was her responsibility to make sure he didn't pay too high a price for that mistake.

Now she realized the men she'd been sent to spy on were equally dangerous.

And wouldn't take kindly to being spied upon, judging by the numerous security measures she'd seen thus far.

They'd been the only vehicle on the boat, and once it had docked, several armed men had materialized out of the tall, reedy grass on the banks to secure the ferry and tie camouflage tarps across the deck and wheelhouse. Clearly, there wasn't going to be a return trip to the mainland anytime soon.

The wind off the ocean had whipped her long skirt and coat about her legs. And though the sun was shining and the temperature was several degrees warmer than the frozen home she'd left behind, she'd shivered.

She'd been shaking by the time her short, skinny escort had wrapped his hard fingers around her upper arm to lead her into some trodden grass along what she now realized was an unmarked path. He paused at a tall, wire mesh fence, hidden in a line of scrubby trees at the top of the sandy incline.

The man pulled a walkie-talkie from his pocket and pressed a button. Another man's voice answered, demanding identification. Even with her limited English, she could tell they were speaking some type of code. Once approved, Tasiya heard a staticky hum from the fence that seemed to charge the air around it and stand the hairs on her arms on end. She started when the hum ended in an abrupt silence. With an "All clear," the man pulled her beside him through a gate. Then there was another call, and the hum resumed behind her. Tasiya realized they'd passed through some sort of electric security barrier.

Such extreme measures to keep people out. Not that she'd expected a friendly welcome. Not that she'd trust anyone who did make a friendly overture.

No one had welcomed her to America or Devil's Fork Island or Boone Fowler's office. No one had asked about her trip or whether she was tired or hungry. No one had said anything beyond, "Show me your passport," or "Get in," or "This way."

She had a feeling Boone Fowler was more used to barking orders than striking up conversations. Tasiya longed for a kind word, a bit of reassurance, a smile, to make her think she could pull this off. Because she had an equally strong feeling that—like Dimitri Mostek—Boone Fowler would have no qualms about taking retribution on anyone who crossed him.

"So we're not supposed to touch you?"

He tossed the letter onto the gray metal desk and looked up, raking his dismissive eyes up and down her figure. Tasiya kept her own gaze trained to the floor. "No, sir."

"That's not a problem for me. I don't do foreign trash." He stood and circled around the desk, stopping just in front of her. "But I do like having a woman at my beck and call."

Tasiya stared at the buttons on his black-and-red flannel shirt. "Minister Mostek said I should help you in any way I can."

"You a decent cook?"

She nodded, not out of ego, but of honesty. "That is how I make my living."

"Good. Anything would be better than that slop Bristoe's been serving us." Tasiya held her breath as his hand moved toward her chin, but he caught himself before making contact. He snapped his fingers instead. Her breath rushed out in a startled gasp and he snickered in his throat. Understanding the command to submit to his will, she steadied her nerves and tilted her eyes up to look into his. "I don't want any of that spicy foreign crud where you can't tell what it is you're eating. Plain cooking. Nothing fancy. Use the supplies we have on hand. Can you manage that?"

Just like Mostek. "Yes, sir."

"Marcus!"

She turned away as he shouted the order over the top of her head. An even bigger man opened the thick wooden door from the outside hallway. He had to stand six and a half feet tall, nearly a foot taller than she. He was built like an ox and seemed to share the same personal habits of a beast of burden. His slick, curly black hair and stained hands needed to meet a bar of soap. And the pool of yellowish-brown tobacco juice that swirled in front of his leering smile before he turned and spat his cud into a corner of the hallway nearly made her gag.

Quickly Tasiya closed her eyes and pictured an image of her father's kind, smiling face. The face of the gentle man who'd read her bedtime stories as a child, and talked about her mother so she wouldn't be afraid of the imaginary creature she'd thought lived beneath her bed.

She was calmer when she opened her eyes, but the big ox with the suggestive grin and large pistol strapped to his belt was still staring at her.

"I heard we had company," he drawled, strolling into the room. "I'm Marcus Smith, Mr. Fowler's newly promoted chief of security. 'Cause I'm so good at what I do. And your name, little lady?"

Little lady? She was five feet, seven inches tall. Of course, everyone must seem little compared to this brute. She fixed her gaze squarely in the center of his chest. "Anastasiya Belov."

"She's a gift from our benefactor for a job well-done," Fowler explained. "He's impressed that we were able to neutralize the strike force."

"I'm the one who's impressed." The man called Marcus Smith reached out and twined his thick, grubby fingers into the long curls of hair that fell across her left breast. "Nice. Prettiest damn thing I've seen in weeks."

Tasiya curled her toes inside her boots to keep from bolting.

But, surprisingly, Boone Fowler saved her the trouble.

"Hands off, Marcus." He shoved the big man back a step. "She's not *that* kind of gift."

Tasiya winced at the pinpricks of pain that danced across her scalp before Marcus let go of her hair, but she refused to cry out. This was nothing. Her father might be suffering much worse than this. She could endure a few unwanted gropes for his sake.

But apparently Boone Fowler intended to follow his instructions to the letter. "The note says we're not to touch her. Our contact wants her in pristine condition for himself. And since his people are funding our operation, I don't want to jeopardize that relationship. Yet. We have business to attend to, anyway. Or have you forgotten our purpose?"

Marcus bowed his gaze like a chastized child. "I haven't forgotten. I just thought maybe, since you seemed so pleased with my performance lately, that—"

"Keep it in your pants for a few days, okay? We'll use her to free up some manpower to increase security patrols and interrogations."

Keep it in your pants? Another strange Americanism. She might not understand the words, but she had no problem recognizing the lechery in Marcus Smith's eyes, or the blame she read there for being reprimanded by the boss.

"I'm sure you can find other ways to entertain yourself. After all, I intend to break every one of Cameron Murphy's team. I want them begging to do my bidding when we make that videotape and broadcast it."

Breaking someone seemed to have a reviving effect on Marcus Smith's mood. He was smiling as he looked up again. "Murphy's men have been pretty stubborn so far. But I like a challenge." He glanced down at Tasiya, giving his statement a double meaning. "I've got a few tricks up my sleeve to try, if need be. This old pirate hideout is proving to be a very resourceful place."

Fowler nodded, pleased with the answer that Tasiya couldn't quite understand. "I don't care how you get the job done. I just want results."

"You'll have them before we shoot the video next week."

Tricks? Video? Were these the sort of things she was supposed to report to Mostek?

She hadn't yet come up with an answer when

Boone Fowler stepped beside her and demanded her attention. "I've got thirty men here who all need to be fed three square meals a day. When you're done with that, in the evening, we've got seventeen prisoners. You're to take them bread and water. Marcus will show you your room, the kitchen and larder, and the route you're to take when you feed the prisoners."

Three square meals versus bread and water? Compassion had her looking up into those cold, dark eyes. "Only one meal for the prisoners?"

Those dark eyes sneered. "Rule number one around here, Ms. Belov. *Never* question my orders."

"No, sir." Tasiya covered the unexpected flare of sympathy for someone besides her father by quickly lowering her gaze. "I just wanted to be clear on my duties."

"You're not stupid, are you?"

She had no trouble comprehending the insult. But she ignored it and made an excuse. "English is not my first language, sir. I only asked because I wanted to make sure I understood correctly. Three meals for your men. One meal for the prisoners."

"In between, you can clean my office and the latrine. But I don't want you in here without myself or a guard present. As a matter of fact, I don't want to see you anywhere but your room, the kitchen or making your rounds to the prisoners unless you have a guard and my permission." He bent his knees and brought his face level with hers. "Do you understand that?"

"Yes, sir."

"Then you're dismissed." He straightened and returned to his seat behind the desk.

Tasiya swallowed her anger and the urge to blurt out that he wasn't a god. And that if he was as smart as he seemed to think he was, he'd realize he had a traitor in his midst. Standing in his office. A black-haired sheep in wolf's clothing, to put a twist on one of those childhood stories her father had read to her.

Fowler was a lot like Dimitri Mostek. Full of himself and high on power. No qualms about being cruel and manipulative. The only thing lacking were the lusty overtures, and she had a sick feeling that Marcus Smith would be adding that dimension to this living hell.

"This way, sugar," said Marcus, turning sideways in the doorway instead of stepping aside, so that her shoulder had to brush against his chest as she exited into the hallway.

Crinkling her nose at the whiff of stale tobacco and sweat, Tasiya clutched her bag tight against her stomach and hurried past him. She fixed an image of her father's loving face firmly in her mind as she followed Marcus Smith down a spiral staircase of worn, warped stone to the doorless closet off the kitchen that would serve as her home for the next few weeks.

Chapter Two

"Please, Minister," Tasiya whispered into the phone, glancing over her shoulder to make sure no one was eavesdropping on her call. She trimmed the wick on the kerosene lantern on her two-drawer dresser, dimming the light so as not to draw attention to her presence in the room.

By the end of the night, she vowed to at least find a blanket to hang across the arched opening so she could change her clothes without the curious eyes of Marcus Smith or anyone else ogling her. "I want to talk to my father. If he's not safe, I have no reason to do this for you."

"Anastasiya. Darling." Mostek's cultured voice tried to seduce her even across the ocean that separated them. "I like it so much better when you call me Dimitri."

Tasiya swallowed her gag reflex and her pride. "Please… Dimitri. Let me speak to my father."

"Very well." Tasiya drifted toward the corner of

the twin-size bed that took up half the room. She sank onto the hard mattress, hugging her arm around her waist while he spoke to someone on his end of the line. But Dimitri still had a few more words for her. "That wasn't so difficult, was it, Anastasiya? I'm pleased you made it to your destination and are getting acquainted with the men you are working for."

She had no desire to get acquainted with anyone she'd met thus far, but didn't think it wise to share that information with Mostek. "No one complained about the dinner I prepared. In fact, I believe Mr. Fowler has ordered his men not to address me unless it is about my work."

"Good. Your father's well-being depends upon you doing your job there and then returning to be my mistress. I don't want you sullied by American hands."

"How can you—" Tasiya bit her tongue to keep the question to herself. It wasn't her place to understand how men like Mostek and Fowler could do business when they didn't like each other and trusted each other even less.

"How can I want you?" She let Dimitri run with the topic so she wouldn't have to explain her impetuous question. "Because you're a beautiful woman and I'm bored with my wife. I told you I could set you up in style in an apartment here in the city if you'll let me."

"What about my father?" She glanced at the clock beside the lantern, knowing she needed to cut the phone call short and get to her rounds delivering the prisoners' rations before anyone questioned her absence from the kitchen. "What will happen to him when I return?"

"I'll give you enough money that you can support him as well. But I don't want him living with you." She could visualize Mostek's vulgar sneer. "I'll require privacy for my visits."

Not exactly the motivation she needed to successfully pull off this charade.

"Here's Anton. Keep it short."

Tasiya shot to her feet and trained every aural cell in her ear to the precious sound of her father's voice.

"Tasiya?" He sounded tired.

"Papa?" This was what she needed to hear. "Are you all right? How is the cut on your head? Are you eating? Have they hurt you anymore?"

"I'm fine, daughter. They cleaned the wound and put a bandage on it. But I'm worried about you. So far away. So—"

"I'm fine, Papa." He was being held by terrorists who wanted to use him as an example of how they dealt with anyone who dared oppose them. She wouldn't be a burden to him on top of that. "The work here is no different from at home. I cook and clean."

"But these men..." She could hear the fear in his tone. "Are you safe?"

She hurried to the open doorway and looked around the empty kitchen. For now, she could give him an honest answer. "I'm safe." But Marcus Smith had warned her to start her rounds by eight o'clock or he'd show up to escort her himself. It was nearly eight now. She had to go, even though she wanted nothing more than to cling to the sound of her father's voice. "I love you, Papa. We'll be together again soon, I promise."

"I love you."

Those three words would have to sustain her courage. Dimitri Mostek snatched the phone from her father's hand, ordered his men to take Anton back to his room and lock him in, and added a final threat.

"Your loyalty to your father is touching. I hope you will prove as loyal to me."

Tasiya felt as if Mostek had ripped her father from her arms again. But she squelched her fear with a deep breath and kept her voice calm. "I've done everything you've asked of me thus far. I won't disappoint you."

"It's imperative for your father's health that you don't. I'll expect a call from you tomorrow. I want to know everything the militia is doing, the status of their prisoners, anything you can tell me. I also want you to find an American television—"

"A television?" In this drafty old place whose only modern amenities seemed to be its security systems? She'd had to hand-pump the stove to make it work, while a small generator produced electricity for the refrigerator and freezer. He wanted too much. "Where will I—"

"Do not interrupt me again." Tasiya bit her tongue, lest he take his displeasure with her out on her father. "A radio or newspaper will do as well. I want to know what propaganda they are saying about Lukinburg, and what news they have of Prince Nikolai and Princess Veronika."

"I'm to spy on them, too?"

The two royal heirs had remained in the United States after speaking out against their father's inhumane policies in their homeland. Though branded a traitor by King Aleksandr and the Lukinburg press, Nikolai had apparently become the heroic darling of American women and politicians alike.

Providing news of the prince and princess to the king would no doubt bring some favorable reward to Dimitri. "I will try my best."

"You will do these things," he corrected. "Is that clear?"

"Yes."

"Such a good girl. Such a good, beautiful girl." The false charm bled back into his voice. "I'll be thinking of you tonight. In my dreams."

Tasiya cringed at the implication, but checked her response. "Goodbye."

She risked a rare, perverse pleasure in ending the call before he could answer. Hiding the phone inside her pillowcase, she glanced at the clock. Two minutes past eight. Marcus would come looking for her soon.

Her father's life depended on her carrying out Mostek's orders.

Her own life depended on her doing it without getting caught.

Ponderosa, Montana

"WHAT DO YOU MEAN they shot another one? Where the hell are my men?" The tall, black-haired man wheezed, trying to rouse himself from his bed.

"Easy, Colonel." Trevor Blackhaw braced his hand against the shoulder that wasn't bandaged and eased his boss at Big Sky Bounty Hunters back against the propped-up pillows. "You've been home from the hospital all of two hours. If Mia finds out we're in here talking business, she'll have my hide."

Mention of Cameron Murphy's wife, who had just stepped out of the bedroom to put Olivia, their four-year-old daughter to bed, seemed to ease his agitation. "I guess this means you had to cut your engagement celebration short?"

Trevor sank into the chair beside the bed. "Sierra understands. She might be free of the militia's influence now, but none of us will rest easy until Boone Fowler and his men are back in prison where they belong."

Cameron rubbed at the scruff of beard that had sprouted along his jaw in the days since barely surviving a chemical bomb attack by the Montana Militia for a Free America at a nearby mall. Though he'd suffered critical burns and some temporary damage to his lungs, there wasn't a damn thing wrong with his intellectual capabilities or leadership skills. "Tell me what we know."

Trevor picked up the grainy black-and-white photographs he'd brought in to show his boss. "An army search-and-rescue team found one deceased soldier down in Swamp Lejeune at the ambush site. Michael Clark," a fellow bounty hunter whose background in army intelligence made him an expert detective, "dates the second photo about a week after the initial capture. The army ID'd the victim as one of theirs, but it's too dark to get any kind of fix on the location."

"What about where the photos were processed?"

Trevor shook his head. "Clark's still trying to trace the source. It passed through a lot of hands before reaching us."

"And there's no way to track them from the ambush site?"

"Lombardi and Cook are in North Carolina now. But Lejeune training base covers thousands of acres over a variety of terrain. They found some heavy-vehicle tracks, but the trail went cold at the New River. Fowler's men could have choppered out, taken a boat, landed a seaplane. They could be camped out next door or halfway around the world."

Cameron crumpled the sheet and blanket inside his fist. "Fowler's on American soil, I guarantee it."

"Both his victims were military, both were part of the covert strike team that was running training ops for an intel incursion into Lukinburg. The executed prisoner photo was delivered in Washington, D.C., with Fowler's usual demand—if the UN insists on sending our men into Lukinburg, then he'll find a way to stop them."

"By killing off hostages one by one?" Cameron shook his head. "Terrorist tactics aren't going to change the government's mind."

Folding his long, olive-skinned fingers together, Trevor leaned forward. "He's probably sending a subtle message to you, too. What he's doing to these soldiers, he intends to do to your bounty hunters."

The bad blood between Cameron Murphy and Boone Fowler went back a long way. "Dammit, Blackhaw—Fowler murdered my sister for his cause. How many other innocent lives has he erased in the name of what he calls patriotism? He's taken potshots at every one of us—hit us where it hurts the most. Why can't we get this creep?"

"We will. Campbell, Powell, the sarge, Riley Watson, Brown and the others—we've all sworn to end this bastard's reign of terror. Fowler's the one who made this war personal. But we intend to finish it. I promise you that."

A painful breath rasped through Cameron's lungs.

Though his dark eyes remained sharply focused, his battered body was fading toward much-needed sleep. "How are we gonna do that if we can't find him?"

"I've activated every contact we have around the country. There's a Special Forces unit waiting to assist us the minute we know anything. Don't think for one minute your men—the men we fought with down in San Ysidro and in Africa and the men you hand-picked to work for you now—are sitting in a cell somewhere twiddling their thumbs." Trevor tucked the graphic photos inside his jacket and stood. "If I know Sergeant Martin and the others, they'll find a way to contact us."

Cameron nodded. "Then let's be ready to roll."

TASIYA SMOOTHED HER PALMS down the length of her cream-colored sweater and steadied her nerves before slipping the elastic band of keys Marcus had given her around her wrist. Then she unlocked the wheels of her stainless steel cart and pushed it out of the kitchen into the breezeway that separated the refurbished quarters housing the militia members from the prison section of the compound.

She passed back through centuries of time as she unlocked a thick wooden door and entered the long passageway that housed the prisoners. In this part of the stronghold, little had been done to reclaim it from its colonial past. The uneven settling of the stones paving the floor created an uneven, repetitive clanking sound that chafed her nerves as her cart bounced over bumps and into ruts.

With no central heating and few covered windows, the chilly night air off the ocean drifted in and caught in the dark, dank corners. The breeze swirled her skirt around her knees. She'd brought one pair of denim jeans with her, which she suspected were going to become her new uniform if she couldn't shake the damp chill that permeated her skin.

Behind locked doors she could hear the hum of generators and other machinery, which she supposed had something to do with the island's alarm system. Driven more by survival than curiosity, she didn't test her keys in any door until she reached the rusted iron monstrosity Marcus Smith had shown her earlier. After unlatching a modern steel padlock, she scraped the dead bolt across its hinge. The door itself groaned from weight and age as she shoved it open and entered the prison proper.

Foul, musty air stung her nostrils and made her eyes water. It was inhumane to keep a man in these conditions, but then she supposed kindness and compassion weren't on Boone Fowler's list of virtues.

Besides the padlock she'd slipped into her pocket to keep from being trapped inside herself, the only visible hint of technology was the single electric wire that ran the length of the stone walls to illuminate a bare lightbulb every twenty feet or so. And she suspected that had more to do with security than with the prisoners' comfort.

Unintelligible snippets of conversation teased her ears and bounced along the walls, but the prisoners fell silent as she approached the steel bars that separated her from the men she was feeding. They all watched her with assessing, unfriendly eyes. Three soldiers in one cell. Four in another. Then three and three more.

They took the small loaves of bread and cups of water she poured for them with a variety of comments at seeing a woman, and a few jeers as they mistook her for a member of Fowler's militia. But hunger quickly overrode their defiance, and they sat down to eat with a pitiful gusto that reminded her of some of the poor families she'd seen in Lukinburg.

Another key unlocked a second iron door. In this long, twisting catacomb, there were four isolated cells, each one separated from the other by thick stone walls and steel bars.

Here the men sat, bound by leg irons and wrist manacles, one to each cell like condemned murderers. These men didn't wear uniforms like the others, but civilian clothing.

The first one had unusual blue-green eyes that looked right through her without blinking. She idly wondered if the blood on his torn shirt was his own or someone else's. He never moved until she had passed on by. The next one stood up when she approached. Despite the bruising and swelling around one eye, he was a handsome man. He nodded a silent thank-you, then watched her every move until she'd rounded the corner out of sight. The third was deep in his own thoughts. And pain, she suspected, noting a dozen or so cuts across his roughly shaved head. Tasiya quickly set the bread and cup of water just outside the bars on the floor in front of his cell and moved on.

When she turned the corner to the last, most isolated of all the chambers, Tasiya hesitated. The lightbulb here had burned out, leaving the only illumination to the bulb twenty feet behind her, and the moonlight that streamed in from what must be the cell itself.

Tasiya silently cursed her luck. She could either travel all the way back to the kitchen for a flashlight, or she could swallow her fear of the unknown enemy around the corner and follow the wall with her hand until it opened up onto the cell itself.

Weighing the options of retracing her steps through the dungeonlike chambers past sixteen prisoners versus checking on the welfare of one man made her decision a quick one. If she could face down the guns of Dimitri Mostek's men, she could certainly handle a shadowy passageway and an unarmed man who was locked safely behind bars.

The stones were smooth with age but sticky with moisture and dust as she trailed her fingers across them. Leaving her cart behind, Tasiya headed toward the shaft of moonlight. When she reached the end of the wall, she peeked around into the cell.

She caught a silent breath.

On the other side of those shiny steel bars stood the hardest-looking man she'd ever seen. He wore only a pair of jeans that hung loosely enough on his hips to reveal a strip of the white briefs that hugged his waist. He stood with his back to her, his arms reaching above his head. He was fiddling with something at the base of the window, doing something with the rusty iron brace at his wrist. He wasn't any taller than her father's six feet of height, but he was massive across his shoulders, arms and back. Twice as broad as her father. Muscled and formed in a way that reminded her of tanks and mountains.

He was all male from the short clip of his dark brown hair to the flexing curve of his powerful thighs and buttocks.

And even in the moonlight that mottled his skin, she could see he was horribly disfigured.

Raised, keloid scars formed a meshwork pattern from his waistband up to his left shoulder, where the dimpled terrain of a faded burn mark took over and disappeared over onto his chest, up the side of his neck and down to his elbow.

Tasiya pressed her fingers to her lips to stifle a gasp. Her stomach clenched and her heart turned over in compassion. My God, how this man had suffered.

To her horror, he froze at her nearly inaudible gasp. With precise deliberation, he lowered his arms and slowly turned.

Shrinking back against the cold stone wall opposite his cell, Tasiya stared. The front view was nearly as harsh as the back. She could see, now, that the shadows that dappled his skin weren't all tricks of the dim light, but from bruising, as well. The old burn injury covered nearly a quarter of his chest and one side of his neck and jaw. His chin was square and pronounced. One carved cheekbone was bloody with the slash of an open wound. And the swelling around his left eye distorted the shape of a face that would have been harsh and forbidding under any circumstances.

Without a word he took a step toward her. But when Tasiya, trapped in a circle of moonlight, flattened her back against the wall, he stopped. His mouth opened as if he wanted to say something, but he shrugged instead. Tasiya's gaze instantly darted to watch the fascinating ripple and subsequent control of all that muscle.

When she realized he'd stopped and was even retreating to the rear of his cell to alleviate her fear of him, Tasiya's breath seeped out on a deep, embarrassed sigh. This man knew he was frightening to look at, imposing to get close to. Others had cowered from him before.

What a lonely, terrible existence that must be.

Sensing some of his pain, Tasiya looked up into his face.

The only thing not forbidding about the prisoner was his eyes. Enhanced by the glow of the moon, they were a cool, soothing shade of gray that reminded her of the quiet, wintry skies of her homeland.

And they meant her no harm.

Unlike the lechery she'd seen in Marcus's and Dimitri's eyes, the cold condescension she'd seen in Boone Fowler's expression, or the blank, preoccupied stares she'd seen from the other prisoners, this man was making a point of putting her at ease.

Responding to that unexpected civility, Tasiya summoned her courage and retrieved her cart. She wrapped the last small, crusty loaf, which couldn't be more than a snack to a man his size, in a napkin and poured some water into the last metal cup. Then she knelt down in front of the steel bars and laid the bread and water just in front of them, the way she'd been instructed.

When she heard the rattle of his chains as he moved to pick up his meal, she shot to her feet and backed well out of arm's reach. Compassion or not, he still made two of her, he was still a prisoner, and he still frightened her.

But in her haste to put distance between them, she'd kicked the cup over and spilled the water. Tasiya watched the puddle quickly seep into the cracks between the stones on the floor.

She couldn't leave the man without water.

She glanced up at him. He was staring at her, with ever-watchful eyes, but he wasn't condemning her. He glanced down at the cup, and she knew what she had to do.

Shaking her head at her own skittishness, Tasiya picked up the pitcher of water from her cart. She had far greater things to fear from men far more handsome than this one. Good looks didn't make a hero. Scars didn't make an enemy.

This was her job. This was for her father.

"I am sorry," she whispered, picking up the cup and pouring him fresh water. "Here."

With a show of bravery, prompted by human compassion, she reached through the bars herself and held the cup out to him. He stared at it for a moment, as if he didn't understand the gesture. Long, silent moments passed. But she waited until his agile, nicked-up fingers closed around the cup. She quickly pulled away as he gently took it from her grasp.

"Thanks."

The deep-pitched voice startled her. The husky tone resonated in that big chest and washed over her like a warm caress.

Tasiya looked into those wintry gray eyes and felt the first human connection she'd known in the four days since Dimitri Mostek had kidnapped her father. She didn't know if making that connection with this beast of a man should be a comfort or an omen. But she sensed that when he looked at her, he saw *her.* Not the *foreign trash* hired to cook and clean and be forgotten. Not a blackmailed mistress-to-be. Not the tool of betrayal.

Her.

"You are welcome."

He retreated to his cot and sank onto the bare mattress to eat and drink.

Tasiya quickly replaced the pitcher and turned her cart to leave.

"I'm Bryce Martin," he said between big bites.

She stopped midstride. He wanted to make personal conversation with her? No one else, not even her employers, had. The idea was almost as disconcerting as the darkened hallway and the threats she'd received.

Turning back to his cell, she watched him take a long drink. The ripple of muscles along his throat fascinated her. How could one man be so much… man? The visible proof of all that physical and mental strength was daunting. She didn't need any female intuition to sense that Bryce Martin was a very dangerous man. And that she should be careful around him.

She quickly returned her gaze to gauge the trustworthiness of those assessing eyes. "I am Anastasiya Belov. Tasiya to most."

"Your accent's foreign, i'n't it?" His wasn't like any of the others she'd heard here in America yet, either. She detected a lazy articulation in his bass-deep drawl.

"I am from Lukinburg. In Europe." She wasn't revealing any secrets with that much information.

He stuffed the last bite of bread into his mouth and stood. She tilted her chin to keep those gray eyes in view, her heart rate doubling as his size and scars moved closer. His wrist chain grated across the bars as he thrust the empty cup between them.

The keys at her wrist jangled as Tasiya snatched the cup and hugged it to her chest, dodging back a step to avoid contact. Bryce Martin scowled, as if her aversion to touching him neither pleased nor surprised him.

"Next time, Tasiya Belov," he warned, "be more careful 'bout stickin' your hand inside the monster's cage."

Chapter Three

The monster's cage?

Smooth move, Sarge. Had he really said that out loud to that woman? No wonder she'd high-tailed it out of here last night.

Bryce sat on the edge of his cot and twisted the crick from his neck. Squinting into the dust motes that filled the rays of morning sunshine, he wondered what kind of hell awaited him today.

Especially after he'd gotten an unexpected glimpse of heaven last night.

Tasiya Belov was a damn sight prettier than that scraggly Bristoe fella with the dirty hands and playground taunts who'd brought his bread and water the past seven nights. The insults and tough talk didn't faze him—Bristoe was a misguided kid trying to prove himself a man. But it sure was nice to finally get a taste of food that was clean and water that was fresh.

It was nicer to get a look at Tasiya.

Bryce rubbed at the skin chafing beneath his wrist

manacles and thought himself twelve kinds of fool. He should have come up with something decent to say to her, or kept his big mouth shut the way he usually did. Then, at least, he could have enjoyed the view a little longer. All that curly hair—blacker than the night around them—falling nearly to her waist. Skin that was as pale and pearlescent in the moonlight as her lashes were thick and dark. Lashes that surrounded wide, slightly tilted eyes the shade of rich, robust coffee.

Or maybe that was just the scent he got off her. Homey. Normal. Like his grandma's good cookin'. Far removed from any of the crap that was going on around here. Something about Tasiya's fairy-tale beauty and quiet ways had breached the cool reserve he wore like a suit of armor. He didn't allow himself to be attracted to many women. By age thirty-three, he'd wised up to that futility. But Tasiya Belov, with the exotic eyes and accent, had gotten to him before he could distance himself from a man's basic, male reaction to a beautiful woman.

So, of course he'd warned her off.

His chains jangled as he crawled onto the floor and squared off to do a set of push-ups. For years he'd used physical activity to dull the aches and longings and regrets of his life. What he couldn't burn out of his system this way, he tried to ignore.

Bryce knew he wasn't any great shakes to look at. The burn scars were old news; he'd had them since he was a kid, from the car accident that had killed his folks. The shrapnel scars that marked the end of his military career were more recent, more shocking to the unfamiliar eye. And the condition he was in now made his appearance even less appealing than usual.

It was a fact of his life. He was a big, scary-looking man. It made him a formidable enemy, a boon to his second career as a bounty hunter working for his former military commander, Cameron Murphy. He used his intimidating countenance to his advantage; few of the criminals he'd brought in expected the big guy to be so smart, or so good with his hands. And yeah, if it came down to it, he could outbust just about anybody in hand-to-hand combat.

He'd had years to learn to accept his fate. It shouldn't bother him.

But when Tasiya had looked at him with those wide, frightened eyes, he'd felt like a monster.

Yep, she'd had to muster up some real guts to hold out that cup of water. As if treatin' him like a human being was some kind of apology—like *she'd* done this to him. Or maybe it was defiance that had made her reach out to him. But what was she taking a stand against? Him? Boone Fowler? Her own fear?

And what the hell was a beautiful woman from Lukinburg, of all places, doing here on this godforsaken island? The Special Forces unit he and his buddies from Big Sky had been ambushed with had been secretly prepping for a covert surgical strike into Lukinburg. The UN wanted to oust their despotic king and restore democratic rule there. Bryce's former unit was supposed to be the first team in—to gather intel and remove a few key leaders.

So how had Boone Fowler's militia gotten wind of that attack when the team had been under a communication blackout for days?

He did one last push-up, shoving himself up and bracing his weight over his arms. An image of a willowy woman with frightened eyes blipped into his thoughts. Surely not. A Lukinburg spy on the militia's payroll? They'd never go for it. The whole point of Boone Fowler's life—beyond his quest for vengeance against Cameron Murphy and the Big Sky team who'd put him in prison before his escape a few months back—was to cleanse America of any foreigners. And to keep Americans off foreign soil and out of foreign business.

So where did Tasiya fit in?

Dammit. He was thinking about her again. He was curious. Worried. *Swift one, Sarge.*

Bryce clapped his hands together as he pushed to his feet to do a round of squats. The noise startled some movement in the corner of his cell. He slowly sank to his haunches and smiled.

His little mouse friend was back, scoping out the nooks between the stones, scrounging for crumbs. Bryce's empty stomach growled right on cue.

"You're outta luck, buddy," he teased his furry roommate. They both were.

He was doing his best to stay in peak physical condition in case the opportunity for escape presented itself. But his insides felt as if they were rubbing together. A little extra food would go a long way to maintain his strength and keep his thinking sharp. If there were any crusts of bread around, he'd have gone after them himself.

Bryce stilled as the mouse scurried between the steel bars and disappeared into the darkness of the passageway beyond.

Smart mouse.

Crossing to the locked cell door, Bryce wrapped his fists around the cold, unyielding steel and pressed his forehead to the bars to peer into the shadows.

That's what he should be doing, searching this place.

But not for bread crumbs.

Let's replay this escape scenario again. He needed to get outside to get the lay of the place. Scoping out the location of the other prisoners and ascertaining a sense of schedules, the number of militiamen at the compound and security protocols could secure a way off the island. Bryce had no doubt they were somewhere off the eastern coastline of the U.S. They hadn't been transported by air, and after he regained consciousness on the boat they'd been tied up in, they'd traveled only a couple of hours. Not long enough to get them out of the country.

And it had to be the ocean. He recognized the smell of the salt in the air. In the still of the night he'd identified the pummeling of waves hitting land with a force too powerful to be a lake or river's edge.

But knowing he was on an island in the Atlantic was hardly enough information to mount an escape attempt. And if he couldn't get out of this hole to investigate for himself, then he needed to make a connection with someone who did have the freedom to move about the place.

Tasiya Belov.

A tight fist gripped his stomach and squeezed. He hated the idea of using her. But it made better sense than digging the mortar from around the bars at the window and climbing out into who knew what kind of situation.

He'd spotted the armload of keys around her wrist and suspected they could get him into nearly every place he needed to go. They could get him out of these chains, at any rate, and that would give him the ability to move about the compound with less chance of being detected.

That had been his first thought, grab the keys. But, short of using brute force against the woman—which wasn't his style—that wasn't gonna happen. That left convincing her to befriend him, to run a few errands for him. Of course, he had no idea whether or not he could trust that she'd bring back the truth. Skittish as she seemed, she might run straight to Boone Fowler and tell him what the monster had asked of her.

Yeah, that'd go over real big in the escape-and-bring-these-murdering-bastards-to-justice department.

That left charming the woman.

A nearly impossible feat.

Long days out in the hills of the Missouri Ozarks where he'd grown up—hunting, fishing, camping—and quiet evenings spent on the porch with the grandparents who'd raised him didn't go a long way toward developing a man's sweet-talkin' ways.

Maybe one of the other bounty hunters, Aidan Campbell, Jacob Powell or Riley Watson—strike that, Craig O'Riley was the alias he'd been using when they were captured—were thinking along the same lines. They had the sweet words and the deceptive smiles and handsome faces he lacked. Hell, the way Powell ran his mouth sometimes, he could wear down a body's resistance, make a woman happy to concede to his will. And O'Riley was the master of undercover work. He could don a persona and make anyone—man or woman—believe every word he said.

So how was a former army sergeant who knew more about weapons and explosives than he knew about conversation and seduction supposed to get close enough to Tasiya Belov to gain her trust and enlist her help?

He wasn't.

He'd have to find another means of escape.

And he'd have to find it soon.

Bryce had been staring down the hallway long enough for the shadows to lighten and take shape. His cell was at the dead end of a passage that doubled back on itself. He knew that route led to a series of locked iron doors, one of which was the interrogation room—four stone walls that housed all the twisted toys of the Inquisition. From this vantage point, all he could see was an electrical wire and broken lightbulb tacked up between the stones.

But he could hear the enemy coming. Since they had the guns and he wore the chains, there was no need for stealth. Bryce backed up to the center of his cell and shook loose the muscles in his arms and legs, mentally bracing himself and prepping his body for the hours to come.

Marcus Smith and a pair of bully sidekicks lined up outside his door to pay him a visit.

"Ready to talk today, Sergeant?" Marcus spat his chaw through the bars on the floor next to Bryce's bare foot.

Bryce didn't shift his gaze from those icy blue eyes. Satisfying Smith's power-hungry need to control him wasn't on his to-do list. Smith was buttin' heads with a man who'd already endured the worst the world had to offer. His boys and toys couldn't break him.

Bryce's only response was the silent promise he made.

Ready to get what's coming to you? Because it will come. Maybe not today or tomorrow. But the days of the Montana Militia for a Free America are numbered.

Bryce and his fellow bounty hunters at Big Sky were damn well gonna see to it.

"DID YOU GET A LOAD of the big guy today?" Even with the buzz of other conversations in the room, Tasiya couldn't tune out Marcus Smith's booming voice. She couldn't ignore the lecherous fascination of his eyes, either. His cold blue gaze followed her as she moved from one table to the next to pour more coffee. Thank God she was out of arm's reach and he was busy regaling his men with stories. "Sits there and stares at you. Never says a word. Pisses me off."

"At least he doesn't get you off track with all his smart-ass remarks." Steve Bristoe, the skinny blond man who didn't seem to mind that Tasiya had replaced him in the kitchen, stuck a forkful of apple pie in his mouth and continued talking. "That Craig O'Riley is gonna say the wrong thing one of these days and I'm gonna really let him have it."

Marcus held up his mug, indicating he wanted her to return to his table for a refill. "Maybe it's time to execute another one of the soldiers. If physical force won't turn them, we'll have to find another way. We'll put one innocent life on each of their heads until we have those Big Sky bozos eating out of our hand."

Execution? Was that the kind of atrocity Dimitri Mostek and his unknown boss were financing here? Would he put a stop to the killing if she reported the militia's activities? Or would he applaud their work?

Tasiya swallowed the lump of dread in her throat and wiped all emotion from her face before stepping into Marcus's personal space. In fewer than forty-eight hours she'd already learned that Marcus Smith, with his yellow teeth and dirty hands, didn't think the no-touch rule applied to him. Unless Boone Fowler was around, of course. And since the militia leader preferred to take his meals in the privacy of his office instead of in the mess hall with his men…

A large, meaty palm attached itself to her backside. Tasiya nearly stumbled as Marcus pulled her even closer. "That's it, sugar," he said, as though his hand on her butt provided some sort of assistance in her duties. "Fill it all the way up."

Even when his words were seemingly innocent, or didn't quite make sense in her translation, his tone always made her feel dirty. The same way Dimitri had made her feel. This is what she'd sentenced herself to by agreeing to Dimitri's plan. A life in which she jumped at the touch of a man's hand, a life in which she turned off her emotions so as not to draw attention to herself and her discomfort, a life in which she would never know a man's kindness or love.

But, for her father, she would do this. He was all she'd ever had. For Anton Belov she would do anything.

"Thanks, sugar."

With the slightest of nods, Tasiya turned out of his grasp, unable to stop herself from wiping at the warm spot he'd left on the back of her jeans.

"Whoa, pretty thing, where you runnin' off to so fast?" His hand at her elbow stopped her escape.

"I have work to do in the kitchen."

This time, Steve Bristoe paused midchew to take note of the grubby hand on her sweater, then looked up at Marcus with a question in his eyes. He wanted to know how Marcus could get away with this infraction. But the black-haired giant was meaner and tougher than Bristoe could ever aspire to be. He was clearly the most feared man in this room. One look from Marcus, and Bristoe quickly turned his attention back to his dessert. With Marcus staking such a proprietary claim on her, there was no one in the room who would come to her defense.

Tasiya twisted against his grip, making an effort

to defend herself. "There is food in the oven I must see to."

"Now you hold on a minute, sugar." The instant she saw how her struggles amused him, Tasiya forced herself to relax. Her quick concession to his will wiped away his grin. "I'm trying to pay you a compliment. I want you to clear these things from the table and bring me another piece of that delicious pie."

"There is no more pie."

His grip tightened, demanding she look at him. "I don't like that answer."

"It is the truth. You have eaten everything I prepared."

"Then prepare some more."

Tasiya shook her head. "But the time..." She pointed to the open kitchen door. "The bread I have baked for the prisoners will burn."

Marcus stood up. Towering over her, he bellowed his fetid breath in her face. "Who the hell cares about them?"

His commander did.

"Mr. Fowler's instructions were to feed them every night. To help them keep their strength—"

"Yeah, yeah, I know all that. He wants them alive, but they don't have to be healthy. You take care of all our needs first. And then you can feed whatever the hell you want to those traitors." He pinched her arm. "Are we clear on that?"

Tasiya bowed her head. "Yes."

He released her and threw his hands up in the air as if reprimanding her had taxed his patience. "Now get this mess cleaned up and don't defy me again."

For a moment Tasiya couldn't stem her temper or find her courage. She opened her mouth, but the right words wouldn't come.

It was a moment long enough for Marcus to shove his plate into her empty hand and swat her rump to speed her toward the kitchen. "Tomorrow night, know that I'm expecting two desserts."

She stumbled over her own feet in her hurry to put as much distance between her and Marcus Smith as possible. Temporarily beyond the sight of that big baboon, she dumped the dishes into the sink and ran cool water over a towel. Angry beyond words, feeling frustrated and helpless, she could do nothing more but silently curse Marcus and Dimitri Mostek. She was trapped by her love for her father in a completely horrible mess in which she had no one to rely on but herself.

Patting the towel across her flushed face and holding it against her nape beneath the French knot of her hair was the only comfort she could give herself, the only outlet for the feelings she couldn't express. She allowed herself five minutes of relative privacy. Time enough to shut off the ovens and let her temper cool along with the loaves of bread. Time enough to fix her emotionless mask back into place, pick up a plastic tub and return to the dining room to begin clearing the tables.

The smells of tobacco and liquor stung her nose as some of the men lit cigarettes and doctored their coffee from flasks in their pockets. A few headed out into the breezeway or checked the pistols at their sides and returned to their posts. Those remaining went back to trading stories, plotting strategies and ignoring her as she worked.

"Hey, listen to this, Marcus. We're on the radio." A short, stocky man she knew only as Ike shushed the room when he turned up the reporter's voice on his battery-powered radio.

"The nationwide manhunt continues for the eight prisoners who escaped from The Fortress prison in Montana where, like Alcatraz, escape was once thought to be impossible. The man believed to have spearheaded the prison break, Boone Fowler, the reputed leader of the Montana Militia for a Free America, is also sought as a suspect in a recent nerve gas incident at the Big Sky Galleria mall..."

"We're famous."

"Is the boss hearing this?"

"They'll never find us here."

"Shut up. I want to listen." Marcus silenced the men.

Tasiya began quietly stacking and clearing dishes from the tables to hide how intently, she, too, was listening to the American news report. "In other news, Crown Prince Nikolai of Lukinburg—at a speech in Kalispell, Montanta—spoke of his gratitude to the American government and its people for their support in helping to bring peace and prosperity back to his country."

After a crackle of applause, she heard the familiar, cultured voice of the man who would defy his king and father to save the country she loved from ruin. "Kalispell, Montana is quite delightful in November. It's almost as pretty and picturesque as Ryanavik Mountain in my nation, Lukinburg. Can you envision the same…"

Tasiya paused with a handful of silverware, frowning at the eloquent oratory. Ryanavik was the name of a lake outside St. Feodor, not a mountain. A native of her homeland would never make such a mistake in geography. Was Prince Nikolai taking poetic license to create an analogy pleasing to the Americans? She dropped the silverware into a mug and reached for the wad of paper napkins at the center of the table. But Lukinburg had so many beautiful mountains, why not—

"Turn that damn crap off!"

Boone Fowler stormed into the dining hall, picked up Ike's radio and hurled it across the room. It hit the stone wall and shattered, silencing Prince Nikolai and any protest from the men in the room.

Like the others, Tasiya froze. Her heart, thumping against the walls of her chest, was the only sound she could hear.

With the pinkie of his left hand, Fowler brushed aside a stringy lock of hair that had fallen across his forehead. But as calm and controlled as that tiny movement was, there was nothing soft or gentle about him as he paced the length of the room. "You men are getting weak and lax. Basking in your own glory. We are fighting for our country, not ourselves. Our campaign is not about our egos and making the news. This is about the truth that I have taught you again and again."

"America for Americans," Ike mumbled dutifully.

Fowler braced his hands at his hips and nodded, slowly turning to make eye contact with each man in the room. "America for Americans," he articulated through the clench of his jaw. "I've trained you all to be better men than this. I've trained you to believe in the cause as much as you believe in me."

He reached out and put a hand on Ike's shoulder. Tasiya, clutching the trash from the table to her chest to hide her own trembling hands, didn't for one second believe Fowler's contact was meant to be a comforting, fatherly gesture. Yet Ike looked up into his leader's black eyes as though receiving wisdom and reassurance from a saint. "I believe in you, sir."

Fowler nodded, then stepped away. "I've devised a plan we must follow to the letter. I've given you orders and I expect them to be obeyed. I haven't let you down yet, have I? I showed you the truth about how our government is betraying our citizens, I gave you something to fight for. Is there any room in that plan to bask in personal accomplishments?"

"No, sir." The timid responses echoed across the room.

Fowler turned. "Is there?"

"No, sir!" they answered with more force.

"America for Americans!" one man shouted. He repeated the slogan and others joined in. Soon they were clapping their hands and pounding on the tables. Tasiya never felt more isolated and unwelcome in the world than she did when the chant reached a feverish pitch.

But as a nervous sweat broke out across the back of her neck and chilled her spine, Boone Fowler seemed to relax. A smile sliced across his thin beard, though the satisfaction never warmed his eyes.

This impromptu rally for their patriotic cause was not unlike the protests in support of King Aleksandr in her own country. But if anyone dared voice a dissenting opinion against king or crowd, the state police would show up. Or else minions like Dimitri Mostek and his security force would pay a more-private visit after the fact.

These men were afraid of their leader. And he'd used that fear to brainwash them into obeying him.

If this was democracy, it was truly a frightening thing.

"Marcus."

"Sir." Marcus jumped to Fowler's side.

The cheers began to fade and were replaced by excited chatter. Tasiya laid the napkins in the tub and tried to make as little noise as possible sliding the chairs back into place.

"I have the prisoners' speeches written for the video. I want an update on your progress with them today," Fowler ordered. "Report to my office in twenty minutes."

"Yes, sir."

Fowler turned to the hapless Ike who was already on his feet, with his shoulders back and his chin tipped up at attention. "I want you to go to the communications center and doublecheck the accuracy of the wire I just received."

"But Simmons is on duty, sir."

"Don't argue with me. I want your expertise to verify it."

"Yes, sir." Ike scooted out the door, pulling out a ring of keys as he disappeared into the breezeway.

"The rest of you—I want a complete sweep of the island. Check every inch of the security grid. I want to know if so much as a pelican has breached the perimeter today."

A chorus of 'Yes, sir' and the scramble of feet and chairs left Tasiya standing alone at the center of the room.

"And you—" She flinched when Boone Fowler

pointed straight at her, yanking her from anonymity into the spotlight. "Bring me coffee in my office. Black. And plenty of it."

"Yes, sir." She needed no excuse to linger. Propping the loaded tub on her hip, she turned and hurried out to the kitchen where she dumped out the dregs and started a fresh pot. But she could still hear Fowler talking to Marcus Smith.

"I need to know if any of the prisoners have made contact with anyone on the outside."

"Impossible, sir. The bounty hunters aren't even allowed contact with each other."

"Good. Now here's what I want you to do."

Apparently, the two men had left the room. Tasiya could hear nothing now but the silence of just how alone she was.

She glanced quickly at her watch. If she hurried, by the time the coffee was done brewing she could make her call to Dimitri about the executions and Prince Nikolai's speech, along with what she'd gathered about Boone Fowler escaping from prison and orchestrating some sort of terrorist attack in Montana. Hearing her father's voice would replenish her strength and give her the courage to venture into Fowler's office and face the man one on one.

Fifteen minutes later, Tasiya had to bite the inside of her lips to keep her nerves from screaming out as she carried a tray into Boone Fowler's upstairs office.

Dimitri had denied her the chance to speak to her father. Whether the excuse that Anton was asleep was the truth or a lie hardly mattered. She'd been denied the one thing that could sustain her through this hellish sentence of servitude. Now she was left to wonder and worry if her father was all right. Had Dimitri's men harmed him? Was he locked up the way those poor prisoners here on Devil's Fork Island were?

Dimitri's compliment on her ability to ferret out detailed information had done nothing to boost her morale. And she couldn't very well tell him how Marcus's unwanted advances angered her or how Boone Fowler's temper frightened her. If Dimitri learned that his prize mistress had been soiled in any way, he might take his disappointment out on her father.

So Tasiya's goal was to slip into Fowler's office, set the tray on his desk and disappear just as quickly as she came in.

But this just wasn't her night.

Fowler must have seen her reflection in the glass as he leaned against his office window and gazed out into the moonlit sky. "Pour for me."

Tasiya hesitated for a moment before setting the tray down next to a wrinkled sheet of paper that looked as if it had been crushed into a tight ball, then spread out flat and smoothed back into shape. She could do this. She'd fixed a full meal for thirty men and served them in two shifts without a mishap until Marcus Smith got her in his sights. Boone Fowler didn't care about such things, certainly not with her.

Drying her nervous palms on the legs of her jeans, Tasiya asked. "You said black?"

"Yes."

She picked up the mug and the steaming pot. As she poured, her gaze strayed to the words on the page that had been discarded, then reclaimed. It looked like some sort of press release. The wire he'd mentioned to Ike? Is this what had Fowler so upset?

"Cameron Murphy released from Montana hospital. Bounty hunter expected to make full, if lengthy, recovery. Timing critical."

Bounty hunter? Like Bryce Martin and the other three prisoners she'd heard the militiamen talking about?

Who was Cameron Murphy? The timing for what?

"Can you read that?"

Tasiya gasped, startled by Boone Fowler's voice behind her. She quickly set down the coffeepot and gripped the mug with both hands before she spilled something. But the warmth that seeped into her fingers couldn't dissipate the chill of being caught poking her nose in where it wasn't welcome.

She uttered the first lie she could think of. "It helps my English to read."

"You didn't answer my question." He breathed his suspicion against the back of her neck.

The coffee in the mug splashed up the sides as she started to shake. His brand of intimidation was even more frightening than Marcus's ranting threats. "I can read the words, but they do not all make sense."

She had to get out of here. She spun toward him. "Here's your coff—"

But he was already stepping around her. "Maybe if you stuck to your own—"

Her hands smacked against his chest. The coffee sloshed over her fingers, scalding them. Her grip popped open and the mug crashed to the floor, splintering on contact. The hot liquid splashed Fowler's jeans and spilled over his boots.

Tasiya gaped at the spreading stain, soaking into suede and denim. "I'm sorry. I'll get another cup. A towel." The man was too still. This was too dangerous. She looked up into the cold void of his eyes and knew she was in trouble. "I am sorry."

"You…stupid…" She tried to retreat, but her hips hit the desk. She turned, grabbed the paper napkin off the tray and squatted at his feet to sop up what she could. He never touched her, but his words were like a slap across the face. "Get up. Get away from me."

Tasiya lurched to her feet, but he cornered her against the desk, preventing her from doing the very thing he asked. "Please."

"Please what?" She squinted her eyes against the foul words he slung at her. "I don't owe you any favors. You're a clumsy foreigner poisoning the land

I love. Your incompetence reminds me of every foul, stinking reason I have to do what I do." He snatched the napkin from her fingers. "Now get out of my face! Go! Get out!"

Shuffling to the side, Tasiya scooted away. As soon as she was clear of the desk, she turned and ran.

His threats chased her out the door. "That's right, you witch. Run. Run!"

"Hey, sugar. What's your hurry?"

She didn't bother sliding to a halt as Marcus Smith emerged at the top of the stairs in front of her. She shifted directions to run right past him. "Leave me alone."

But his bear-size paw latched on to her wrist and hauled her up to his level. "Now that ain't nice—"

"Don't touch me!"

Tasiya jerked her arm away. Her hand flew back and hit the wall, scraping knuckles against stone and shooting a jolt of pain straight up to her elbow.

The sharp ache cleared the fog of panic that had consumed her long enough to shove Marcus aside and dart down the spiral staircase.

"Hey—"

"Marcus!"

Boone Fowler's summons kept Marcus from pursuing her. But Tasiya didn't stop running until she reached the relative security of her tiny room off the kitchen. She unfurled the blanket she'd hung across the opening, sank onto her bed and hugged her pillow to her stomach. Burying her face in the pillow's muffling softness, she screamed until her throat was raw and her energy was spent.

She was less than a human being in this place. Without kindness. Without security. Without respect.

By the time she could think clearly again, she looked at the clock. It was going on eight o'clock. She had seventeen hungry prisoners to feed.

Men who'd been chained, caged, tortured, beaten. Men who might be executed on Marcus Smith's whim.

It was empathy, more than duty, compassion or even fear, that finally prompted her to rise to her feet and dry her eyes. Tasiya straightened her bed, re-pinned her hair and walked into the kitchen with a determined stride. She fixed an unsmiling mask on her lips and buried her emotions in the deepest hole she could find.

She was a prisoner, too.

Only, her chains were the greed and lust of powerful men. Her cage was the deal she'd made with the devil to save her father's life.

Chapter Four

Bryce's hands stopped their diligent work as he tipped his head to listen to the food cart clanking over the uneven stones in the passageway.

She was coming.

That better not be his pulse rate kickin' into a higher gear. Bryce's sigh of self-disgust ached against his tenderized rib muscles and stirred the plaster dust at the base of the window. He had to move past this fascination with the woman. He had to focus.

But he'd been thinking about Tasiya's visit all day long. He'd thought about that silky waterfall of raven-colored hair when Marcus and his thugs had him chained in the interrogation room, pointing out every antique torture device they could use on him before resorting to good old-fashioned fists. He'd thought about those dark, exotic eyes instead of reading the standard hostage script Marcus had pushed in front of his face.

Even now he could close his eyes and remember

the normal, out-of-place scents of cooking and coffee that had clung to her skin and clothes.

There was something racing through his veins he couldn't control. An excitement. Anticipation. It made him itchy inside his own skin.

Man, wasn't this a disturbing development?

It wasn't like this was a date. It was only dinner. Hell, it was scarcely that.

When he heard Tasiya's cart round the corner, his years of training were the only thing to rouse Bryce's survival instincts enough to brush away the loose plaster at the window. He'd been digging with the iron brace around his wrist so he blew away the telltale bits that had collected there, too. Then he used his toes to cover his tracks by nudging the dust out of sight into the cracks in the floor.

He rolled the stiffness from his neck and turned to face the bars of his cage.

Escape.

He forced the word into his brain, forced the memories and reactions out of his system. He put himself firmly in the moment and completely focused on the task at hand.

His goal was to get her to take a message to one of the other bounty hunters. Powell or Campbell or O'Riley could strike up a conversation with her. They were smart enough to see that she might be the key to getting out of here, too.

If he could get her to take a message.

But Tasiya Belov wasn't in the mood for talking.

Bryce frowned. Something about her was different tonight. Not just the elegant way she'd swept all that hair up onto the back of her head. Not the jeans she wore that looked just as feminine against the willowy curves of her body as the conservative sweater and skirt she'd worn last night.

Nah, this was something in her posture. There was a brittleness to her carefully precise movements as she set aside the flashlight that had guided her here, wrapped the bread and poured a cup of water from her pitcher. He saw a blankness in her expression that he recognized from battlefields—from Maria, stranded in the middle of that San Ysidran minefield with mortar shells winging her way, bringing certain death.

Fear.

Helpless, paralyzing fear that could only be dealt with by denying the expression of *any* emotion.

Son of a bitch.

What had happened to her? Bryce drifted forward, forgetting for a moment that he might be the cause of that fear.

Tasiya froze. Her gaze careened from the cup she was setting on the floor to his feet inside the cell. Bryce stopped in his tracks.

He retreated, and she slowly stood and turned his way.

She wasn't making eye contact. Instead she stared

at the middle of his chest. But he had a feeling she wasn't seeing the old scars or the new bruises.

She wasn't seeing him at all.

"You okay?" The deep, rusty sound of his voice startled him almost more than it startled her.

Tasiya blinked, and a spark of light and focus gave her eyes life as she raised her gaze to his. She hugged herself, rubbing her hands up and down her arms as if she'd just woken up from a troubling dream and didn't quite know where she was. "You do not say much, do you?"

Not an answer, but at least she was talking. "Nope."

"The other prisoners...say more."

"I reckon."

She tilted her head at an angle and squinted, drawing a fine line of confusion above the bridge of her nose. *"Reckon?* I do not know that word."

Maybe that's all this was. She was having a little trouble with the language, misunderstanding things, feeling isolated—homesick, even—by the frustrating process of learning to communicate in a foreign language.

And he thought he could draft her as a messenger?

That's when Bryce saw the knuckles of her right hand against her pale-blue sweater. The porcelain skin was swollen and discolored with darkening blotches of deep purple and violet.

The blood in Bryce's veins steamed. Her distance tonight wasn't about words at all. "Who hurt you?"

Tasiya glanced down at her hand, as if embarrassed or frightened that he had seen it. She quickly tucked the betraying appendage beneath her arm, out of sight. "I hit it against a wall."

She must have punched the wall pretty damn hard.

Or somebody had punched it for her.

A protective anger churned inside his stomach. It had always been this way for him. If somebody was hurtin' and he could help them... Well, hell, what else was a big brute like him good for?

His grandma had said that soft spot of his would always keep him human, no matter what the world threw at him. Seemed like it never caused him anything but trouble, though. It complicated things when they should be simple, like telling Tasiya to ask the other bounty hunters whether or not they were being beaten every day in the same interrogation room.

That alone should be enough of a clue to let them know his condition, a bit of the militia's routine and get them to start comparing notes about the prison's schedule and layout. Plus, it would get them to thinking about striking up a relationship with Tasiya so that she might willingly—or without knowing it—aid them in an escape attempt.

But this wasn't simple. A woman getting hurt while he was around didn't sit right with him. Even chained up in a damn cage, he couldn't bring himself to use Tasiya the way he needed to.

Not when somebody else was already using her.

He'd have to move on to plan C or D, or whatever letter of the alphabet it took until he could find a way out of this place with every bounty hunter and surviving Special Forces soldier in one piece. Maybe he could devise a plan that might even help Tasiya. He shook the thought out of his head and tried to focus on his own mission again—get the hell out of here and take down Boone Fowler and his militia in the process. But it was too late. He'd already passed into complicated territory.

Tasiya retreated to the far side of her cart as Bryce crossed to the bars to pick up his bread and water. He needed to eat and drink and send her on her way before he started thinking crazy things and making foolish promises.

But his grandma had known Bryce better than he knew himself. He sat on his cot, demolished the bread in a few bites. Then he washed it down with the water and said, "You get into any kind of trouble, come see me and I'll do what I can to help."

Bryce let the words fall into silence. They drifted across the moonlit shadows to the woman whose eyes gleamed like polished mahogany against the pallor of her skin.

Their gazes locked through the ghostly moonlight—hers, seeking, searching, disbelieving...his, merely stating a fact.

Finally Tasiya released a deep, perplexed sigh.

She smoothed her palms against the denim at her thighs, steeled her posture and walked up to the bars that separated them. That tiny line of confusion that added dimension to her beauty was back in place as she wrapped her fingers around the bars and leaned in. "Why would you want to help me, when your enemy shows you no mercy?"

Interesting. She wasn't interested in how a man in chains could help her, but *why* he'd want to. Bryce stayed put, respecting her caution, admiring her courage. "You my enemy?"

She considered the question for several moments. "I do not know. You do not feel like an enemy. But it is not wise to trust in this place."

"Nope." She was being smart. There wasn't a man in this compound who didn't have an ulterior motive, himself included. Hell, he hadn't yet figured out why she was here on the island. He licked the crumbs from his fingers and rose to his feet. After stuffing the napkin inside the mug, he held it out to her and explained, "Helpin' folks is what I do."

She wrapped her fingers around the mug, linking them together even though they never touched. "You have a funny way of speaking, Bryce Martin."

Like calling him by his first and last name wasn't an odd way to talk?

But her serene smile hit him like a punch to the solar plexus, and for a moment he forgot how to breathe, much less take offense. God, she was beautiful when she smiled. As though a light went on inside her and spilled over into his dark world.

Bringing a smile to her strained expression made him less self-conscious about his hillfolk drawl, less guarded about his fearsome appearance, less aware of the band of keys on her arm that were so easily within his reach.

But before Bryce could move past that awkward, adolescent rush of pleasure and take advantage of her trusting proximity, his stomach interrupted. A deep, low-pitched rumble protested being teased with a snack when it was looking for a full-course meal.

Tasiya's gaze dropped down his bare torso. Her cheeks heated with color. Bryce wished Marcus Smith hadn't taken his shirt so he and his men could jeer at his deformities. He should be able to hide himself so Tasiya didn't have to see the scars, didn't have to fear the bulk of him.

He should forget about her and her safety and her smile and grab the damn keys.

But Tasiya had taken the mug and backed beyond his reach before he could reconsider.

"You are still hungry, aren't you?"

Bryce shrugged, damning that soft spot inside for caring what happened to her and complicating his escape. "I'll live."

"A few bites of bread is not enough to sustain a man your size. It is not enough to help you heal from your injuries."

The rations they'd been feeding him weren't enough to sustain *her*. "I'll get by."

She stacked the mug on her cart. But Bryce was mistaken in thinking she'd been making polite conversation. "There is dried fruit in the pantry. I could add it to the bread I bake tomorrow—to give you vitamins, a more balanced diet. There are different grains that are more filling."

He eyed her bruised hand. She wanted to defy Boone Fowler's orders? "Don't do anything that's gonna get yourself into trouble."

She nodded as if he hadn't spoken. "I will bake this bread tomorrow. For you and your comrades. To keep up your strength."

"No."

"You would help me if you could. I will help you."

"Don't do it," he warned, fearing repercussions beyond his control. "Fowler will know."

"Good night, Bryce Martin." She pushed her cart down the passageway.

"Forget about the bread. Watch your own back." Bryce yanked at the bars, wishing he could pull them apart and stop her. "Tasiya?"

But Tasiya Belov, her noisy cart and her surprising stubbornness had already disappeared around the corner.

"PAPA?"

"Daughter, it is good to hear your voice."

Anton's weary sigh concerned her. "You sound tired."

"I am fine," he reassured her. "I think they give me something in my food to make me more docile."

Tasiya released the blanket that now covered her door and paced to the far corner of the room. She'd seen no one in the kitchen eavesdropping on her, but she wouldn't risk anyone overhearing the panic that sprang into her voice. "You are not cooperating with Dimitri's men?"

He dropped his voice to a whisper she could barely hear across the miles. "I cannot stand what he has done to you. Maybe we cannot stop his bullying ways, but I do not intend to make his rule over our lives an easy one."

"Papa…" Hadn't she promised to defy Boone Fowler's bread-and-water rations order for the prisoners? It wasn't much in the way of rebellion against the rules and oppression here, but it was one little stab at independence that might keep her from going completely mad. However, hearing that her injured father might be taking a similar stand against Dimitri Mostek worried her. She hugged an arm around her stomach, but found little comfort. "You must be careful."

She'd witnessed the penalty for not cooperating with a superior here. Verbal abuse. Humiliation. Even violence. She squeezed her eyes shut and remembered the horrible welts and bruising she'd seen last night on Bryce Martin's ribs. Though they'd all been tortured in one way or another, it seemed as though he was being punished more than the other prisoners. Isolated in the last cell. Kept in the dark. And perhaps because he was able to endure more abuse, Fowler's men inflicted more.

It pained her to see such a physically able man as Bryce being hurt that way. To think of her more fragile father enduring such cruelty… "Please do everything they say. Let me take the risks, Papa. I am young and strong. I can do this. Knowing you are safe is what gets me through each day."

"Is it really so awful there?"

"It is lonely." She bit her tongue to keep from blurting out how her encounters with Boone Fowler and Marcus Smith had alternately shamed and frightened her. Anton didn't need to worry about that. "But I am fine."

"Is there no one there you can talk to?"

You get into any kind of trouble, come see me and I'll do what I can to help.

Bryce Martin wasn't exactly what she'd call a confidant. But in the dark shadows of the night, when she'd felt vulnerable and alone, when she'd ached for a kind word—for hope—he'd noticed. He hadn't said much, but the depth of his voice had resonated across every shattered nerve, calming her, grounding her. He seemed solid as a mountain to cling to, yet just as forbidding.

There was a kindness to his perceptive gray eyes that had washed over her like a gentle spring shower. A sadness, too, as though the ugly marks on his body were etched even more deeply inside.

He'd called himself a monster at their first meeting, and she'd believed him. But last night she'd seen a glimpse of the heart within the beast. And that paradox, as much as the anticipation of speaking to her father, had given her the strength to survive one more day.

But how could she explain to her father that she was drawn to such a man, and still ask him not to worry?

"I am fine, Papa," she repeated. "Do not test Minister Mostek's patience. Please."

A self-satisfied laugh grated against her ear. "Excellent advice, my dear Anastasiya."

Her father had been taken away from her again. Determined not to give verbal vent to her frustrations, Tasiya began to pace, three steps this way, three steps back. "You did not let me say goodbye to him."

"*You* should not test my patience, either," Mostek warned. "You had your chance to talk. Now tell me what Fowler and his people are up to."

She shoved her fingers into the hair at her temple, massaging the twinge of a headache that had formed the instant Dimitri returned to the line. For a moment, she considered setting the phone back on the charger and disconnecting the call. For a moment. "They talk about a video they will make next week."

"Good. They are staying on schedule. My superior will be pleased."

"Minister..." Tasiya stopped her pacing, swallowed her pride and begged. "Dimitri. There is no place I can go here. I cannot leave Mr. Fowler and his men. I promise I will still call you...but can't you let my father go free? Aren't I payment enough for his transgression?"

The silence on the telephone line worried her. When Dimitri began to speak, she worried even more. "My darling Anastasiya. While it pleases me to hear you offer yourself so freely, you must remember that this is not my decision alone. The man I work for does not overlook those who would cheat or deceive him. You should be counting your blessings that your father is still alive."

"But the king does not even know my father—"

"The *king,*" he emphasized, "has put me in charge of this project and has granted me discretion to handle it as I see fit. I will not take the chance that you would seduce one of the American infidels in order to bring about your escape. By keeping Anton close to me, I'm confident you will keep the men there at a distance."

Tasiya quietly gnawed her lip until his outburst dissipated. "I have no intention of sleeping with any man here," she stated quietly. She had no intention of sleeping with Dimitri, either. But that was another trial she would deal with when—and if—she survived this one. "Will that be all? I must attend to my duties here before I am missed."

"Tell me again about this note you read in Boone Fowler's office that upset him. I do not want him to be distracted from his purpose, either."

Though the name Cameron Murphy meant nothing to her, apparently it had some significance for Dimitri. With the clock ticking toward eight o'clock and the bile rising in her throat at every slimy innuendo from Dimitri's lips, Tasiya answered his questions. She dutifully repeated his instructions for listening to tomorrow's American news reports, ignored the kiss he blew across the line and rang off.

BRYCE STOOD ON TIPTOE in the darkness with his hand fisted around the bar at the window. He'd dug enough mortar from the base that he could twist it back and forth now, starting the painstaking process of loosening the bar from its upper mount. Removing one bar still wouldn't create a space large enough for him to crawl through to the outside, but the bar itself would give him a weapon, a tool.

The digging would go faster. He could pry himself out of these chains. He could defend himself if he got the opportunity to make a run for it.

It would give him the first advantage he'd had since getting tossed into this place.

He froze at the muffled sound of footsteps in the passageway. Ignoring the tender twinge that ached along the right side of his ribs, he breathed in deeply, silently—mentally and physically bracing himself for another visit from his captors.

Then he heard the distinct metallic clank and rattle of Tasiya's food cart bouncing across the paving stones.

Make that his second advantage.

The wary tension in Bryce's muscles eased at the familiar sound. His breath seeped out on a slow exhale and he dropped flat on his feet, brushing away and hiding the evidence of his handiwork as he turned to wait for her arrival. He was almost grinning with the keen anticipation of seeing her again. But a scratch at his whiskers on the unscarred half of his jaw gave him a sobering reminder that while her face might be a sight for weary eyes, his was not.

The rattle of metal cups and rhythmic thump and bump of the cart fell silent before she reached his cell. She'd stopped several feet away, near the turn in the passageway. Or had she been stopped?

Bryce's senses buzzed on alert, listening for some other sound in the shadows. Items moved, shifting on the cart, as though someone was searching among the napkins and baskets. Son of a bitch. He clenched his hands into fists and crossed to the door of his cell, wishing he was a super hero so he could pull the bars apart and go help her.

"Tasiya?" he whispered, so softly that his voice was swallowed up by the shadows.

If Fowler or Smith or some other yahoo had stopped her…if they suspected she'd used their rations to feed more to the prisoners, that she was doing something kind for him…if they'd chosen a dark corner so far removed from the rest of the prison that no one could hear her scream …

He heard a soft gasp. The grind of metal. The tinkling shatter of delicate glass breaking. A word in another language he could only describe as a curse.

"Tasiya!" His voice boomed off the rock walls. Hell. Let Fowler's men make a connection between them. If she was getting into trouble, then it was *his* fault. They should punish *him*. "Tasiya?"

He peered into the darkness, unable to make sense of the moving shapes. And then a sharp pain pierced his retinas. He had to blink and turn away as an unexpected light flooded the hallway.

After so many days and nights in relative darkness, the artificial light reflected off the smooth stone walls, filling the space in front of his cell with a cold, harsh glare.

But when the reassuring thump of the cart resumed, Bryce shaded his eyes with his hand and forced himself to look. It wasn't that bright, really, but it took several moments for his eyes to adjust before he focused in on Tasiya, wearing jeans and the long, cream-colored sweater she'd worn the night of their first encounter. She appeared to be alone, unharmed—and well beyond arm's reach.

Bryce's concern for her petered out on a resigned sigh. He was still standing at the cell door. He'd been imagining the worst, frantic to get to her, to save her from whatever had gotten its hands on her. But *he* was still the monster she feared.

A little frisson of useless resentment fired through his blood. He looked beyond her to the lone lightbulb, weakly shining from its mount at the end of the passageway. He purposely challenged the caution in her eyes by wrapping his fingers around the bars and staying put.

"I thought someone was after you."

Loose black curls danced across her face as she turned to glance over her shoulder, just now realizing how her scuffling sounds in the darkness and the clumsiness of a broken lightbulb might sound. She quickly turned back to him and tucked one of those curls behind her ear. "I am all right, Bryce Martin," she stated. "Even Mr. Fowler would not begrudge me a light to illuminate my path."

Bryce continued to lean against the bars, and Tasiya still kept her distance. But his resentment was gradually replaced by acceptance. It had always been this way, and Tasiya's misgivings about him weren't gonna go away just because he seemed to be developing an overzealous sense of protection where she was concerned.

She looked mighty pleased with herself over changing a lightbulb. And while that added bit of confidence was a welcome change to the fear that had haunted her expression last night, Bryce felt compelled to remind her of the risk she had taken, and the danger she might be in as a result.

"You ever think maybe they want to keep me in the dark?"

"Yes."

Startled by the bluntness of her reply, Bryce looked deep into her eyes. Hell. She was dead serious. She got the whole torture thing. Maybe she wasn't as naive about the dangers surrounding them here as he'd originally thought.

"Well," he released the bars and retreated, giving her the distance she needed, "it doesn't bother me none."

As soon as he moved, Tasiya began assembling his meal. "It should bother you. It is wrong for one man to have so much power over another. You have no shirt, no blanket, no shoes. They treat you as if you are..."

She pinched her lips together, searching for the right word. But Bryce could translate for her. "Not human?"

Her pitying gaze locked onto his and she nodded. She set his bread and water on the floor and backed away. Bryce rattled forward like the ghost of Jacob Marley in Dickens's *A Christmas Carol,* dragging his chains along with him. They were a visual and aural reminder of the burdens he carried through life, a reminder that Fowler and Smith—and even Tasiya, with her reluctance to get too close—saw him more as a monster than a man.

But it wasn't a topic he cared to discuss at the moment, despite the polite need to apologize he could see dancing through Tasiya's shifting feet and the stricken expression in her eyes. Pity was an emotion that had never done him any good. He'd rather deal with her fear, or have her ignore him altogether, than waste his limited emotional expertise trying to ease the guilt of someone who pitied the way he looked or was treated.

So, Bryce silently retrieved his meal and settled on his cot. He broke apart the crusty loaf and saw that, true to her word, Tasiya had added some wheat bran to the processed flour, and filled the inside with moist red and blue bits his nose quickly identified as cranberries and blueberries.

But even if he was done talkin', Tasiya had more to say. "In my country, they treat political prisoners this way. The king would break down his people's spirits so that they do not complain about poverty or the bullying police. We are not allowed to speak out or better ourselves unless we..." Her voice and gaze trailed away to a distant place, and Bryce wondered if she was remembering some event in particular or if this was a philosophical argument. "In Lukinburg I could not even have this conversation with you. If someone heard me say these things..."

"No one can hear us back here." On his short walks from his cell to the interrogation room and back, he hadn't passed any occupied rooms or cells, so there was no one around to eavesdrop. He'd heard the hum of generators through layers of walls and locked doors. But whatever they were running on all that power, it wasn't listening devices or video cameras. Security at this end of the compound, at any rate, was all iron and stone, without one high-tech doodad in sight. "Say what you want. I won't tell."

"Is that why they beat you?" she asked, in a soft, hesitant voice. "To get you to tell them things?"

"I won't tell," he reiterated, closing the subject. If he could keep Big Sky secrets, he could keep hers, too.

He pressed his nose to the bread's soft interior and savored the rich aromas. His grandma would have served it slathered in butter or honey or both. But he didn't feel he'd been deprived of anything when he sank his teeth into the first delicious, crunchy, chewy bite. He moaned in his throat at the first real flavor that had enriched his life since he'd been taken prisoner.

He opened his eyes and sought Tasiya's gaze. This he could discuss. "You made this?"

She nodded and drifted closer to the bars that separated them. "I am a cook in my home country."

Bryce took another bite. "You're a damn good one."

"Thank you."

He had to look away and concentrate on the second half of his bread. If she smiled that prettily at one lame compliment from him, just think what she might do if a more charming man plied her with a bunch of the right words. Thoughts of escape, ever present in his consciousness, surged to the front of his mind. How would she respond if *he* could come up with the right words?

"Anybody give you any grief over doctorin' up the recipe?"

She wrapped her fingers around the bars and leaned closer. He could see they were long and dexterous fingers, blunt tipped and businesslike in their practical elegance. He could also see she hadn't quite gotten his question. "I am not sad to do this for you. I enjoy preparing food."

"No, I meant..." Bryce gave up on that line of discussion. "I appreciate you doin' it."

She rested her cheek against the steel bar and smiled again. "You like to eat?"

Two hundred forty pounds of muscle and bulk wasn't an obvious indication? "It's one of my favorite pastimes."

That line of confusion furrowed between her eyebrows.

Pastimes. Yeah, this was goin' real well. Communication was so not his area of expertise. He rubbed his palm over the scars and stubble of his jaw, searching for a simpler way to rephrase. "My grandma was an excellent cook. I enjoy it when I find food as good as hers."

"Your grandmother was a cook?" That seemed to interest her.

He nodded. "Not a professional. But we ate better than just about anybody in the Ozarks."

"The what?" He'd lost her again. "Oze…?"

Yeah, right. Try explaining the bastardization of a French Arcadian word about a tribe of Indians to a woman who spoke whatever Russian dialect it was they spoke in Lukinburg.

Time to change the subject if he was ever going to get this messenger thing to work. He popped the last bite into his mouth and picked up his mug. "So what brings you to this place? Is there some kind of trouble at home you're trying to get away from? Can't be much better in this place. I know Fowler doesn't cotton much to foreigners."

"Cotton much?"

She shrugged, narrowing her eyes in a quizzical frown. Her stiff, self-conscious posture pulled her sweater taut and thrust the curve of one small breast between the bars. Of course, he had to notice that. Too damned observant for his own good. Look away, Sarge, he warned himself as his blood thickened and pooled behind his zipper as if she was dressed to seduce and that innocent movement had been some sort of intentional come-on.

Closing his eyes to break the spell she seemed to

cast over him, Bryce stood up to get his common sense circulating again. "I wouldn't think he'd want a woman around here."

"He doesn't mind if I am serving him."

Bryce swallowed the last of his water in one long gulp, doubting if Boone Fowler made any distinction between a servant and a woman who was subservient to his needs. "So what does a gig like this pay?"

"Gig." The line between her eyes deepened. "I do not understand."

Shaking his head, Bryce turned away. He was getting as frustrated with the language barrier as she was. But, refusing to surrender just because a task was tough, he faced her again. "How much money does he pay you to work for him?"

"Money?"

"You know what money is, right?"

"I know." Her porcelain cheeks flushed with color. Her eyes were looking everywhere but at him now. "He does not pay me."

Since he doubted she shared Fowler's fanatical views on American isolationism, and she wasn't in it for the money, that left only a handful of reasons why Tasiya could be here—and none of them were good. Bryce moved imperceptibly closer. "Why *are* you here?"

The question had her so agitated she forgot about keeping her distance from him. "I am paying off a debt."

He slipped even closer. He could smell the scents of baked bread and spices that clung to her hair and clothes.

He could smell the fear on her, too.

"What do you owe Fowler? What the hell business does he have in Lukinburg?"

She snatched the mug from his grip and spun toward her cart. "I have to go."

Uh-uh.

"Tasiya." Bryce reached through the bars and grabbed her wrist.

She jumped at his touch, turned back and tugged and twisted for her freedom. "Let go!"

He wasn't hurting her, but he needed her to stay and answer the question. "Just hold your horses. Please."

Then, just as abruptly as a light switch flipping off, she went still and dropped her gaze down to his belly button. Though there was such a determined lack of focus in her eyes that he was sure she wasn't looking at the abs or the bruises. It was a practiced pose of submission, as if she'd responded that way to a man's touch a dozen times before.

Ah, hell. He liked this response even less than her eagerness to get away from him.

Bryce's big hand easily spanned her arm beneath her sleeve. His sensitive fingers noted that her skin was as cool and velvety soft as it looked. And the pulse beating beneath his fingertips raced with a madness that belied her distant, aloof posture.

"Tasiya," he whispered, giving her arm a gentle nudge. "Look at me." Long, tense seconds passed before her shoulders lifted with a trembling sigh and she tipped her chin. Curling black tendrils fell away from her pale cheeks as she blinked her eyes into focus. "I'm not going to hurt you. I know it looks like I could, but I wouldn't do that."

She tried to latch on to something she saw in his eyes, but couldn't quite bring herself to make that leap of faith. However, her wide, unadorned lips moved with a succinct articulation that could be understood in any language. "I am not supposed to be touched."

Bryce instantly popped his grip open, releasing her. He took a step back, holding his hands up in apology. He imagined his questioning frown only added a fearsome quality to his concern. "Is that your rule or somebody else's? I just wanted you to finish the conversation. I wasn't puttin' the moves on you."

She understood *that* phrase well enough, judging by the sudden color that flushed her cheeks. But she didn't answer the question. She was suddenly too busy organizing the empty mugs and baskets on her cart and wheeling it around.

"I am sorry. The hour is late. I must clean up and get to bed. They require that I prepare breakfast quite early." Now that he'd let her go, she'd forced a brightness into her tone and pasted a taut smile on her mouth. But at least she had the guts to look him in the eye as she prattled on. "For Mr. Fowler's men, unfortunately. I am sorry to mention food when I know you are hungry. I will see what else I can bring you tomorrow. Perhaps a shirt and socks as well. It is cold here at night."

"Forget all that. Just do me a favor, will ya?"

Man, she was ready to bolt. He suspected years of polite good breeding and fear of drawing more attention to her obvious discomfort were the only things still keeping her here. "If I can."

"Check on my buddies for me. Jacob Powell. Craig O'Riley. Aidan Campbell. Tell 'em I'm okay—"

She frowned and looked straight at the puffy, fist-size bruise on his rib cage. "But you are not."

"Tell 'em I'm okay," he insisted. "Find out how they're doin'. Just tell 'em Sarge asked."

"Should I not tell them the truth?"

She could say whatever she wanted, just so long as she got one of them talking. "I've been hurt worse than this. Trust me."

Tasiya paused at those last two words, considering them, and then—though it didn't surprise him—dismissing them.

"Good night, Bryce Martin."

And then she was gone. A noisy, graceful wraith with ebony hair, a compassionate heart and a truckload of fear and distrust balanced on her narrow shoulders.

Bryce scrubbed his hand across his jaw, damning his body's interest and his conscience's concern over her. He'd been in this medieval island hell for over a week now. He should be concentrating on nothing else but finding a means to escape, or a way to contact his colleagues at Big Sky Bounty Hunters in Montana so they could mount a rescue.

But no, he stood in the gloom of a cell made a little more bearable by the unexpected kindness of a single lightbulb, and inhaled the sweet, womanly smells that still clung to his hand from where he'd touched her.

"Son of a bitch." Tasiya wasn't the only thing he'd touched.

The sentimental aura vanished. Bryce blew out a disgusted sigh and called himself every sorry name in the book. He'd had his hand on her keys... the keys to his freedom. Forget about trying to communicate and using her as a messenger. If he'd been thinking straight—if he'd been thinking with his head instead of other, more easily distracted parts of his anatomy—he'd have snatched them off her wrist.

But no, he was a dope with a soft spot who'd let an opportunity to escape slip through his fingers. Literally.

With no one to blame but himself for the sentence of another night in this cell, he returned to his tedious work at the window. Tasiya Belov better get interested in conversing with one of the other men.

Because he was gettin' a mite too interested in these late-night chats himself.

Chapter Five

"Mr. Fowler, you gotta hear this!"

Tasiya dodged out of the way as Ike rushed past her into Boone Fowler's office. Wearing headphones, wires and antennae, the short, squatty man reminded her of a trained chimp who'd been readied for a launch into outer space.

But Tasiya didn't laugh at the humorous picture Ike made as he set up an old military-emblemed box loaded with buttons and knobs on the edge of the desk. She hadn't allowed herself the luxury of laughter since her father had been taken hostage. And the only time she'd given in to so much as a smile had been late at night in the farthest corner of Boone Fowler's pirate-prison-turned-militia-camp. In the private shadows, where a quiet, battered man spoke in funny phrases, and where the kindness of his eyes offered a respite from the trials of her day.

As always, in the four days that had passed since the night she'd changed the lightbulb, when her thoughts turned to Bryce Martin, she felt combative urges of dread and anticipation.

She was saddened that he'd been so horribly disfigured, and a little afraid of whatever unknown events had scarred him so. He was hurt and cold and hungry, and she could do so little to help him. More than that, she felt guilty because she had to lie. He'd been so endearingly sweet, trying to carry on a real conversation with her, hinting at a grandmother he loved and an appreciation for simple pleasures. Even when she'd felt stupid and frustrated, not comprehending his American slang, he hadn't given up on trying to communicate with her.

But then everything had taken a personal turn. He wanted reasons why she was here, truths that could only get her or her father killed. She couldn't tell him about her double life as a slave and a spy. She couldn't be his friend. He couldn't be her confessor. Those desires were too dangerous to even contemplate.

But as much as she needed to keep her distance from that formidable strength, as much as she feared that his odd, deep-pitched voice could trick her into revealing more than she should, as much as she knew that trusting the wrong man—trusting any man—could be fatal, Tasiya still wanted to get closer to him.

Tightening her fists around the broom in her hands, she swept the dirt out of the cracks beside the office door. But she couldn't sweep aside the uncomfortable realization she'd made about herself.

When Bryce Martin had reached beyond the confines of his cell and touched her, she'd been startled. For a moment, that had been Dimitri Mostek's hand on her. Or Marcus Smith's. She'd been repulsed. Afraid.

But then the difference in his touch had registered. The surprising restraint of all that muscle power binding her wrist had stunned her. She'd known the oddest sensation of comfort. His grip, though unbreakable, had been as gentle as the cool refuge in his wintry eyes.

Tasiya closed her eyes and breathed deeply, remembering how she'd felt something seductive in the casual stroke of his thumb against her pulse. For a few brief moments, Tasiya Belov had been a real woman—with thoughts, choices, freedom, desire. And she'd wanted nothing more than to squeeze her way through those bars and be wrapped up by all of Bryce Martin—to sink into his warmth, to be surrounded by his strength, to be shielded by the deep understanding of life, danger and hardship that branded his skin.

"Should she be here, boss? This is business."

Blinking her eyes open at Ike's accusatory question, Tasiya quickly resumed her be-neither-seen-nor-heard posture. She swept the dirt into a dust pan and dumped it into the trash beside the desk. Then, picking up the trash can and gathering her cleaning supplies, she hurried to the door, intending to slip out and leave them to their secrets.

But Fowler snapped his fingers. "Foreigner. Wait."

Tasiya turned and dipped her chin, avoiding eye contact the way she'd learned he preferred after a week on Devil's Fork Island. "Yes, sir?"

He rose and circled his desk, crossing to take the trash can from her hand. "I want to inspect this before you leave, in case you're trying to steal anything."

Tasiya's feathers ruffled beneath her sweater. But she chewed the inside of her lip to keep her indignant response to herself. What could she possibly want to take away from this place? A rifle or pistol from the padlocked gun cabinet? Sure, she'd stand a real chance of breaking in and escaping against thirty armed militiamen. Was he worried she'd abscond with one of the hateful diatribes she'd seen him penning at his desk? Even if she wanted a souvenir, she couldn't take it. She could barely move the furniture to sweep beneath it without his ever-watchful devil eyes boring holes of suspicion into her back.

"I have taken nothing, sir," she stated calmly. "I really should get to the kitchen to begin preparations for dinner."

"You'll leave when I tell you to."

"Sir?" Ike urged. "The radio? It's broadcasting now."

"Put it on speaker," Fowler ordered. He stared

down at her a few moments longer. "You can dust in here until I'm ready to dismiss you."

She'd done that before she'd swept. But she knew this was more about control than cleanliness. "As you wish."

"Exactly."

Leaving that word hanging in the air like the threat it was, Fowler carried the trash can back to his desk and had the gall to rifle through it. Inuring herself to the insult, Tasiya leaned her broom against the wall and pulled the dust rag from the pocket of her jeans. She went to work moving the heavy volumes of notebooks she now knew to be various maps from across the United States and dusted the clean shelf beneath them.

In the center of the room, Ike peeled off his earphones and reconnected a couple of wires. "I picked this up off an FBI comm-link first. But it's already on military bands, ham radio reports and Internet chatter. Network news will be picking it up soon."

Fowler grabbed a pencil and notepad to add to his copious notes. "Fill me in."

"News from Montana. Somebody tried to kidnap Veronika Petrov."

"Princess Veronika?" The name was out of Tasiya's mouth before she could stop it. Fair-haired Veronika Petrov was the darling of the Lukinburg people, although the king's daughter had been kept out of the spotlight, even presumably out of the country, for most of her life. "Is she all right?"

Fowler glared Tasiya back to her dusting without an answer. He turned to Ike. "You said *tried?*"

Tasiya moved the cloth across the books, but her attention was on Ike's response. "Her bodyguard was killed. But it seems some guy came out of nowhere and busted it up. He shot one of the perps outside a restaurant in Bozeman. Apparently, this good Samaritan stuffed her in his truck and took off even before the cops could get there."

Couldn't the man in the truck be the real kidnapper? A backup plan? Why would anyone attack the princess in the first place? Veronika had nothing to do with her father's politics back home, and nothing to do with her brother's rebellion here in the States.

From the corner of her eye, Tasiya saw Boone Fowler twisting the pencil between his fingers and thumb. "Let's hear it."

Ike turned a knob and the room filled with the sporadic, staticky sound of two men having an official-sounding conversation.

"...one man in custody. He's not talking. Claiming diplomatic immunity."

"And the two DOS?"

"We identified one man as her bodyguard. The other man dead on the scene fits the same description as our perp. Black hair, olive skin. No ID. But if he could talk, I bet he'd be spouting immunity in the same accent."

"So we think this is a Lukinburg plot?"

"Too soon to say. Aleksandr has a lot of enemies. Or it might be an attempt to silence the Crown Prince. Could be part of the nationalist movement—another one of those militia attacks."

"That son of a bitch." Tasiya dared a look at the growing fury in Boone Fowler's eyes. Was he condemning the authorities on the radio? The king? Prince Nikolai? "I would never use foreign trash to do our noble work."

"But that's good PR, right, boss?" Ike gestured toward the radio. "I mean, they know who we are if they're talking about us."

"Shut up."

From the radio came: "What about the guy who drove off with the princess?"

"Montana plates and a general description are all we got. Tall. Blond. Knew how to use a gun. Far as we can tell he's a local hero. Maybe an off-duty cop? We're combing—"

Fowler slammed a button on the radio, silencing the two men. "Local hero?" He crushed the pencil in his fist, spraying the shards across his desktop and the floor as he stalked across the room. "I'll bet Cameron Murphy has something to do with this."

Tasiya's attention quickly shifted gears. Cameron Murphy was the name on the memo that had ignited Fowler's temper a few days ago. Why would the militia be interested in the kidnapping of a foreign princess? Why was Cameron Murphy's name so upsetting to Boone Fowler?

And why was that connection of such interest to Dimitri? Tasiya's breathing went shallow with dread as she thought of her phone call to Minister Mostek tonight, and how he'd grill her when she told him about the radio report and Fowler's reaction to it.

Ike tenderly gathered his gear away from further abuse. "I thought Murphy was out of commission."

"He doesn't work alone, you idiot. That's why four of his men are in my…" Fowler's voice trailed off in intensity, but he countered with the pinpoint attack of his cold, black eyes. "Foreigner."

Tasiya jumped at the snap of his voice. But she buried her trembling inside as she slowly turned to face him. "Yes, sir?"

"Don't pretend you weren't eavesdropping. I dislike people who pretend to be stupid. But you know as well as I do that there is no way off this island. And if I thought there was any chance of you telling someone what you've heard around here, I'd be cutting out your tongue right now." He strolled up to her and pulled out a long, thin pocketknife. With the press of a button, a sharp, skinny blade popped open in front of her eyes.

Tasiya gasped and automatically retreated half a step before butting up against the bookshelf and discovering she had nowhere to go. Again he avoided touching her as if he found that contact as loathsome as she. But he had no qualms about twirling the knife blade into a tendril of her hair and playing with it so that it tickled her ear.

"I will not say anything," she lied, knowing Dimitri would be expecting her call.

"Oh, but you will." He flicked the knife from her hair and mimicked a slicing motion through the air in front of her throat before pointing it straight at the tip of her chin. "You'll tell *me* everything you know about Veronika Petrov."

Tasiya clenched her fingers around the shelf behind her to keep them from shaking with fear or striking out in anger. There wasn't much to tell about the princess. "She is a few years younger than me. Very beautiful in the pictures I've seen. Well liked in my country."

"Does she have any political enemies?"

"I do not think so. King Aleksandr does not allow women to be involved in politics."

Fowler laughed, but the sound grated along Tasiya's nerves. "Maybe the old bastard's smarter than I thought. What about personal enemies? Does she have some famous boyfriend she's dumped? She ever cause a scandal?"

"I've only seen Princess Veronika a few times in my life, in official royal portraits. She does not make public appearances. Mostly, she has been away at school. In Paris, I believe."

The knife point wavered back and forth, slowly

searching for a target. "She doesn't like living at home?"

Tasiya swallowed hard and tried to focus her hatred on the knife, instead of risking the impotent fury she longed to glare into Fowler's eyes. "How would I know? I am a cook, not a confidante to the princess."

"Don't get uppity with me, foreigner." He pressed the knife into her chin and tilted her face up to his. "I don't tolerate back talk from my men. I won't tolerate it from you."

Tasiya gnawed the inside of her lip to keep from crying out as she waited helplessly for the blade to break through the skin and draw her blood. But then, just as she closed her eyes to brace for the pain, he lifted the blade. Maybe Fowler had remembered Dimitri's direct order to keep his "gift" in pristine condition, or perhaps he believed that just the threat of cutting her was intimidation enough.

"Now. Answer the question. The UN claims that Lukinburg is a country worth saving. But if it's really so hot, why doesn't the princess go home where she's safe?"

Tasiya swallowed her fear and contempt and answered as evenly as she could. "King Aleksandr has been very vocal about his children choosing to remain in this country and defy his rule. I am not sure he would welcome them home."

"So you think she staged her own kidnapping? Maybe to get Daddy's attention?"

"I do not know."

"You think the king was trying to force her home since she wouldn't go voluntarily?"

"Again, I do not know."

"What *do* you know?" He snorted in disgust and flipped the blade back into the knife. "Don't move."

Tasiya dared to do little more than breathe as Fowler strode back to the desk to pick up the notepad he'd tossed and to find a surviving pencil.

He gave Ike a command while he scribbled something on the pad. "Find out everything you can about the kidnapping attempt. I need to know who's behind it. Kidnapping the princess isn't on my agenda. If somebody's trying to interfere with my schedule or smear my name, I want to know about it. And get me an update on Cameron Murphy's condition."

"Yes, sir."

"Go." Fowler nodded toward the door. Ike wasted no time scooping up his gear and hurrying out in his waddling, bow-legged gait.

"Foreigner." He ripped the top page from the notepad and folded it in half. He held the paper out to her as he turned. "I want you to deliver a message to Marcus Smith for me."

Tasiya nodded. She tucked the note into her jeans and gathered her cleaning supplies, as anxious to be out of there as Ike had been. "Where will I find him?" she asked.

Please don't say his quarters. Marcus Smith was

one of the few men who had his own private room at the compound. He'd invited her to visit more than once, but she'd always found an excuse to avoid spending any one-on-one time with the man. Groping hands in the mess hall she could grit her teeth and ignore because, with an audience, she knew he couldn't completely disregard his boss's order about keeping his hands to himself. But behind the privacy of a locked door, she'd be on her own. And Tasiya knew she'd have no ally to help stop the lecherous brute then.

"He's working in the interrogation room. In the prison wing." Fowler pointed toward her wrist. "Take your keys. You'll find him."

Ponderosa, Montana

TREVOR BLACKHAW SAT in the communication bunker hidden beneath the Big Sky Bounty Hunter headquarters building and listened to the impatient man on the phone.

He swiped a weary hand through his long, black hair and couldn't help thinking how wonderful Sierra's fingers had been last night, tangled up in his hair and massaging his scalp before they drifted off to sleep in each other's arms. But the past several days had allowed them little time to savor their recent engagement.

He'd nearly lost her to the craziness surrounding

Boone Fowler and the escaped prisoners, terrorist attacks and the unknown maniac behind it all whom they'd dubbed The Puppet Master. Trevor wasn't going to lose anybody else he cared about. He was going to get his team out of wherever the hell Boone Fowler had taken them and keep fighting until his world was safe again for the woman he loved.

However, this was a complication he hadn't expected.

Propping one boot up on the edge of the console, Trevor waited for a pause to reiterate his advice. "Joe, there's nothing we can do right now. I talked it over with Murphy. We both agree that the best thing you can do is just lay low for a few days until we can figure out how the kidnapping attempt is related to the UN resolution to invade Lukinburg—or if there even is a connection."

He could well imagine Joseph Brown pacing circles around his beloved black pickup truck—or whatever vehicle he'd gotten to replace it by now so he couldn't be found. "Whoa. You mean me and Princess Poor Little Rich Girl are going to be stuck alone together indefinitely? I'm a tracker, Blackhaw. Don't you have someone better suited for bodyguard detail?"

"You're the one who saved her pretty ass." Normally his colleague was all business, setting aside his emotions when it came to getting the job done and hauling in his bounty. But this evening Joe was so worked up that Trevor couldn't resist the tease.

"Yeah, well for as much trouble as she is, it's not all that pretty."

"So you've been lookin'?"

Joe's denial was both colorful and revealing. Interesting. So Joseph Brown, the born-again bachelor who'd sworn off women since a messy divorce, had the juice for the princess. "I just happened to be in Bozeman, following up on a rumor about a militia connection when those two guys jumped her."

"She was lucky you were there."

"Maybe."

Trevor had no doubt Veronika Petrov was in safe, capable hands. Instead of giving Joe any more grief over an apparently unexpected and unwelcome attraction, Trevor went back to business. "You got a safe place where you can take her?"

"I know a place. If she'll follow orders." Trevor could envision the scowl that matched Joe's voice. "I swear to God that woman's never met a man, child or animal she didn't want to meet and make friends with. I nearly lost her at a gas station. I sent her to the john and told her to come straight back to the truck. I knew we hadn't been followed, but after ten minutes, when she didn't show up, I went looking for her. I found her in the garage, talking to the mechanic."

"From what I hear, women aren't allowed a lot

of freedom back in Lukinburg. Maybe she's just feelin' her oats here in the States, away from all those restrictions."

"Yeah? Well my job would be a hell of a lot easier if she'd lock herself in the barn and stay put."

Trevor grinned. There was only one man on the team he knew could be more stubborn than Joseph Brown, but it sounded as if Joe was giving the Sarge a run for his money. "Good luck, buddy. Keep us posted, and if you need anything, call in."

Resigned to his princess-sitting duties, Joe eased into a more professional tone. "Will do. Hey— how's the colonel?"

"Beat-up and worn out, but in a better frame of mind now that he's at home with his family. He'd be a lot happier if we could hear some news about Sarge and the other hostages."

"We all would. Let me know if there's anything I can do at my end. You can reach me on this secure line."

"Just keep the princess safe. We'll bring our boys home. I promise."

"ALL RIGHT, MR. MARTIN. Let's try again." The mock pleasantness in Marcus Smith's voice underscored the soft rustling sound of a piece of paper being unfolded. Again. He thrust the worn letter with the familiar scribbles in front of Bryce's face. "Read it."

The blockhead needed a shave and a breath mint, and just wasn't getting the idea. Bryce looked beyond the page, beyond the ice-blue eyes, and stared at 6-12.

Smith nodded to the man on Bryce's right.

Damn, this was gettin' old.

The blow to his gut hit like an explosion in his side. Pain radiated outward in aftershocks that clipped the top of his thigh, his back and lungs before fading into one dull ache in the middle of his body.

Bryce concentrated on his breathing, taking slow, shallow breaths that would keep him conscious and cognizant without hyperventilating or putting any added pressure on the burning ache in his torso muscles. Wincing, he swallowed a curse. Oh, yeah, one or both of those bottom two ribs on his right side had cracked.

Pulling his gaze away from 6-12, as he'd dubbed the chipped, moldy stone—sixth row from the top of the wall, twelfth block over—that had been his point of focus for two weeks, he let his peripheral gaze sneak a peak at Bristoe and Hodges. Marcus Smith's two goons had switched to brass knuckles this week, probably because their own hands had taken a beating after so many days working out against his tough hide.

Bristoe hit like a girl, probably the only reason Bryce's left side was in better shape. Hodges had either boxed Golden Gloves or grown up on the street, though, because each blow was on the mark—the same mark—time and again. But Hodges's glass eye, probably the result of all that boxing experience, would give Bryce a maneuvering advantage—if he ever managed to free himself from these chains.

That was getting to be a big *if.* He was trussed up like a pig at the slaughterhouse, with his wrist chain suspended from a rusty O-ring in the ceiling. Bryce's feet touched the floor, easing the pressure on his chest and preventing suffocation. Marcus Smith knew his business. He didn't want his prisoner to pass out or die during an interrogation—he just wanted him to experience lots and lots of pain.

Try burying your parents when you were eight, your grandparents when you were twenty-one. Try living through second- and third-degree burns over half your body, skin grafts, shrapnel wounds, startled gasps and rude comments because you were an ugly son of a bitch. Try living with loneliness nearly every day of your adult life. Bryce knew more about pain than Marcus Smith ever would. He could handle this interrogation.

He fisted his hands where they hung above his head, then splayed his fingers and wiggled them to keep the blood circulating through his arms. For a few seconds he considered letting the tingling pinpricks of numbness settle down into his wrists and forearms. Maybe if he lost the sensation in his arms, he wouldn't notice the raw skin chafing beneath the iron manacles.

Of course, if his arms went numb, he wouldn't be able to keep subtly twisting the O-ring. Bristoe and Hodges were good little soldiers who only took orders. And Smith was so close to his boiling point that he hadn't noticed the little crumblings of mortar dust that had snowed from the ceiling every now and then—ever since Bryce's very first day in the interrogation room.

Smith huffed with impatience, wadded up the letter and chucked it at Bryce's head. Bryce ignored the painless blow and spared little more than a blink when Smith got up in his face and hollered. "Dammit, Martin, you are gonna talk!"

Bryce sought out 6-12.

"Your buddies from Big Sky have already broken," Smith spat in his face. "They've read their letters. They're ready to make the tape."

Bryce doubted it.

Smith's meaty hands curled into fists at his sides. He let his hot breath wash over Bryce's face and tried to stare him down, waiting for some kind of reaction, anything he could jump on and use against Bryce. Bryce suspected that Marcus Smith would like nothing better than for the two of them to head outside and duke it out until only one of them was left standing. He was tempted to give Smith the satisfaction. But with who knew how many other militiamen to back up his enemy, Bryce doubted it would be a fair fight.

It was a good measure of the power Boone Fowler held over all his men that Smith reined in his pride and testosterone and stuck to their plan. As self-titled security chief, Smith was charged with *convincing* each of the Big Sky Bounty Hunters to read a letter on videotape. The tape would condemn the UN's resolution to send troops into Lukinburg, and apologize for any role they had played in interfering with the Montana Militia for a Free America— including imprisoning their leader and pursuing him as a criminal instead of honoring him as a patriot.

Fat chance.

Bryce kept his expression as craggy and unmoving as 6-12.

Marcus Smith stormed across the room. He picked up the wadded paper and spread it flat against his thigh before speaking again. "Tell me your name."

That he would do. "Bryce Martin."

"Who do you work for?"

Uh-uh. Rank and serial number were the only other information he'd share. And since Bryce was no longer military, he was done talking.

"Read this letter."

Old 6-12 was becoming a good friend.

"I can put you on the rack." Smith pointed to the rickety wooden structure whose antique pulleys would give out before Bryce did. "I'll put you in the stocks." At least Bryce would get the feeling back in his hands. "I'll whip you with that cat-o'-nine-tails on the wall." The guy talked too much.

"Read it!" Marcus commanded, striding back and waving the paper in Bryce's face. "You will answer my questions and you will read these words."

Bryce shifted his position, adjusting his arms and squinting as a shower of dust sprinkled over them.

Smith nodded. Bristoe's punch scraped the skin, but did little damage inside.

Bryce was finding 6-12 again when a metallic knock echoed through the room.

Scratching his fingers through his thick beard, Smith answered. "Enter." A key turned in the lock and the rusted iron door groaned on its hinges. "Well, well, well, what have we here?"

The insidious delight in Smith's voice was enough to prick Bryce's curiosity. But he fought the urge to look.

He didn't have to.

When the door opened into the room, he caught a whiff of home-cooked heaven. He knew it was Tasiya, even before she spoke. "Mr. Fowler asked me to deliver this message to you."

"Come on in, sugar. You'd better wait right here until I find out whether or not I need to send a reply." Smith swung the door open wide, giving Bryce a clear view of Tasiya's raven-dark curls piled at the back of her head, her creamy skin and dark eyes that widened and locked instantly on him.

Bryce's pulse rate tripped into a higher gear. He didn't want her here. She didn't need to see this place, didn't need to see him like this. A spot deep inside him, softer than the one Hodges had been working over, began to ache.

Though he tried like hell to concentrate on 6-12, he couldn't miss each dart of her eyes to every bruise, every bloody scrape, every lock and chain that held him in place.

She pressed her lips together around her hushed gasp. But that slightest of sounds seemed to fill the chamber's dank, heavy air and settle deep into Bryce's conscience. Marcus shifted his attention from the note and saw her distress. Even worse, those sick blue eyes saw the flinch of Bryce's reaction to her shock.

Go away. Bryce risked making contact and silently warned her with his eyes. This was not gonna be good.

Marcus Smith smiled. "You wanna watch me work?"

Shaking her head, Tasiya tore her gaze away from Bryce and stared at the buttons on Marcus's shirt. "I only came to deliver the message." Her bottom lip quivered before she drew it quickly between her teeth. "What are you doing to him?"

"Why don't you see for yourself." Marcus

reached over her shoulder and pushed the door shut, trapping her. Bryce's blood caught fire and surged in his veins. He jerked against his chains, fighting to stay in control.

"No." Tasiya clawed at the iron ring behind her back, caught hold and opened the door. "My duties. I have dinner to prepare."

But Marcus's hand reached over her and slammed it shut with a dire inevitability that shook through her.

Bryce's fingers splayed, then fisted above his head, giving vent to his frustrated need to shield her from this nightmare. He watched her shut down her emotions like that night at his cell when she'd been terrified of something she feared more than him. Her body went still except for the quiver in her chin as she clenched her jaw too tight and put on a brave show. Bryce counted the raging heartbeats pounding in his ears as she averted her gaze and pretended she didn't mind Smith moving closer, tangling his beard with the curls at her forehead.

When the big bastard grinned at her discomfort, Bryce made his first mistake. "Let her go, Smith."

With his hand still braced on the door behind Tasiya's head, the big man slowly turned. He raised a bushy eyebrow in triumph. "So—your mouth works after all, eh, Sarge?"

"She doesn't need to see this."

"I think maybe she does."

Tasiya's panicked gaze flew up to Bryce's the instant Marcus turned his back on her. But Smith never stepped away, keeping her backed into the corner without enough room to open the door. Bryce drilled Smith's icy eyes. He didn't want to give the security chief any more of an advantage than he already had.

Smith flipped open the note she'd delivered, barely taking his focus off Bryce to read it. "I think we finally found the key to making him talk, boys."

Hodges's and Bristoe's rowdy taunts were nothing but white noise in the background. Bryce knew where the real threat in the room lay—and that threat was too damn close to Tasiya.

He swallowed his pride, his plan and the bitter taste of capitulation in his mouth. "Let her leave and I'll say whatever you want me to."

Smith gestured with Fowler's note, obviously a revised set of instructions from the head honcho. "Tell me about Cameron Murphy. We left him for dead at the Galleria Mall. Is he still alive?"

"He was in the hospital when I left Montana."

"He still calling the shots at Big Sky?"

After two weeks in his solitary prison cell, Bryce had no clue about the status of affairs at Big Sky. He only knew his loyalties were with the colonel. "I still work for him."

"Not what I asked, Sarge." Smith clicked his tongue with a pitying reprimand. "Who's making the decisions for them now? Do they have the man-power to mount a rescue?"

Why don't you let me go and I'll ask. But the sar-castic response on the end of Bryce's tongue never came out. It wasn't his way. "Send Tasiya back to the kitchen first."

"She's fine where she is." Smith nodded once and Hodges nailed him in the ribs.

"No!" Tasiya cried out as Bryce swallowed a curse and fought to master the pain spiraling through him.

"Let her go." He ground out the words on the deepest breath he could manage.

"Are you gonna read this letter now? Like you mean it?"

"When she's gone."

Smith turned his face to the side and spat out his chew. It was the only respite Bryce got before his captor gave the order to attack.

"No!" Tasiya screamed as Hodges and Bristoe pummeled him with their fists. There was no dis-guising the terror on her face now. Bryce dodged and braced as best he could. He strained against his bonds, but without his hands, he made an easy punching bag.

Marcus Smith laughed, and Tasiya snatched at his arm, begging him to listen. "Make them stop!"

Bryce took an easy shot and kicked Bristoe in the gut. But while one man doubled over, the other rammed his brass knuckles into Bryce's exposed back, knocking him off his feet. He pulled against his chains and righted himself, but the fists kept coming.

"You are killing him!" Tasiya shouted. Instead of making a break for it while Smith watched the fight, the crazy woman shot forward, trying to help. "Stop it!"

Marcus grabbed her around the neck and shoved her up against the wall. "You watch, sugar."

"Let her go!" Bryce ignored the coppery tang of blood in his mouth. "I'll read it. I'll read the damn letter!"

Smith nuzzled his lips against Tasiya's ear, holding her by the chin and pinning her with his hip so she couldn't look away. "Listen to him. Now he wants to cooperate." He glanced over his shoulder at Bryce. "I don't care what you have to say now. My boys can have at ya until they get tired."

"Stop!" she cried.

Tears glistened in her eyes. And while they had no effect on Marcus Smith, they tore Bryce up a lot worse than Hodges's fists. "Tasiya!" *Close your eyes. Look away.* "Let her go!"

"So you can take a beating, but you can't stand to have the little lady watch it? Oh, man, this is rich," Smith laughed. He wrapped his arm around Tasiya's waist, pinning her arms and picked her up. Then he set her down in front of him, squeezing her chin and forcing her eyes toward Bryce. "The view's better from here."

"You son of a bitch!" A shower of dust rained down from the ceiling and stuck in the sweat and blood on Bryce's skin.

He saw a flash of Tasiya's straight, white teeth and suddenly glimpsed a rebellious spirit inside the demure cook he'd never have suspected. With a twist of her neck, she sank her teeth into Smith's hand.

The big man yelped, cursed and threw her across the room.

"Tasiya!"

She smacked into the wall and bounced off, landing on her hands and knees.

Bryce fisted his hands around the chain and pulled with all his might.

Smith followed her across the room, his hand raised to strike as she pushed herself to her feet.

"Tasiya!" Chips of mortar and stone crashed down from the ceiling as Bryce ripped out the O-ring. Before his bellowing voice faded away, he'd looped the chain around Smith's neck and jerked him away from Tasiya. He spun around, sticking Marcus in front of him to absorb the next blow from a startled Hodges. "Run!"

Dammit, she wasn't moving. He couldn't maintain the advantage for long. He shoved Smith into Bristoe and Hodges, knocking them into the rack and off their feet.

"Bryce Martin?"

"You can't help me." He grabbed her by the wrist and hustled her toward the door. "Just go."

"But—"

Angry hands yanked him away and slammed him into the wall, knocking the air out of his already tender lungs. "Please, dammit!" he wheezed. "Get out of here!"

"Please, dammit," Marcus mimicked.

Bryce summoned the strength to ram his fist into Marcus's mouth, drawing blood and shutting him up—and igniting his temper.

Smith wiped the blood from his lip, called him the devil and worse. And while his thugs held on, he hit Bryce low in the gut.

As Bryce's knees buckled, Bristoe and Hodges took him the rest of the way, pinning him stomach-down on the cold stone floor. A crack of sound that could only be the cat-o'-nine-tails snapped in the air. "You're done, Sarge. You don't have to say another word."

"No! Mr. Smith—please!"

But all of Smith's rage was focused on Bryce now, and Tasiya's presence was blessedly forgotten.

Bryce raised his head, warning her away with his eyes, apologizing for the stark terror he saw in hers. He could only mouth one word. *"Go."*

"I am so sorry." She backed into the door, fumbled in her hurry to find the handle. "I am so sorry."

She threw open the door and ran.

Bryce breathed an odd sense of relief that she was gone, that she'd been spared the hell that was about to claim him. He could endure this now that she was safe. He wouldn't add to the fear in her eyes.

Her footsteps and sobs faded as the whip hit his back, all nine of its claws ripping their way through his skin.

Chapter Six

"Maria? Maria!"

Bryce shivered at the fiery pain that burned through his feverish body. Maria was dead. Seventeen innocent civilians were dead because he hadn't been quick enough to save them.

There were too many mines. Too many damn mines.

And the mortar fire.

The command to retreat.

Ordered to save his own hide and let them die.

"Sarge? You've got to pull through this. You're a fighter. I need you on my team."

Colonel Murphy's voice. He'd always obeyed that voice. But he couldn't do it. He didn't have the strength in him anymore.

He was in the hospital. Lying on his stomach with his face looking through a hole to the green linoleum tile on the floor beneath him. He'd been lying here for weeks while the doctors battled infections *and waited for enough skin to grow back so they could stitch him together.*

"You did your best, Sarge. We'll have another chance to get the bad guys. I promise."

Bryce nodded, but he didn't believe. Murphy was here. Powell and Trevor Blackhaw, too. Campbell. Brown. They'd all been in to see him.

He should rise to attention. Salute. But all he wanted to do was roll over and be done with the pain. He wanted to be done with giving a damn about things that could never be his.

He wanted to be done with living and losing.

"Bryce Martin."

They were taking away his career—nerve damage, loss of flexibility—an honorable discharge and a couple of medals? They were taking away the last thing he cared about, denying him the one place where it didn't matter where he'd come from or what he looked like.

"Keep fighting, Sarge."

"I can't."

It hurt too much. Inside and out. The pain burned through him. Cut him to the heart as easily as the shrapnel cut through his skin.

"Bryce Martin."

Something cool touched the back of his neck. Soft words he didn't understand murmured a gentle rhythm against his ear, scattering his bleak thoughts.

"No, sir," he answered with less strength. "Can't fight... No reason to..."

"Do it for yourself," the colonel ordered. "Do it for your men."

"No." It hurt too damn much.

"Shh."

Sweet relief traveled across his shoulders and down his back, giving him the first real comfort he'd known in weeks. The fever in him cooled along with each gentle touch, each hushed word. The anger in him abated.

"Bryce Martin."

Bryce awoke without opening his eyes, slowly sifting his way through hazy layers of consciousness.

He frowned into his pillow. Why would the colonel call him by his first and last name?

"Shh." The cool balm settled at the back of his waist. "Rest easy. Shh."

His breathing eased at the tender command. He never knew Colonel Murphy had such a soft, sexy voice.

Bryce's eyes snapped open.

Murphy talked like a soldier. Nobody talked soft and sexy to Bryce Martin.

His muscles tensed with confusion as Bryce tried to sort through the images in his brain and place himself in his surroundings. Which were memories? What was feverish illusion? Where did the nightmares from his past end and his present reality begin?

A foggy mist of light and shadow told him nothing but that it was night. So he listened to the world around him—ocean waves splashing a rocky shore in the distance, a gentle trickle of water closer by. He sniffed the musty odor of damp ticking, and the more pungent smells of citrus and ointment.

Was he back in the hospital? Did that hushed, heavenly voice belong to a nurse?

"Are you awake, Bryce Martin?"

Trilled *r*s. Succinct articulation. The homey scents of yeast and spice.

An instant awareness cut through the shroud of fever, pain and confusion. *Hell.*

He wasn't in any army hospital.

Colonel Murphy wasn't whispering in his ear.

"Tasiya?" His voice was a ragged croak. He tried to get his arms underneath him, to push himself up. But his muscles were weak, wobbly.

And her hands were surprisingly strong against his shoulders. "Do not move. You should rest."

But he'd been whipped. As if he wasn't already hard enough to look at, she was sitting on the edge of his cot beside his prone body—in his cell—tending the wounds on his back. "You shouldn't be here."

She oughta leave. She oughta run as far away from him and his hell as her long legs would take her. He should make her leave. But her tender hands—the cloth and cool water and salve she used—felt so good against his skin.

"I am not leaving until I am finished. This is my fault."

How could Marcus Smith being a son of a bitch possibly be her fault? Bryce turned his head on the mattress to glimpse her from the corner of his eye. "You're not responsible. I had it comin' to me sooner or later. I'll be—"

"Do not tell me you have faced worse than this and survived." She leaned forward so he could look straight up into those stern brown eyes. "You are facing this because of me. You are hurt now because of me."

Such a sharp tongue. But he understood the difference between anger directed at him and a misguided woman being angry *for* him. Other people didn't stand up and fight for Bryce—especially a slender slip of a woman. The men he'd fought with and worked with watched his back, but no one defended him. Most figured he didn't need the help.

But Tasiya Belov was fired up—in her own reserved, ladylike way. If he had the strength, he'd smile and thank her for the uncustomary honor. But he needed to conserve whatever energy he had left. "Marcus Smith and his ego did this. Don't feel guilty."

"I did not know it would give him such pleasure to see you suffer." Bryce followed her precise, efficient movements as she rinsed the cloth in a basin of water made pink with his blood. When she faced him again, some of the fight had gone out of her. Her eyes seemed darker, sadder, full of regret. "If you were not such a gentleman, you would not be so hurt."

A gentleman? Was the translation between them that far off? "He used you to get to me. I shouldn't have let him."

Tasiya resumed her work without comment, folding the cloth and laying it over his tricep muscle. Some of the nerves there hadn't functioned since he was a kid, so he felt no sting from the lemony soap she used. But he could feel the light, sure pressure of her fingers as she doctored the laceration there, handling him like a baby instead of a man twice her size.

A woman's gentle touch was as foreign to him as the weakness that consumed his body. He'd lived a hard life, had never really done relationships. What he knew about women had to do with sex, generally the quick, no-strings-attached kind. He didn't even have buddies who were women. A few co-workers, but that was all business. Jacob Powell's fiancée had tried to talk to him a couple of times, and he appreciated the effort, but friendly banter was just awkward for him.

He knew his mama had loved him, but he'd been an unscarred, untested boy then. His grandma had loved him for the young man he'd become, but theirs had been a secluded life.

All this talking, all this tenderness from Tasiya was…perplexing. In the end, all Bryce could do was be who he was. "How long was I out?"

"You have not gone anywhere."

"I meant, how long have I been unconscious?"

"Oh." She pulled her hands away, clutching them together in a self-conscious gesture. Bryce wished he could withdraw the question. He should have just shut up instead of making her self-conscious about the language barriers between them.

But Tasiya was made of sterner stuff. "Mr. Smith's men brought you here before dinner. You did not waken when I brought your food, so I..." She glanced over her shoulder at the steel bars that had separated them for so many nights. "I came in to help you. It is nearly three in the morning now."

He tried to roll onto his side, to at least hide the worst of his injuries from her. "You need your sleep. I'll be all right."

But her firm hands guided him back down. She squeezed some ointment from a tube across the tips of her fingers and dabbed it over the cuts, stubbornly refusing to be shielded from his ugliness. "There is no doctor here, but I know something about taking care of wounds like this. My father was once..."

Bryce waited expectantly to learn more about her, but she didn't complete the sentence. Reading the distant sorrow in her eyes, he didn't want her to. He knew Tasiya Belov was no stranger to hardship. That wasn't right. But Bryce didn't know how to make things right for her, how to make whatever scared her go away. He couldn't even get things right for himself.

"Tasiya?"

"I am almost finished." She rose and carried the cloth and basin out into the passageway. She set the items on the floor, and for the first time he noticed she'd sneaked in to see him without her noisy cart.

Sneaking couldn't be good for her safety.

"Finished with what?"

"Bathing you."

She meant cleaning the cuts and welts, of course. Then Bryce realized that he smelled a heck of a lot better than he had yesterday. His face and hands had been washed and he...

He clenched and released his muscles, all the way from his nose to his toes. He ignored the stabs of pain and took note of the breezy sensations in between. Lordy. *Now* he was wide awake. His jeans were unzipped and hanging low on his hips, his briefs pulled down just short of indecent. The dainty, practical miss from Lukinburg had been quite thorough in her washing. His skin heated up, but not with the fever from his open wounds.

A new kind of feeling that had nothing to do with pain, and everything to do with the thought of Tasiya putting her capable hands on his buttocks and other interesting places that hadn't been injured, charged his blood with a uniquely masculine burst of strength. Propping himself up on his elbows, Bryce managed to drop his legs over the side of the cot and push himself up to a sitting position.

The uneven floor swam before his eyes. "Whoa."

"What are you doing?"

Bryce laid his forehead in his palms and tried to shake off the dizziness. Metal scraped against metal, and hurried footsteps brought her back to him. He swayed into her hands, but they latched onto his arms and steadied him until the light-headedness passed and he could open his eyes.

"I must have lost more blood than I thought." Or he was still recovering from shock. He patted at her fingers and lifted his gaze to an eyeful of gently sloping breasts, rising and falling beneath her pale-blue sweater. She was long and lean and, oh, so feminine, making it damn near impossible for his pulse rate to regulate itself when she was this close. Wisely, he averted his eyes before giving in to the tempting urge to rest his head against her. "I'm okay."

The cot shifted slightly as the mattress took her weight beside him. He angled himself away from her, but didn't have the legs yet to put any more distance between her and his libido.

"I heard the men talking at dinner. Mr. Fowler said to give you a few days to heal before resuming interrogation. You must use that time to rest."

They were finally cutting him a break? That probably meant Smith and his goons would be loaded for bear when they got the okay to torture him some more. In the meantime, they'd no doubt be practicing their skills on one of the other hostages.

Bryce should use the uninterrupted time to plot a way out of here—a way to get them all out of here— the bounty hunters, the soldiers. Maybe even Tasiya, assuming she wanted to go.

Right now, though, he could barely manage to pull up his pants. A pinch of pain beneath the elastic told him how far down his injuries went, but he didn't plan on mooning the woman who'd been so foolishly kind to enter the cage with the monster and doctor him up.

Bryce flinched when Tasiya's fingers brushed against the small of his back. But whether she attributed the corresponding flood of goose bumps to pain or understood that his body just wasn't used to a woman's familiar touch, it didn't deter her from straightening the elastic and tugging up his jeans.

He drew the line, though, when she reached around to help him with his zipper. Bryce grasped her wrists and pushed them gently back into her own lap. Wounded or not, there was a thing or two about his male anatomy when he was around her she didn't need to see. "I can get it."

He tried not to be disappointed at how quickly she moved on to a new task—pouring him something that was too dark to be water out of her pitcher and unwrapping a crusty loaf of bread. "I saved you some food." She tore the loaf in two and cradled one end in her lap while she dipped the other into the cup. "It's cold now, but I made some broth to help you regain your strength."

Propping the cup between her knees, Tasiya cradled the soaked bread over her palm to catch the drippings. When she carried it to his mouth, Bryce had to stop her. "I'll get that, too."

Letting Tasiya feed him was just too suggestive for his peace of mind right now. How incredible would it be if her tender attentions were motivated by attraction instead of a guilty conscience? Bryce had lived long enough to know not to ask for the impossible. But his weakened body seemed to have no problem interpreting the touches and the talking and the delicious smells of food and cook as a personal invitation to be aroused.

He sank his teeth into the first rich bite of nutty bread and beef au jus before he realized just how far she'd gone to help him. His chewing slowed as he stared at his naked wrists. He swallowed before trying to gauge the motivation in her expression. "You unchained me."

"I put medicine on the welts around your wrists and ankles. You were already heavy enough to move. It was less awkward to bathe you once I removed them." She was either exceedingly practical or too naive for her own good.

"You should have put 'em back on," he suggested.

That tiny vertical line of confusion and doubt appeared between her brows. "You will not run away from me, will you?"

She must not know how badly he was hurtin'. He

eyed the keys around her wrist. She'd been cautious enough to secure the manacles in the passageway outside his cell, but then she'd been trusting enough to lock herself inside with the keys to his freedom within arm's reach.

"I wouldn't get you into trouble that way."

Yet.

But with that promise, she relaxed and smiled.

Bryce quickly stuffed another bite into his mouth, though the bread and broth had turned bitter. Maybe there *was* something he could do to earn her trust. He could take advantage of the pity she felt for him, the way it lowered her guard and made her believe he was some kind of victim or gentleman. Maybe he didn't need Powell or Campbell to sweet-talk her.

And while she worked off whatever penance she felt she owed him, he could slowly gain her trust. She'd answer his questions out of guilt. And if pity could make her unlock his chains tonight, then a growing bond would make it a piece of cake to steal those keys without resorting to force.

Problem was, he didn't want to leave her company, not just yet. And while he had no illusion of a happily-ever-after with any woman, he was human. He'd never known a woman's gentleness before. He'd never known how much he craved it.

He risked a glance into her dark, mysterious eyes and allowed himself one moment to dream. Would her hair be as silky to the touch as it looked? As rich and heavy in his hands as it was a feast to his eyes? What would her lips taste like? They were pink and full, with enough attitude to make them interesting—like sweet, tart raspberries ripe for the plucking. What would she feel like in his arms? Strong? Delicate? Would she melt in a puddle of shy femininity? Or would she be as practical and efficient and sure of herself as the woman who'd stripped him down and washed him from head to toe?

Bryce snatched the bread and cup from her lap and turned away, damning the useless needs that heated his blood and made him hungry for more than a batch of fried chicken and mashed potatoes. This wasn't a fairy tale, and he wasn't gonna be anybody's prince—not out of love or pity.

He just needed some time to heal. Then he needed to use her and not look back with longing or regret.

TASIYA WONDERED what dark thoughts had put such a scowl on Bryce Martin's harsh face. She swore that his beautiful gray eyes had sparked with desire, that they'd shared an inexplicable warmth and closeness in the cool, dim air of his quiet cell. But maybe it was only an apology she had read there. She'd had so little experience with men who made her feel anything, it was hard to be sure.

Perhaps her presence here embarrassed him. The men she knew liked to be strong. And with the exception of her father, they seemed to possess a brutal urge to show off their power and lord it over others.

But Bryce Martin had needed her. At least, he'd needed a nursemaid to help him before he risked infection, perhaps even death, in this forgotten cage in the middle of the ocean. Since he'd taken the horrific beating to protect her, Tasiya felt honor-bound to repay the favor by bringing him food, clothing and medicine and tending to his needs.

She could have left an hour ago, been less thorough in her caregiving. But conscious or awake, Bryce Martin was a calming presence. Well, *calming* might not be the right word. She moved her gaze past the raw strips of skin that had been peeled from his broad back and studied the intriguing stretch and flex of his bottom each time he moved to find a relatively comfortable position or to finish the rest of his late-night snack.

Tasiya smiled to herself at her surprisingly naughty thoughts. She'd learned he was muscular all over—warm to the touch, too—even on parts of his body that she rarely got to see on a man.

If she looked past the surface of his skin, past his square, craggy face, he was really quite a fine specimen of a man. Tasiya's smile quickly faded. She couldn't ignore the old scars or the new ones he would bear from this ordeal. And she couldn't ignore his face, because that would mean avoiding his eyes. There was such strength in his wintry irises. Such depth. Such beauty.

Those eyes, and these quiet moments together, had become as necessary to surviving her sentence here on Devil's Fork Island as keeping her secret from Boone Fowler was. That's where the calm feeling came from. Bryce Martin was a mighty mountain who could withstand the storm spinning around them. It was only natural to seek shelter beside him.

Even in his weakened condition, Bryce had a hearty appetite. In no time he'd polished off the bread and drunk the last of the broth and a cup of water. With a flattering thoroughness, he licked the last crumb and drop off his fingers and thumb. "I'll bet you could even make a brick taste good."

She liked the musical cadence of his voice, even if his words didn't make sense. "Why would you eat a brick? Is that an Americanism?"

"It's a compliment." He handed her the cup. "Good stuff."

"Thank you."

Unlike Fowler's men, Bryce didn't make fun of her ignorance or berate her when she couldn't quite grasp the intricacies of American slang. Maybe his funny accent, *hick,* she'd heard Marcus Smith say, helped him understand how difficult communication could be—and made him sympathetic to how lonely a soul could get when not allowed to express herself.

Tasiya carried the cup and pitcher into the passageway and picked up a man's shirt and the manacles she'd taken off his body.

Whatever verbal shortcomings Bryce lacked, there was little that his eyes missed or failed to communicate. She felt him watching her as she draped the heavy chains over her arm and sorted through her keys. When she dropped them to the floor, she sensed the shift in his focus. As she stooped to retrieve them, his gray eyes stared at the keys with an intensity that had matched his silent warning to her in the interrogation room. When he lifted his gaze to where the door stood ajar, Tasiya quickly rose and pushed it shut.

He was thinking escape, wasn't he? Debating whether or not to take advantage of her visit. Maybe she was wrong to trust Bryce too quickly. Wasn't freedom every prisoner's dream?

If she could be free—if she could free her father—wouldn't she be willing to take advantage of Bryce?

But freedom wasn't an option for her. Even survival didn't look all that promising if she managed to allow one of the prisoners out of his cell.

Surely Bryce was too injured to try anything. And as cruel as it seemed, once she put him back in his chains, he'd be even less likely to try to bolt. She truly didn't think he would harm her—his actions and his eyes had told her that. But if Fowler and Smith found out what she'd done tonight, *they* would have no qualms about punishing her.

Tasiya slipped the keys deep into the pocket of her jeans, just in case she was wrong about Bryce Martin. "I do not know if Mr. Fowler only sent me to make things worse for you, or if it truly was important for him to find out about this Cameron Murphy who upsets him so."

Bryce didn't seem put off or surprised by her own subtle interrogation. "Maybe both."

"Why does he hate him?"

"Colonel Murphy—the man I work for—put him in prison once. We intend to do it again."

The chains weighed heavily in her arms. Neither one of them needed to explain that thus far, the only person who'd successfully captured anyone else was the man Bryce and his friends were after. "What did Boone Fowler do?"

"Killed Murphy's sister. Plus a bunch of other innocent people. He masterminded a plot to escape from a Montana prison, orchestrated more terrorist attacks in the name of patriotism, killed two innocent soldiers and stuffed the rest of us into this hellhole to be used as pawns in whatever scheme he's planning next."

Tasiya clutched the shirt that Fowler had insisted would be treatment enough for the wounded prisoner. Why waste first-aid supplies when he could simply hide the wounds from the camera? Let the guy sleep it off for a few days, Fowler had ordered—if he could stand and talk, they could find him.

But she wasn't used to hearing such bile in Bryce's voice. The man he'd described wasn't all that different from Dimitri Mostek and King Aleksandr. The emotions Bryce revealed weren't all that different from the resentments and frustrations locked up inside her.

Not for the first time since coming to America, she battled with her conscience. How could she allow men like Bryce to suffer so that her father wouldn't have to?

She crushed the faded cotton in her fists. Maybe it was only a rationalization to ease her guilt, but she *was* helping him. She couldn't set him free, but without her help, he and his friends would surely starve. Without her help, he might not recover from his beating.

It was enough of an excuse to fix a polite smile on her face and walk back to the cot.

"Let us not talk about him anymore. Here." She shook out the khaki shirt—the biggest one she could find. "It is clean. You need something to protect your wounds."

She helped him into it, easing it slowly over his back and shoulders. Even that much effort seemed to tax his strength. He rested his elbows on his knees and leaned heavily against them. Tasiya breathed a little easier about him attempting an escape.

She held out the chains next. "I must put these back on you. I do not want anyone to question how you removed them." But his skin was still so raw; it hurt her just to look at it. "Perhaps only the wrists."

He pushed himself upright and spread his feet apart on the floor. "Better do 'em both. I don't want Fowler or Smith suspicious about you…bein' kind to me." Tasiya reluctantly snapped the manacles around his wrists, then knelt in front of him to lock his ankles together. "You better head on back to wherever you're bunkin' out, too. I don't want anyone to come lookin' for you and find you here."

But Tasiya didn't want to leave just yet. "No one comes into the kitchen where I sleep. And the sentries are posted outside the building at night. Unless I make too much noise and wake someone…"

Despite her hesitancy to trust and her guilt at deceiving him, Tasiya didn't want to be anywhere else. Though she could never tell him why, he understood the things she was feeling. Cocooned by the night, in this remote corner of the compound, she'd found a soul mate. So Tasiya gave herself another job to delay her departure. Rising in front of him, she reached out and helped him button his shirt. "Tell me about your Oh-sark."

Bryce's big fingers stopped on the button above where she had paused. He lifted his face, and their gazes locked together.

Maybe she'd found something else, as well.

Tasiya was sinking, deep and fast, into the gun-metal depths that seemed so like home to her. The heat from his body seeped into her hands and she felt herself leaning. Or perhaps he'd inched closer. His gaze dropped to her mouth, and her lips parted as the breath inside her swelled with anticipation. He caressed her lips with his eyes, awakening every female instinct inside her with the raw desire stamped in his features.

She was struck by the bold notion of closing the gap between them and pressing her lips to his. She wanted to crawl into his lap and burrow inside him, to soak up his heat and be sheltered by all that strength. She wanted to kiss him. To be kissed by a man as wild and rugged as the snow-capped mountains of her homeland. She wanted to be taken from her world of vicious words and violence and simply be a woman that a man wanted—the way Bryce Martin's eyes said he wanted her.

She curled her fingers into a handful of shirt and skin, and let her eyes drift shut. Just one kiss…

But Bryce had a saner notion in mind.

She blinked her eyes open as he pried her hands from his chest and pushed her away.

"It's Ozarks," he stated, emphasizing the *z* and the *s*.

"What are Ozarks?" she asked, carefully mimicking the word. She wondered if she should be feeling grateful rather than disappointed that Bryce had kept her from making a fool of herself. And she'd been afraid of trusting him!

"It's a place." Tasiya sat down beside him as he rolled up his sleeves. "Ancient mountains, worn down to rugged hills and exposed rock. In southern Missouri and northern Arkansas."

Those were states she knew from her studies. Gradually she began to relax. The more he talked, the more she reminded herself of why she'd been drawn to him in the first place. "They look like your Rocky Mountains, then? I have seen them in pictures."

"Nope. The Ozarks are green."

"What makes them green?"

"Water."

"We have many beautiful lakes outside our capital, St. Feodor. Where does your water come from?"

The tension seemed to be easing from Bryce, too, as he talked about his home. He leaned forward over his knees again, away from her. But it seemed to be a posture that gave him some relief rather than an intentional snub. "Rivers. Man-made lakes. Natural springs. There's a lot of underground water there. A lot of caves carved out by water."

"The foliage there must be very lush."

"Yep."

Behind his back she smiled at his funny word. "Are there flowers? Grass?"

"Trees mostly. Lots of 'em everywhere you look.

Oak, maple, elm, locust. With lots of good cedar. It smells fresh and clean out in the woods."

Not much like this place, in other words. "Green is the only color of your Ozarks?"

"Nope. On the hillside, if you look close among the taller, darker trunks, in the spring you'll catch a glimpse of white or pink flowers. Those are the dogwood trees. In the fall, all the leaves change colors. Bright red. Gold. Orange."

The subtle longing in his deep-pitched voice spoke to the kindred soul inside her, as though he knew what she needed more than she knew herself. She shouldn't fantasize about passionate kisses. This strange, budding friendship was already more than she could ask for. "Your Ozarks sound very beautiful."

"Yep."

"I should like to get permission to see it one day. Where do you get a travel voucher in your country?"

"You don't have to get permission. You just go. The United States isn't like this place." He shrugged, then winced as if the gesture had caused him considerable pain. Tasiya found herself holding her breath along with him until he slowly exhaled and could speak again. "You can go wherever you want, whenever you want to."

He didn't have to register travel dates with the Ministry of Security? Report in at the local town hall upon his arrival? "You did not need travel papers to go from Missouri to Montana?"

He shook his head. "I needed a change of scenery so I up and went. That's where the job was."

"Even a woman could do this?"

He huffed a sound that might have been a laugh and angled his head to look at her. "Hell, yeah."

"Incredible."

Her father had told her similar stories about his childhood, how he remembered taking drives to visit his grandparents in the country. Sometimes they enjoyed themselves so much that on the spur of the moment they would decide to stay the night—or a whole weekend. But that was before the reign of Aleksandr Petrov and the restrictions on travel she had always known.

Curious at how casually Bryce talked about moving from place to place, Tasiya tucked one leg beneath her and scooted closer. "Tell me more about your country. The Grand Canyon. And New York City."

"Ain't you talked out yet?" He'd spent what little strength he had left, no doubt.

"The men here ignore me as if I do not exist except to serve them. I hear no 'Good morning.' No 'Good night.' No 'How are you feeling?' No one else tells me what a beautiful country you have."

"That ain't right." He turned away and stared out into the passageway. "But talkin' i'n't my best thing."

Tasiya frowned, unseen behind his back. Did he honestly have no idea of the effect he had on her?

On impulse, she leaned forward and kissed his cheek. "You do it beautifully, Bryce Martin."

She fished her keys from her pocket and headed for the door, hoping she didn't look as startled by that little kiss as he did. The urge to offer him a kindness—to thank him for his solace—didn't surprise her. The fact that she wanted to offer him so much more than a peck on his whiskered cheek did.

As she reluctantly locked the steel bars behind her and gathered her things, the rattle of chains diverted her attention.

Bryce wobbled on his feet, bracing one hand against the wall for balance. But he was standing.

"'Night, Tasiya Belov."

She nearly burst into tears at his sweet chivalry, knowing that this wounded giant had truly listened to her, despite his pain. A forbidden bond had been forged between them this night, inside this horrid prison where they were both held captive.

They'd traded comfort for comfort, strength for strength.

And for the first time since that fateful night in Lukinburg when terrorists had shattered her world, Tasiya had hope.

"Good night, Bryce Martin."

Chapter Seven

TASIYA CLUTCHED the collar of her jacket together and huddled against the mist blowing off the water.

Devil's Fork Island was small enough that, from the port between the old stone fortress and the newer fiberglass docks, she could see the two long inlets that formed the trident shape giving the island its name. But the island was large enough that when the ferry chugged around the tip of the westernmost peninsula, the jetty and dock blocked it from view.

The landscape where she'd stopped to breathe in fresh air and remind herself what the sun looked like was wild and barren of animal life except for the large sea birds that fed and nested along the shoreline. And while the prison compound stood like a weary, yet unbending sentinel on the windward side of the island, here, along the half-mile path, Tasiya felt as if she might be standing in the middle of an unspoiled nature preserve. If she closed her eyes and tipped her face to the warmth of the sun, she could almost imagine what it was like to be free.

But the strident hum of the electronic security fence rebooting around the perimeter was a harsh reminder that she wasn't free. Maybe she'd never truly been free. Growing up in the increasing oppression of Lukinburg society, she hadn't been allowed to continue beyond basic schooling to become a chef. She couldn't travel from place to place—wherever she wanted, whenever she wanted, the way Bryce had described living in America—without being documented at a checkpoint. Not even to visit her mother's and grandparents' graves in the countryside outside St. Feodor. All she could do was work a menial job or become a man's mistress.

His victim or his slave.

Shaking with a suppressed anger that blotted out the November chill, Tasiya opened her eyes and looked around. There wasn't a guard in sight, and a quick check of her watch said she still had ten minutes before she had to report back to the kitchen.

Such a generous privilege, she noted with sarcasm. After fifteen days of reliable work, Boone Fowler had granted her permission to walk down to the docks unescorted to deliver a list of supplies she needed from two men heading to the mainland. But he'd given her a strict time limit on her freedom, and reminded her that there was no way on or off the island without being detected. How were time limits and restrictions any different from the life waiting for her back in Lukinburg?

Seized by a rebellious urge after twenty-seven years of being the dutiful citizen who knew her place, Tasiya left the path and hiked up a shallow slope to the edge of a rocky drop-off overlooking the island's western shore. In vain, she peered along the horizon, seeking some sign of the beautiful, free America Bryce had described. But there was no land, no civilization. The stormy gray Atlantic sluiced over the rocks below, then ebbed and rolled into waves that seemed to throw themselves against the matching sky in the distance.

Not that she'd have any chance of reaching the mainland on her own. She couldn't swim that far. The island's ferry and two speed boats were heavily guarded. And since she hadn't seen any sails or heard heavy engines or sounding buoys since she'd arrived, she guessed they weren't on any shipping lane where she'd have a chance of flagging down a passing tourist or tradesman for help.

Tasiya grasped the corkscrew tendril the wind plastered against her cheek and tucked it behind her ear. There was no sense depressing herself by noting how far she was from America proper, or how much farther she was from Lukinburg and her father.

Her only ally was the battered giant locked in solitary confinement.

The kindness and resolute determination beneath

Bryce Martin's gruff manner and harsh exterior had awakened something deep inside her. An urge to fight back, to do more than resign herself to a life of servitude and discontent. And while she would not jeopardize her father's life, she wouldn't sit idly by and let Bryce be slowly tortured to death, either. Above all, she would not let Boone Fowler and Marcus Smith break the big man's spirit.

Letting her attention slide back to her immediate surroundings, Tasiya began forming a modest plan. The foliage on Devil's Fork Island had all been beaten down to a sandy color, including the sturdy, thigh-high grass that clung to the gritty soil and rippled in the breeze like an extension of the sea itself.

Reminded of the reeds that grew around Lake Ryanavik, she reached down and plucked a blade. The whole shaft, from tip to roots easily came loose in her hand. She rolled the three-foot stalk between her palms and tried to snap it in two. A satisfied smile curved her lips. With the daily beating it took from the elements, of course it grew to bend and not break. It was fibrous and strong, yet pliant to the touch—perfect for basketweaving.

One of Tasiya's most useful homemaking skills was making do with whatever she had on hand. With an island full of this unique grass, she could make a basket to carry the bread and water to the prisoners, instead of pushing that noisy metal cart and worrying that she was waking every militiaman and shouting her presence everywhere she went. With a basket, she could move quietly through the passageways and worry less about paying a late-night visit to her friend in the last cell.

The five minutes she had left before Fowler sent a guard after her wasn't much time. But the grass came away easily in her hands, and if she couldn't gather enough now, she could make up an excuse to come outside again to finish her work.

Or…she spotted a clearing at the bottom of the rise close to the beach where bundles of the grass had already been uprooted and cast aside.

Shifting the grass she'd already collected into one hand, she made her way down along the edge of the drop-off, carefully avoiding the slippery rocks and a certain tumble. Like walking through molasses, the sandy ground sucked her boots into its grip, forcing her to shorten her stride and push off at every step. She was breathing hard by the time she reached the clearing.

As she hit the flatter ground, she idly wondered why Fowler's men would create such a muddy mess. The grass surrounding the turned-up soil had been trodden and destroyed. Perhaps it had something to do with the security system. Or maybe it was nothing more than a place to bury their trash. Tasiya herself had come up with the idea of burning any leftover garbage she couldn't use in the wood heating stove at night. Perhaps such a practical idea was beneath Boone Fowler's grandiose scope. Certainly, Steve Bristoe wasn't bright enough to think of such a thing for himself.

Grinning at the idea of having outsmarted her captors, and reminding herself that coming back late would make her just as foolish, Tasiya quickly gathered the bundles of discarded grass and laid them in her arms.

Beneath the last bundle, the first real shot of color she'd seen in the landscape caught her eye. Dark green and russet brown. A leaf, perhaps? But how could an autumn leaf of such a rich hue bury itself in the sand on Devil's Fork Island?

Squatting down to investigate, Tasiya saw that the mottled colors weren't natural, but a pattern on a tiny corner of cloth sticking up from the ground. She shifted the grass to one arm to pick up the material, but it was stuck. She dug away some of the wet, sandy soil on either side, wrapped all five fingers around it and gave it a good tug.

About six inches of mud-caked cloth ripped up through the soil. Enough for her to recognize a camouflage pattern. Tasiya frowned. The soldiers who'd been captured along with Bryce and the other bounty hunters wore uniforms of this material.

Why would someone bury a uniform?

With a new sense of urgency and half-formed revelation of fear, Tasiya dropped the bundles and used both hands to pull. Mud and gravity worked against her, but with a determined heave she pushed with her legs and yanked until the ground gave way.

Tasiya flew back and landed on her bottom. But she hardly noticed the discomfort of mud and water soaking through her jeans.

She could only shiver and stare.

She'd unearthed a man's cold, dead hand.

Biting her lip to keep from screaming out loud, she scrambled to her feet. But mud and panic and the heels on her boots kept her from finding her footing, and she slipped. Windmilling her arms and fighting for balance, she stumbled backward. Between leather soles and slick rocks she went down hard on her hands and knees.

Allowing nothing more than a gasp of pain, she planted her feet, stood, then cried out in shock as her knees and shoulders were zapped with a jolt of electricity.

Tasiya collapsed to the ground, shaking. But she was less concerned about her body's temporary paralysis than she was about the sudden, loud, blaring alarm she'd triggered when she hit the invisible security fence.

"Oh, God. Oh, God," she whispered, her tongue tasting like copper in her mouth.

Each howl of the alarm grated along her nerves like a vicious shout in her ear. But she could feel herself breathing again. And though the feeling hadn't returned to the tips of her fingers and toes, her larger muscles were beginning to work. The sight of that stiff, crumpled hand sticking up through the ground warned her of what she must do.

That dead man would be her if she was discovered here.

Pulling herself up to her hands and knees, Tasiya crawled across the rocks like a drunken woman. But with every inch, she gained speed, clarity, control.

She could hear Fowler's men shouting in the distance now. She gave her fingers no choice but to cooperate as she pushed the hand back into its resting place and scooped the sand and soil back over it. Booted feet were tromping through the grass now, closing in on her position. She was running out of time to hide her discovery.

Tasiya lurched to her feet, grabbed one of the sheafs of grass, swept it across the sand to cover her tracks, then tossed it over the exposed fingertips. Snatching up the remaining bundles, she scrambled up the hillside.

For the few seconds she climbed, she debated whether it was smarter to run and put distance between her and the body, or whether running would only make her look suspicious. But the decision became a moot point as she cleared the rise and was greeted by voices shouting "Halt!" and the black steel barrels of three rifles pointed straight at her.

Tasiya cast her eyes to the ground and froze.

"What are you doing out here?" Steve Bristoe, the

skinny blond man who'd been so inept in the kitchen, seemed much more sure of himself on guard duty.

She bit down on the hateful resentment shouting inside her. Bristoe was one of the men who'd beaten Bryce and held him down while Marcus whipped him. Her lungs swelled painfully in her chest as she tried to calm her breathing and keep her head. "I went for a walk. I was gathering grasses to weave a basket and I fell. I am sorry about the alarm."

Bristoe nodded to the other two men. "Walk the perimeter to make sure she's the only thing to set it off."

As the other two hurried in opposite directions to do his bidding, Bristoe nudged the tip of his rifle through the grass in her arms. Apparently satisfied that she hadn't run off with the militia's silver, he shouldered his weapon.

"Basketweaving?" he asked skeptically.

Tasiya nodded. "The kitchen supplies are limited. I thought I could help by making some items myself."

He might have withdrawn his weapon, but he wasn't letting her go. Wrapping his bony fingers around her upper arm, he jerked her into step beside him. "Whatever smokes your shorts."

Tasiya glanced up. She had no idea what that meant. But as long as he was taking her away from the unmarked grave, she wasn't going to ask any questions.

"WAIT HERE."

Tasiya was well aware of the temperature as she stood outside Boone Fowler's office in her wet clothes. The blustery draft swirling up the spiral staircase raised goose bumps along her skin and made her teeth chatter. But it was nothing like the coldhearted chill of Boone Fowler's voice as Steve Bristoe knocked and pushed open the door to report how the cook had taken herself for a walk, and accidentally tripped the alarm when she fell.

When Fowler's response didn't match the report, Tasiya realized he was holding two conversations— one with Bristoe, and one on his cell phone. As had become her habit of late, when the militiamen talked, she went quiet as a mouse and listened.

"...more money, for one thing. You can't expect me to get the results you're after in only two weeks. I have too many new recruits. Training isn't cheap."

Tasiya hugged her arms around her middle and tried to rub some warmth into her body without drowning out the terse posturing in Fowler's voice.

"You don't worry about what I have on videotape. It will be very persuasive, I promise you." Dimitri would no doubt want to know about this conversation. "When the time is right, you'll get your money's worth, I promise you.

Just what kind of message did Fowler want to

send? Did his method of *persuasion* have anything to do with the dead man?

"Uh-uh, pal. You don't screw with *my* timing. Was it your idea to kidnap the princess?" Tasiya turned her ear to the doorway, wishing she could hear who was on the other end of that line. She wondered if that person was as displeased as Fowler seemed to be. "The whole world's lookin' for her, and I don't need that kind of scrutiny." He paused. "No. No one has any idea where we are. Now why would I tell you? That'd be one more person I'd have to trust." She huddled tighter within herself at the evil in Fowler's laugh. "Not any more than you trust me. Good. I'm glad we understand each other."

He snapped his fingers, and Tasiya quickly stepped away from the door when she heard Bristoe headed her way. But Fowler's voice still carried into the hall. "I'll expect a deposit in my account tomorrow. The usual amount." With an insincere friendliness he added, "Always a pleasure."

Tasiya pressed her back against the cold stone wall and closed her eyes, breathing a sigh of relief that she'd gathered information without getting caught. At some point Dimitri would hear whatever news he wanted to hear from her and hopefully release her father. Though the thought of returning to Lukinburg and beginning her sentence as Dimitri's mistress was growing more unappealing by the minute.

"I didn't know you were into mud wrestling, sugar."

Snapping open her eyes, Tasiya looked straight up into Marcus Smith's leering smile. The leisurely stroll of his gaze along her sticky clothes sickened her as if he'd groped each clinging curve with his meaty hands.

"He'll see you now." Steve Bristoe's startling grip on her arm was almost a welcome relief.

But Marcus pointed a finger and shook his head. "Hands off, Bristoe." He wagged his finger, and the younger man let go. "The little lady's not to be touched."

Every bruise on Tasiya's body, whether from the rocks this morning or Smith's hand at her throat last night, throbbed in protest at the hypocritical order. She might not be familiar with American customs, but she was painfully familiar with the lustful need to punish and control shining in Smith's yellowed, solicitous smile. He wasn't being gallant, he was staking his unwelcome claim on her.

"Bristoe!" Fowler yelled from his office. "You're wasting my time."

Smith nodded over his shoulder. "Go back to your post. As security chief, I'll take care of her."

Screaming *no!* would do her little good. Bristoe was already jogging toward the stairs, clearly intimidated by the bullying ox.

"After you." Marcus Smith moved close enough for her to smell the sweat clinging to his clothes, close enough for his stale, tobacco-steeped breath to wash over her face. But he didn't touch her. He didn't have to. She understood the mockery in his defense of her. She understood the threat of retribution somewhere down the line if she ever dared speak out against him or interfere with his treatment of the prisoners again. "Move it, sugar."

With a dutiful nod, Tasiya slipped past him and entered Boone Fowler's office. Smith followed right behind her, making sure she walked right up to where Fowler perched on the edge of his desk.

The militia leader patted the folded-up cell phone beside him on his left. "I had to tell my colleague we were running a drill." His calculating black eyes bored into hers. "What happened, foreigner?"

Tasiya fixed her eyes on the scruffy tip of his faded beard. "I was returning from the dock when I decided to take a walk. I have been inside for many days. I needed fresh air. The ground was uneven and I fell. I am sorry."

On Fowler's right side lay a black-handled pistol. His men weren't the only ones who had gone on alert when the alarm sounded. "*You* decided to take a walk? *You* needed fresh air?"

As soon as he saw her gaze dart to the gun, his hand snaked out. Before she could draw her next breath, he had the barrel of it shoved up beneath her chin. Using the gun, he tipped her face up to his and demanded that, for once, she look him in the eye. "First I had to discipline Marcus for putting his hands on you, after you tried to come on to him."

Was that Marcus's version of what had happened in the interrogation room? She could almost feel that yellowed smirk leering behind her. Tasiya's stomach clenched into knots since the gun allowed her no other outlet for her rage and frustration.

"And now you're setting off alarms? Do you want me to think you're deliberately trying to sabotage my work?"

Tasiya bit her tongue on the lie she must keep and swallowed her pride. "I am only one woman. How could I possibly hurt you or any of your men?"

Fowler considered her response for a moment. She held his gaze, daring him to believe her. Either the direct approach had appeased him or he was tired of dealing with someone he'd labeled inferior. Shrugging aside the life or death moment, he removed the gun and got up to lock it inside the gun cabinet that framed the wall behind his desk. Growing shamefully accustomed to spying by now, she took note of where he stashed the key in his top drawer.

When he strolled back to face her, she quickly averted her eyes so he wouldn't know what she'd seen. "Just so long as you remember that, foreigner. You have no power over me. No one does. Not even our illustrious government. Gift or not, understand that I will do whatever's necessary to keep it that way."

Even kill a man and hide him in an unmarked grave?

"I understand." More than he knew.

"Now go get cleaned up before you touch my food. Marcus, you're with me. I want to start taping tomorrow."

THE WOMAN NEEDED to talk.

Bryce sat on his cot, eating the broth-soaked bread and cheese Tasiya had brought, and watched her pace off the length of his cell as she recounted the events of her day. Mostly, he watched the soft folds of her skirt catch around her long, strong thighs and tease the curve of each shapely calf. Three steps one way hinted at the womanly shape beneath her drapey clothes. Three steps back, and he caught a glimpse of creamy skin.

Though his stamina and flexibility had been severely compromised by the whipping, he noted that he must be regaining some of his strength. How else could he account for his body's healthy response to the mental debate of whether he liked the view better coming or going?

Certain parts of his anatomy didn't seem to care that he was supposed to be recuperating. Every precise movement of that articulate mouth, every careless bounce of those midnight curls, every spark that glittered in those exotic eyes triggered an answering pulse beat in his veins. The night air coming off the water was cool, but his temperature seemed to rise another degree with each detail he noticed about her. And judging by the rising heat pooling behind his zipper, he was noticing a lot more than he should.

Coming or going didn't matter. He drained half the cup of water she'd poured and wished it was icy cold. No matter how he looked at Tasiya Belov, there was something to like.

And if she'd shown any interest in him beyond the need of a sounding board, Bryce might have forgotten his plan for tonight.

He had only a few days of solitude, with minimal supervision from the militia, to make something happen. And whether she knew it or not, Tasiya was going to help.

"I think if I was a man, he would have shot me." Tasiya had finally stopped. She stood at the window, hugging her arms around herself and staring up at the waning moon.

Bryce stopped chewing. He scrambled for the emotional detachment he'd been practicing all day, choking the bread past the lump of rancor in his throat. "He pulled a gun on you?"

His voice sounded remarkably calm, considering the damage he wanted to do to the man who'd threatened her.

Her slim shoulders lifted with a deep breath. "He held it to me right here." She faced him and pointed to the deadly target beneath her chin. "He has three rifles and several pistols in the cabinet in his office. One day it's a knife, now a gun. For a man who cannot stand to put his hands on me, he seems to have a very—" Bryce gritted his teeth as she searched for a word he was pretty damn sure he didn't want to hear "—disturbing...way of making contact."

When had Fowler pulled a knife on her?

Screw emotional detachment.

Finding out where a cache of weapons was located barely registered through the impotent fury firing in Bryce's veins. He set aside his last bite and pushed himself to his feet, forgetting for a moment that Bryce Martin on full charge could be a pretty terrifying thing as well. "Did he hurt you?"

"No." Tasiya flinched. Her eyes widened like saucers. Their focus darted from corner to corner of his tiny cell, no doubt taking note of the fact that he stood between her and the door.

No, Fowler didn't hurt me? Or no, don't come any closer, you big brute?

Bryce curled his toes into the floor and fisted his hands to keep his protective anger in check. He turned to the side to let her know she could pass by without fearing him, that she could leave at any time. He had to show her with his body that she didn't need to fear him since he knew that *reassuring* wasn't an expression his face could make. "I'm sorry."

Tasiya's brow furrowed as she searched for something in his craggy features. He couldn't tell what she saw until she spoke. "You startled me is all. You are not like Boone Fowler. The man has no heart. He cares about causes, not people. I am the one who is sorry if I made you...uncomfortable."

"Hell, you can't hurt me."

Her eyes were touched with some of that pity he'd planned to take advantage of. But the tight set of her mouth and the flush of color on her cheeks made her look as if she was mad enough to spit. "Just because you can withstand pain does not mean it should be inflicted upon you."

Tasiya's succinct words chipped away at that brittle shell of self-protection he wore like armor around his heart. She was defending him the way his grandparents used to, back when kids had teased him on the playground or a girl had reneged on a prom date when she got a better offer.

It just meant she had a kind heart, he reminded himself. She was a good person, nothing more, nothing less. But her insistence touched him. The fact she took a couple of steps toward him meant even more.

Still, he had to remember *he* was the protector here, not her. "He's got no right to treat you that way."

"He thinks because I am a woman, because I come from another country, that I am too stupid to know what he is doing. He does not believe I have the courage to defy him."

Defy? Bryce didn't like the sound of that. That was his job. "Maybe you'd best not—"

"I will show him." She was hugging herself again, rubbing her hands up and down her arms to dispel excess energy or warm herself. His own hands itched to do that for her, but he suspected keeping his distance right now would do a lot more to calm her than touching her would. "I am smarter than he knows. I bring the prisoners extra food and inventory the supplies so he does not know they are missing. I have found out secrets about this island."

"What secrets?"

"There is a body buried here. On the western shore at the edge of the grass. One of the soldiers."

The kid they'd executed two weeks ago. Hell, she'd seen that?

"I wondered what happened to him. I saw him the night he was...murdered. Damn." Bryce squeezed his eyes shut, unable and unwilling to forget the ominous crack of a single gunshot and the sight of that lifeless body being videotaped by a laughing cameraman.

The subtle scents of yeast and shampoo teased his nose just before he felt a tug on his shirt. Bryce blinked his eyes open to find Tasiya straightening the open placket. About a size too small, the shirt wouldn't button without rubbing the cloth across the cuts on his back, so he'd let it hang open.

But that didn't stop her from tucking it together

and smoothing it across his skin. What? Did she think he was gonna catch cold now? It wasn't a hug or a smile, but her matter-of-fact attentions eased some of the pain and anger inside him. "I would think your army would want to punish Mr. Fowler for that."

"They'd love to kick his ass." So would he. "Honey, you gotta watch talkin' back to Boone Fowler. Don't give him any excuse to hurt you."

Bryce shivered, whether from the stroke of her fingers or the realization that he'd just crossed a very dangerous line, he couldn't tell. *Honey?* Where the hell had that come from? But Tasiya didn't seem to notice. Maybe she didn't understand the significance of the word—or what her gentle touches were doing to his efforts to keep his distance from her.

Her hands were on his neck now, straightening his collar. "Do not worry. My rebellion is silent. I know my place. A woman cannot speak out against a man. My word would not be good in court. But I will—"

"Your place?" He wrapped his fingers around her wrists and pulled her hands away. Touching her soft skin sent him one step farther across that line, but Bryce wasn't paying attention to the warning signals. "Where does Fowler get off treatin' you like some kind of second-class citizen? Why couldn't you testify in court?"

She shrugged as if she'd uttered something that

was common knowledge and he was a dolt for not knowing it. "I am a woman."

"Men and women have equal rights here in the United States. Your word's as good as any man's. A damn sight better than Fowler's, I'm guessin'." A new understanding dawned. "That why you don't always look me in the eye? 'Cause I'm a man and you're a woman?"

Automatically her dark eyes shuttered and her gaze dropped to the middle of his chest. She pulled her hands away and held herself in a subservient posture that busted at that soft spot inside him. "Should I not be so bold with you?"

"Hey." He nudged her beneath the chin, splaying his tanned, roughened fingers against her paler, velvety skin, finally touching her the way he'd wanted to. Her eyes glittered like polished mahogany when he tilted her face up to his, and the night air warmed up a good ten degrees between them. "I know I ain't handsome, but I like a person to look me in the face when they talk to me."

"Your face isn't…" Her forehead crinkled in mute apology and the right words tried to form on her lips. *Oh, no, woman. Don't tell me it ain't ugly.* A lie now would spoil the tenuous bond he felt with her. "You have very beautiful eyes. The color reminds me of the mountains and the robust winters in my homeland. I feel…safe…when I look into your eyes."

Though the words were a little too poetic for his

taste, her soft, melodic voice sounded genuine. She hadn't called him handsome, hadn't said anything remotely provocative. But Bryce felt the admission deep beneath the scars that had hardened him inside and out.

"Thanks." He pressed a chaste kiss to that frown mark on her forehead, resting his lips there for a moment until he felt the tension in her relax. Then he pulled away. "That might be the best compliment I ever had."

Bryce's voice sounded deep and growly in his own ears. But he was standin' a might too close to her clean smells and amused smile to retain much objectivity about where they were, who he was and what he had to do.

Right now Bryce wanted only one thing. And the drowsy sigh in Tasiya's throat said that maybe she wanted it, too.

He slipped his hand beneath the ebony fall of hair behind her ear, cupping the back of her head and tangling himself in the silky weight of springy curls that caught around his fingers and teased his palm. The curious way she focused on his mouth made him hungry to taste her.

Go slow, he warned himself, dipping his head. Their eyes met for one hesitant moment, asking permission, granting it. And then he touched his lips to hers.

She was warm and soft and pliant beneath him. And Bryce thought he'd gone to heaven.

It was just a little kiss at first. He was every bit as mindful of his size and scars and not wanting to frighten her as he'd been with that modest kiss to her forehead. He'd suspected she hadn't had much experience—as controlled as her life had been, as old-world and ladylike as she behaved—why else would she even consider him a candidate to strike up a friendship with?

But then Tasiya inhaled a stuttered breath. Her lips parted and she braced her palms against the center of his chest.

"Kiss me like I was an American woman," she murmured against his mouth, brushing her lips across his in a tiny sampler of kisses.

"Tasiya…honey…" He met each kiss with a grateful one of his own. He touched his tongue to the fullest part of her lip and traced the rim. She tasted so good. He'd bet she tasted even better along the smooth, damp warmth inside her mouth. He swallowed hard, reining in his desire. "In this country we're equals, remember? If you want something, or you want me to stop, just say so."

"Don't stop." She almost whimpered with the protest. "I don't know how, but I want…more."

She caught his bottom lip between hers and suckled, sending a jolt of pure energy straight to his groin. This was a woman who didn't know how to kiss? If she ever figured out what she was doing, he'd be in serious trouble.

Bryce curled his left hand into a fist at his side to keep himself from grabbing her, plunging his tongue inside and taking everything she was offering. As far as he could tell, the woman was a natural talent. But if she was looking for a man to teach her the seductive intricacies and delights of kissing, then his normal bull-in-the-china-shop technique probably wouldn't get the job done.

Yeah, he'd had sex. But cuddling? Kissing? Tender foreplay? They just weren't in his dossier of experience with women.

And this one—strong and innocent and eager to explore—got into his blood and fired him up. He wanted more, too. Soon. Now. But he was too big, too strong, too damn lonesome for the physical acceptance she offered. He'd scare her off for sure if he gave in to the flashfire of hungry need that was burning him up from the inside out.

In his condition, *slow* should be about all he could do, right?

Slow, slow, sl—

"Bryce Martin," she gasped. Her hot breath fanned across his cheek in an urgent plea. She moaned low in her throat, curled her fingers into his shirt, kneaded his skin and demanded he give her what she wanted. "Please."

No slow.

Who was he kidding? He had to be the man he was. Bryce tunneled all ten fingers into her hair, forcing her head back into the basket of his hands so he could plunder her mouth. He thrust his tongue inside, finding hers, touching the tip, twirling them together. He snatched up handfuls of that liquid midnight hair and let the heavy tendrils sweep across his bare forearms, teasing him with dozens and dozens of tiny caresses.

He wanted to feel that hair brushing his naked chest. He wanted to see it fanned across a pristine white pillow while he went down on top of her.

"Tasiya." He groaned her name into the silk at her temple, fighting for a deep breath to erase the images of sex and Tasiya and explosive heat that consumed him. He kissed her again, unable to resist her seeking lips.

She wanted more? He wanted everything.

He slid his fingers down through the length of her hair and discovered the silk didn't end until he reached her waist. He splayed his fingers at the small of her back and tried to pull her closer. "Touch me."

Wherever, however she wanted. He needed her to be feeling at least half of this crazy madness that was steaming out of his ears.

But her hands and arms were wedged between them, keeping them apart. Her fingers tangled in the canvas of his shirt, pulling it across a gash near his shoulder blade. He winced. She apologized.

"I do not know where—"

"I'm fine." He reassured her with a kiss.

She trailed her fingers down the center of his chest, eliciting a groan of pleasure she mistook for another injury. "I am sorry."

"No, honey. Don't stop." He kissed her again, desperate to reclaim her when she snatched her hands away. He could feel his energy ebbing as his frustration grew. But other forces were winging through his body now—adrenaline, desire—giving him a new source of strength and purpose.

She tapped at his shoulders, tugged at one sleeve, looking for purchase but afraid to touch. "I do not want to hurt y—"

"I won't break. I promise."

He took her arms and looped them around his neck. In the same fluid motion, he snugged his hands at her waist and walked into her, pressing their bodies together from chest to knee. Her breasts pillowed against him. He slipped his hands inside her sweater and ran his palms across her cool, smooth back. She wound her arms tighter, sparking a delicious friction between the pebbled tips of her breasts and the wall of his chest as she pulled herself up into his greedy kiss. Equals? Hell. He was playing catch-up.

She couldn't hurt him. Not when it felt this good, this right to hold her in his arms. The only way she could hurt him now was to come to her senses and end the kiss.

Senses. Ah, damn. A nagging voice that had

been with him a lot longer than this hunger for Tasiya reminded him of his mission. He tried to ignore the instincts that had been trained into him from the first day he'd enlisted in the army. The same creed he lived by now as a bounty hunter. *The mission comes first. Your men are depending on you.*

Bryce forgot all about even pretending he knew how to finesse a woman. Bracing a hand against the stones, he drove her back against the wall and wedged his thigh between hers in a desperate effort to ease the ache in every pore that had been ignited, and could only be assuaged by touching Tasiya— by absorbing her into his skin, his muscle, his heart.

She scraped her palms across the short hair at his nape and hummed in her throat as if the needy, coarse action somehow thrilled her. "Bryce Martin," she gasped as he shamelessly rubbed himself against her womanly heat. "I have never—"

He stole her breath with another kiss. He didn't want to talk. He just wanted her. He wanted to feel normal. He wanted to feel her passion. He wanted to pretend that this was real, that she'd be kissing him anywhere on the planet right now—not just in this desperate, hidden corner of the night where two solitary souls had no one else to turn to.

But the voice was insistent. *You gotta do it, Sarge. Forget how good this feels, how bad you want this. Think. Do this before your strength gives out.*

"Whoa." What did she say? *I have never?* Did she mean—?

Get a grip on reality, Sarge.

"Whoa." He whispered the word more firmly against her mouth, drawing on sheer will to turn his lips away from temptation. But burying his nose in the clean scent of her hair wasn't much better for gathering his composure.

"Whoa." He planted both feet flat on the ground and pulled his body away from hers, praying the damp ocean breeze would chill the air between them and cool him off fast.

"What is *Whoa?*" she asked on a breath as raspy and uneven as his own.

Bryce couldn't pull away entirely. He wasn't strong enough to do it. Not yet. His back ached, but there was something inside him hurtin' even more. So he rested his forehead against hers, looking down into those beautiful eyes and kiss-swollen lips as he awkwardly straightened the clothes he'd nearly torn from her back. The stones were too hard, too cold for her tender skin. He pulled her away from the wall and retreated a step himself, finally letting go. He looked her straight in the eye. "It means we should stop. We can't do this here. I can't do this to you. Take a good look at my face, Tasiya. You don't want to do this with me."

She frowned at his crude speech. He didn't mean to reject her or hurt her. He just wanted her to wise up. Devil's Fork Island was too dangerous a place for either one of them to be distracted by false hopes or fairy-tale kisses.

She smoothed her hair as best she could after his hands had had their way with it. "I have never been kissed like that before."

Join the club. But Bryce knew she was talking about being inexperienced when it came to getting hot and heavy with any man. "I shouldn't have—"

"Shh." Despite the innocence of her body, she smiled like a siren as she pressed gentle fingers over his sensitized lips. "Do not spoil it with an apology. I knew who you were when I kissed you. I looked into your eyes and knew that I would be safe. I am not sorry it happened."

As stunned by her acceptance as he'd been by her enthusiastic, untutored response, Bryce could only turn and stare as she crossed to the cot and picked up his chains. "But it is late. I must go. You need your rest."

He held out his wrists and let her snap them shut around him, transforming him from a man into a prisoner again.

But when she was done, she took the sting away by blessing him with a gorgeous smile. "Good night, Bryce Martin."

He couldn't help himself. This was as hard a goodbye as any he'd faced in his life. Without touching her in any other way, he bent his head and stole one more quick kiss. She wisely backed out and pulled the door shut before he could steal another.

With a definitive click, the steel bars locked into place. And after one last, searching look, she picked up her things and walked away.

"'Night," he called after her, watching her every step of the way until the last flip of her skirt disappeared around the corner.

I am not sorry. Hell. She would be soon enough.

Every good, hopeful feeling she'd spawned inside him withered. Bryce cursed himself and turned away from the bars.

He pulled out the band of keys he'd stolen from her and unlocked the manacles from his wrists.

Chapter Eight

Tasiya wasn't sure how it had happened—how thank-yous and comforts had escalated so quickly into a kiss that left her still shaky on her feet as she negotiated the shadowy passageways of the prison wing.

Clutching the water pitcher in the crook of her arm, she stuffed Bryce's napkin into his metal cup and freed her hand to trail her fingertips along the slick, cold stones. That was all it took to recall how feverish she'd felt, pressed between the wall and Bryce's hard body.

His needy hands in her hair and on the bare skin of her arms and back had been as sensuous as the raspy tickle of a cat's tongue and as hungry as a ravenous lion. His mouth had been gentle at first, then most insistent. Then he'd driven her absolutely mad with the need to learn how he elicited every tingle, every shaft of heat inside her. She'd been thrilled to discover that touching him, kissing him, striving to give him the same pleasure in return only intensified the experience for her.

She curled her fingers into her palms and hastened past the corridors leading to the other prison cells, hoping the aftershocks of those last few minutes in Bryce's cell would dissipate before she reached the breezeway and ran the chance of bumping into one of the sentries posted outside.

But her breasts still felt heavy, and prickly at the tips. The intensity of Bryce's need, and the power of her own body's unexpected response, had frightened her at first. Then she couldn't seem to get enough of the way he made her feel. Ultimately she'd been left feeling mysteriously incomplete when he had reluctantly but, oh, so sweetly ended the kiss.

Though it had angered her at first for Bryce to claim that she was kissing him just because she wanted to be with someone, she'd quickly seen through his self-effacing lecture. He was worried that he'd frightened her or had taken advantage. He didn't believe anyone could see through his scars to the good man he was inside. That a woman, that *she* could want him.

Dimitri Mostek, with his handsome face and politic charm, had tried time and again to force a kiss, to seduce her. But though he'd said pretty things and offered her gifts, she'd never felt anything but revulsion for the man. She'd never once been tempted to offer him her trust or her body.

Bryce Martin, a wounded ogre of a man with kind eyes and a unique way with words, had nothing to give but his time and his patience. He spoke of things that made her dream of freedom from men like Mostek and Fowler and Marcus Smith, that made her feel better about who she was and the woman she could become. He listened when she talked. He cared that she was hurt and scared and alone.

And he kissed like...well, Tasiya had little to compare it to. But there was something raw and honest and very basic about Bryce Martin's embrace. That immense physical strength, tempered by his determination to be gentle, then refined into desire in its purest form and focused on her, was enough to make any woman feel as if she was the sexiest, most beautiful woman on earth.

Dimitri Mostek's lust made her feel dirty and small. Bryce Martin's attentions empowered her with confidence and strength.

It was well past midnight now, but Tasiya felt renewed as she passed by the locked iron doors of the interrogation room, the communication center, and who knew what other secret places a man like Boone Fowler might hide. She was too keyed up to sleep, and more inspired than ever to, in some small way, put a crimp in the militia's plans.

She would work for a while on the basket she'd started that afternoon—the one that would allow her to creep about the prison wing and visit Bryce without being detected. She'd also start planning exactly what she wanted to say to Dimitri Mostek when she called him that evening.

Relating the argument over money she'd heard between Fowler and his mysterious partner should clue in Dimitri that the Americans he and his superior were funding were not so loyal as he would hope. They expected the militia to stop Prince Nikolai's speeches and stop the UN from invading Lukinburg and taking away their power.

Instead, the militia was murdering soldiers, torturing men who weren't even in the military, and demanding money from another source. Perhaps that would be enough to convince Dimitri that Boone Fowler was a much bigger liability than her father could ever be, and would shift his attention to the American traitor and let the petty embezzler who'd only wanted to feed his daughter go free.

She wasn't holding her breath that Dimitri would agree to such a thing. But it couldn't hurt to ask. According to Bryce, women in America could ask for anything they wanted—and she was in America, wasn't she?

A serene smile of satisfaction curled her lips as she closed the iron door that shut off the prison wing behind her. The dreadful weight of it creaked into place, and her smile quickly faded. She was no better than Fowler or Dimitri each night she locked this door behind her.

Her silent rebellion and pushy American questions meant little as she closed off Bryce and the other prisoners in their dismal time warp of eighteenth-century barbarism. But what could she do, short of setting them free and sentencing her father and most likely herself to certain death?

Tasiya's entire sense of hope seemed to be closed up on the other side of that door, as well. On this side of the iron barrier, there was no Bryce. She had no friend. There were only watchful eyes and suspicion and loneliness.

For two seconds she considered leaving the door unlocked, to give Bryce and his comrades some chance at escape, to give her an imaginary connection to the men inside. But, ultimately, Tasiya was a practical woman. Nurturing her own kinship to Bryce and the prisoners would only put them at greater risk. If Marcus Smith and his security team found the door open, there would no doubt be a price to pay. And after witnessing the price literally extracted from Bryce's hide for her defiance in the interrogation room, she would not put them at risk again.

Tasiya reached for her keys to open the padlock so she could slip it through the hasp and secure the dead bolt in place before the guard's inspection at dawn. She frowned. Her wrist was empty. "Where...?"

She quickly checked the other arm, refusing to acknowledge the panic that lit a fuse inside her. "What have I done?"

She set the pitcher and cup on the floor and shoved the sleeves up past her elbows. Nothing. She slid her sweater back into place the same way Bryce had done after… A funny little glitch of a memory tried to tell her something.

The fuse shifted direction inside her and raced straight toward her heart.

"He wouldn't." She checked her pockets, the pitcher, the cup. She pushed open the door and retraced her steps across the floor. But she would have heard the keys hitting the stones, wouldn't she?

"He didn't take them," she whispered out loud, needing to hear the reassurance herself.

Her breath came in quick, nervous gasps. She peered into the shadows, beyond the glare from the harsh bulbs, desperately looking for the shiny glint of her missing keys. "I dropped them somewhere, that's all."

One of the men might notice the jingling at her wrist had fallen silent. They'd see the locked padlock on the open door and come looking for her. Without her keys, she couldn't get into the pantry to prepare any meals. By their 7 a.m. breakfast call, the militia would certainly notice that.

The fuse inside her hit its mark and caught fire. Finding those keys was her only option for survival.

After tucking the pitcher and cup into a hidden corner, she raced back through the corridor. She spared a glance for the sleeping soldiers and curious stare of the handsome, green-eyed bounty hunter who rose to his feet as she checked the floor outside his cell.

"You're out kind of late, aren't you?" he asked in

a croaky voice that might have something to do with the ligature marks around his neck. "Something goin' on? You understand me, don't you? You okay?"

For the briefest of moments, Tasiya wanted to ask him if he'd seen his friend, Bryce Martin. But she had a horrible feeling his answer might be yes. She clamped her mouth shut around the question, shook her head and ran down the next corridor.

"Hey, I appreciate the extra rations." But the compliment fell into an empty hallway as she continued her frenzied search.

There were no keys. No hint of anything modern along her path. She didn't want to think that Bryce had used…

But the last place she'd had them was to enter his cell and free him from his manacles and leg irons. Then she'd slipped them onto her wrist. They'd talked and… "No."

Anger hastened her steps, warring with the panic inside her. She whipped around the last corner. The light behind her cast a shadow, blocking what little moonlight streamed into the corridor.

"Bryce Martin?" she called in a heated whisper. She stumbled up to the bars. *No. No, no.* She grasped the steel in her fists and stared into the empty cell.

"No!" She pounded one of the bars with the heel of her palm, then turned and peered into the passageway. "How could you?"

The one man she'd cared about in this place—the

one man she'd thought cared about her—had stolen her keys and escaped.

"Where would you go?" she muttered aloud, already moving back toward the solitary light she'd brought him so that he wouldn't be alone in the dark. Ha! He *was* a beast. He didn't give a damn about her consideration for him. She was a stupid, lonely woman who'd been easy prey for his kind words and abundant strength. He saw that she felt something for him, that she wanted to trust him— and he'd taken advantage.

Tasiya sulked around the corner as resentment gave way to disgust at her own naiveté. She intended to find Bryce and get her keys back, then let him suffer the consequences for leaving his cell. She peered into every shadow. Peeked under doors for any sign of movement.

But *consequences* was a dangerous word on Devil's Fork Island. Memories of a man being beaten until he fell unconscious, a man having his long hair shaved with a rough blade to purposely leave cuts and scars—a young soldier buried in an unmarked grave in the middle of nowhere—clarified every emotion into stark, wary fear.

It hurt that Bryce had used her. But she could understand. Freedom, as he'd taught her, was a precious thing. She'd never known it was worth fighting for. But Bryce had never forgotten.

"Where are you?" Her words bounced along

the stone walls and were swallowed up by the breezy mist.

If Bryce made it all the way outside, the sentries would catch him. Even if he was stealthy enough to avoid capture, he'd eventually hit the perimeter fence. The electric shock would set off the alarm and incapacitate him. Every man would be awake and armed. And he'd be paralyzed while they hunted him down.

Suddenly Tasiya was every bit as afraid for Bryce's safety as she'd been upset with him for using her. She quickened her pace, sharpened her ears to any sound, and doubled her efforts to find him. She still wanted to throttle him, but she'd do it once he was safely back inside his cell, out of harm's way, beyond Boone Fowler's reach.

She heard a thump and turned toward it. "Bryce Martin?"

Tasiya hurried down the corridor, drawn to the sound. "Bryce Mart—!"

Rough hands grabbed her from behind and dragged her into a darkened room.

TASIYA'S SCREAM RANG in her ears, muted by the large hand that covered her mouth. She twisted and kicked, but the hands wouldn't let go. A steel band cinched around her waist, trapping her arms and lifting her clear off the floor before a force, like a large truck, flattened her against the wall.

"Hush." A nearly inaudible warning brushed

against her ear, and Tasiya went completely still, save for the shallow, sucking gasps that thrust her chest and stomach against a now-familiar immovable object.

Tasiya recognized Bryce by size, smell and the sound of his voice just as Ike waddled past the open door, oblivious to the statuelike couple in the shadows mere inches away. Over the bulk of Bryce's shoulder she saw that Ike carried a crumpled sheet of paper in his fist and muttered to himself between yawns. Because he had his headphones on, he thankfully hadn't heard her calling out. But she would have run right into him if she'd continued on her frantic path.

Eons seemed to pass before she felt Bryce's deep breath push against her chest. The prison had fallen silent now, except for the endless drone of hidden machinery that she normally tuned out as background noise.

He removed the muzzle of his hand and let her slide down onto her feet. "I thought you said there were no sentries inside."

His voice, barely a whisper, was as sharply articulate as she'd ever heard it. She matched his volume, if not his tone. "Ike is in charge of communications. Normally, once I lock the door at night, no one comes into this wing until morning. I do not know why he is here."

"He must be sendin' a message. Somethin's goin' down."

She didn't know what direction *down* would be in a one-story building. Only the crumbling look-out tower that housed Boone Fowler's office and bedroom had a set of stairs. But as naive as she'd been about Bryce's intentions with her earlier, she didn't presume to understand him now.

"You must return to your cell," she pleaded. "If anyone finds you, you will be punished."

His fingers hovered close to her temple, as if he wanted to touch her. Instead he clamped his fingers into a fist and released her with a sharp, heated curse. "Not yet. I gotta get the layout of this place. I need to know my options."

Tasiya shivered as he crossed to the door and peeked into the corridor. She hugged her arms across her stomach, unsure whether the sudden chill was part of the close call they'd had, or the fact that she missed Bryce's abundant heat. As her eyes adjusted to the darkness, she could see a screwdriver poking up from Bryce's hip pocket. He'd stolen that instead of a knife or gun?

But a look around the room revealed there were no weapons to be had. It appeared to be little more than a storage facility, with scattered maintenance supplies and crates of spare parts she couldn't identify. "What is this place?"

Bryce spun around and slipped into the shadows.

She could hear him quietly moving things. "Where's the communications room?" he asked. "You know what kind of setup they have?"

Setup she didn't understand. But going to the room where they knew at least one of the militiamen would be waiting for them was clear enough.

"Please. Give me my keys and go back to your cell." She followed the sound of him working across the room. "I will not tell anyone you got out or that you have stolen anything. I promise."

"I'm guessin' all this stuff's stolen. Or bought off the black market. But they'd need a lot of money to do that. Most of it's military issue."

Military? Tasiya picked up something that looked suspiciously like a microchip. It certainly wasn't native to the prison's antique decor. She scanned the room. While she couldn't identify most of the items, their markings—like the radio set Ike had carried into Fowler's office—were all painted in camouflage patterns or labeled with military codes. "Are they planning an invasion?"

It was a rhetorical question, but Bryce answered anyway. "They call themselves a militia. A group of citizens who train to be soldiers. Believe me, Boone Fowler's lookin' for a battle to fight."

"Against you?"

"He made Big Sky Bounty Hunters his enemy when he broke out of prison and started killin' people. He may call it patriotism, but he's just a murderin' thug. Whatever ideals he once had have been perverted into a lust for power."

Like Dimitri Mostek and his superior. Men who used glory of the homeland as an excuse to wield their corrupt authority over Lukinburg citizens. Very dangerous men. Not the sort that one man—even Bryce Martin—could take on, on their own.

"Please." Tasiya circled the crates and touched Bryce's arm. She knew how to put her feelings aside in order to keep someone safe. "You must go back to your cell. I do not want you to be found here."

He stopped his search for a moment and looked over the jut of his shoulder at her. His eyes glittered in the darkness. "You know what a son of a bitch is?"

She'd heard the phrase more than once since she'd been here, and only knew it to be a curse. "No."

"You're lookin' at one." He shrugged his arm away from her and went back to work. "You shouldn't be worryin' about me. I don't deserve it."

"Why? Because you made me think I was special when, in reality, I was merely a tool for your escape?"

He froze for an instant, and even through the dim light from the hall she could see the sadness on his face. But then he shrugged it off and reached for another crate. "Yeah. Somethin' like that."

She could scarcely overpower him, so she had to rely on reasoning with him—or guilting him back to safety. "So you will go to your cell now?"

He didn't answer.

His big fingers moved with surprising agility as he sorted through items and filled his pockets— small metal disks that looked like bottle caps, needle-nosed pliers and a spool of white cord that reminded her of the island grass. "You know if this Ike uses radio waves or a satellite connection? Is he hooked up to a computer? Use a cell phone?"

She was quite certain she didn't know any of those things. When it became clear that Bryce was going to finish the task he'd started before he made any attempt to do as she asked, Tasiya decided that providing some kind of information might speed the process. "I think they monitor military or law enforcement channels. They knew that someone had tried to kidnap Princess Veronika in Montana, even before it was on the news from the networks."

Bryce's hands stopped. She felt his wintry gaze on her in the darkness. "Veronika Petrov? She all right?"

"A man saved her. Now the two of them have disappeared."

"The militia have anythin' to do with it?" He set aside one crate and rifled through the contents of the next one.

"I do not believe so. Mr. Fowler seemed quite angry that the attempt had been made." She didn't mention the knife he'd pressed to her chin as though he'd blamed *her* for the incident. "He said it did not fit with his plan and would bring more scrutiny to him. He wants publicity, but I do not think he is ready for it. Not until the videotapes are made."

Bryce stopped. "What do you know about videotapes?"

"Only that he will start filming them tomorrow."

The outline of Bryce's shoulders sagged. "Damn. I thought I'd have more time."

"More time for what?" Tasiya reached across the crate and laid her fingers across the back of his hand. A shiver of goose bumps rose across his skin and she wondered if this might finally be the way to persuade him. "Please, you need your rest. I do not think your body will withstand any more punishment. And if you are caught, they will surely—"

He jerked his hand away. "I need to get to that communication room. See if I can get a message out."

"Not while Ike is there." She clutched at his sleeve and tried to keep him from doing such a crazy thing. "He wears a gun. They all do. He will shoot you."

But stopping Bryce was like standing in front of a moving train. He easily slipped from her grip and headed to the door.

"Bryce, no!" Tasiya dashed around the crates and hurried after him. But he stopped unexpectedly in the doorway, and she plowed right into the middle of his back.

He didn't cry out, but she could see the flinch in his posture, she could hear his fingernails grating across the stones as he squeezed his fists around the door frame.

She pressed her fingers to her lips to stifle her own gasp, but couldn't stop the sting of tears burning her eyes. Lord, how she must have hurt him. His skin would still be raw, his nerves on fire. She backed away, not fearing his wrath but aware of her own ineptitude at causing him such pain. "I am so sorry."

His shoulders heaved in slow, deep breaths. He dropped his chin against his chest, but he didn't seem to be able to move. Tasiya slipped beneath his arm and gently pushed at his stomach, nudging him back into the storage room, out of sight from Ike or anyone else who might walk past while he was in such a vulnerable state.

He released the frame, leaned his weight on her shoulder and let her guide him back into the shadows. "You're right. Maybe I'm not up to this yet."

With her hands still at his waist, offering what support she could, she looked up into the taut lines of his face. "Please. I will get medicine. Ice. A blanket. Whatever it takes to make you feel better. But you must stop this madness and go back to your cell."

"All right." He nodded, but she knew it was too soon to breathe a sigh of relief. "On one condition."

"What? Anything."

He took her hands and pulled her into the darkest corner where she could only imagine the expression on his face. But his voice was deep and strong with his husky request. "Forgive me for kissin' you."

"There is nothing to forgive." She answered the question too quickly and tried to leave, but Bryce's grip didn't budge.

"There is, and we both know it."

Tasiya wanted him to forget that humiliating embrace. Obviously, it had meant something different to her than it had to him. She ducked her head to stare at the black space where she knew his chest would be. "I know now you did not want to. That it was only a trick to distract me. I understand why you did it."

"I'm up here, honey." He slipped his callused fingers beneath her chin and tilted her face up to his. "You be mad at me all you want. Hate me, if that's what you feel. But I never want you to be afraid to look me in the eye and tell me the truth."

The warmth of his fingertips and his fierce words quickly took her back to the strength she'd felt before realizing he'd stolen her keys. But wasn't that just an illusion? Did Bryce Martin really care? She lifted her chin away from his touch but gamely held her head high. "I do not hate you. I am embarrassed to be so—what is the American word?—gullible? You must think me very foolish to throw myself at you like that."

"No." His hands closed around her shoulders, his

fingers kneading her flesh with a little bit of that controlled desperation she'd found so seductive earlier. "You didn't read the signals wrong. I wanted that kiss more than my next breath. I wanted *you.* I still do." He released her and she could see the silhouette of his fingers splayed out to either side as if she was arresting him for touching her. "But this can't be about what *I* want. I got a job to do. My men are dependin' on me. Maybe you were, too, and I screwed that up. I'm sorry. I'm sorry I hurt you."

"Apology accepted. Now can we go?"

"Slap my face or somethin'. Call me whatever they call a pig in your country."

"I will not hurt you," she vowed, shocked at the notion after seeing so much violence in her life already. "And you are not the son of the bitch. It is no crime to help your friends or do your duty. I do the same thing when I bring you extra rations and care for your wounds. I am only sorry that I confused our comradeship with something more."

"What's goin' on between you and me is a hell of a lot more than comradeship."

"There is nothing going on between us," she insisted, confused to hear him claim he had some kind of feelings for her. "We are two lonely people caught in a terrible situation. Do not worry about it."

"How many men you ever kiss like that before?"

She shook her head. They needed to leave. "Forget it."

He grabbed her by the elbow as she tried to hurry past. He bent his head and whispered in her ear. "I've *never* kissed anyone like that."

Tasiya stopped in her tracks, feeling his breath like a caress that stirred her hair, hearing his ragged words like some kind of promise. She turned her head. His mouth was right there in front of her eyes. A rugged, sensuous line that had shown her kindness and passion, that had made her feel powerful inside and weak in the knees. "What are you saying?"

She watched his lips and waited for his words. But Bryce Martin had his own way of communicating with her. He tugged on her arm, tunneled his fingers into her hair and dipped his head to cover her mouth with his own.

Electricity arced instantly between them, making Tasiya catch her breath. He tongued the seam of her lips and she opened for him, helpless in the face of his unfiltered need. The tug of an emotion too powerful to acknowledge squeezed her heart and filled her with the desire to heal the hurts and distrusts and misunderstandings between them.

She lifted her hands up to frame his face, less aware of the rigid scars at the surface than of the flex of muscle and the pounding pulse beating underneath. Bryce's quick, deep breaths fanned across her cheek as his mouth moved against hers. This kiss was quick, fiery and all too brief.

With a groan from the cavern of his chest, Bryce lifted his mouth. With his passion-hooded eyes looking deep into hers, he pulled her hand from his jaw and slipped something hard and cold into her palm.

His nostrils flared as he worked to regain control of his breathing. Tasiya was too shaken by her own eager response to move away, but she understood the gift as he curled her fingers over her keys and held her fist in his larger one.

"A gesture of good faith."

Tasiya nodded her thanks, unable to speak. She was too busy trying to regulate the pulse still pounding in her ears and decode all the emotions she'd felt in that kiss.

Bryce stroked his fingers through her hair, the only place he touched her now. Maybe he was straightening the tangles from his clutching hands, but Tasiya sensed it was more of a petting, a soothing, an apology. Though which of them needed more comforting right now she couldn't tell.

"You're gonna get hurt if you get involved with me, Tasiya, and that'd kill me. I don't know what you've seen in me these past weeks, but I'm grateful. I will always treasure our time together—even if it was all inside this crazy place."

This was goodbye? How could that be? How could he show her such need and concern one moment, then say such a fatalistic farewell in the next breath? "Bryce—"

But the man finally had something to say, and he wanted her to listen. "I gotta do my job. But I'll find a way to do it without you. So you don't get hurt again. By me, or anyone else. I can live with loneliness and I can live with anger. But I can't live with knowin' I hurt you."

He tucked her hair behind her ear, lingering in the long strands as if savoring a forgotten memory. But then he let her go and grabbed her hand. "C'mon. You can lock me up, and I promise I'll never mess with your head again."

"Mess with my head?" Was that part of caring or escaping?

He grinned at their latest communication snafu, but she noted the smile never reached his eyes.

"Let's go." He pulled her alongside him, keeping her out of sight as he paused in the doorway and checked for any visitors. With the light from the passageway to highlight his craggy features, it was easy to read his austere expression. He was all business now, and she should be thankful. But Tasiya missed the tender, passionate man she'd seen glimpses of tonight.

She believed, now, that he really cared about her on some level. As a friend, an innocent caught up in a dangerous game of survival, a woman he was attracted to. How else could a man be so protective yet feel so guilty? How could he kiss her as if she was a precious, beautiful treasure and then turn around and ask to be forgiven for wanting her in such a deeply personal way? She couldn't help but admire him for his loyalty to his friends and his devotion to freedom and justice.

Why hadn't any other woman seen through all his scars to the good heart he had inside?

Pressing a finger to his lips in the universal sign for quiet, Bryce led her out into the hall. Darting from shadow to shadow, alcove to alcove, he guided her through the twisting halls.

"Where are the other prisoners kept?" he whispered as they crept through the passageway.

She pointed down the darkened corridors as they passed. "The soldiers are there. Your friends, there." She curled her free hand over his grasp on her and asked. "You are not going to try to see them tonight, are you?"

He shook his head. "I promised I'd go back. Besides, I need some time to think of a plan. I do need to make contact with them somehow. Before the tapes are made tomorrow."

They reached the last lightbulb and turned the corner. If he would do this for her, then she would repay the favor. "I will take a message to your friends for you."

"No. It's too dangerous."

He stopped in his tracks, tugging her off balance. But his hand was there to steady her. "You've already done more than you should to help us. It's probably best if you steer clear of me from now on. I have a feelin' things are gonna get pretty rough before this is over."

Steer clear sounded like never see him again. And she couldn't do that. She was falling in love with the man, and he was in danger. Nothing might ever come of her growing feelings, but Tasiya Belov was every bit the fighter Bryce Martin was.

She wasn't the same woman who'd first come to Devil's Fork Island, cowed and afraid of a country she didn't know or understand. She'd made a deal with a real devil to save her father's life. But she wouldn't sink to Dimitri Mostek's level and trade one man's life and misery for another's.

Bryce seemed to think that was the end of the discussion. After she unlocked the cell door, he stepped inside and pulled it shut himself. Tasiya watched him pull the chains from between his mattress and cot and refill the hiding place with the items he'd stolen from the supply room.

She rested her forehead against one of the bars and watched the expression on his face turn grim and resolute as he snapped the manacles around his wrists and ankles. Though her bonds were less tangible than steel and iron, Tasiya understood his driving need to escape and to ensure the safety of the people he cared about. She even suspected she was one of them now.

"Can you really find a way to escape and free your comrades if you are out of your cell at night?"

The question seemed to take him aback. His gray eyes searched hers before he stepped closer. "I think so. But I promise I won't take advantage of you again."

This wasn't about *his* promises. "Can you stop the militia from killing anyone else?"

"I dunno." He came even closer, until only the steel bars and the memory of that goodbye kiss lay between them. "That's a tall order unless I can find a way to contact my boss in Montana and let him know where we are so he can send reinforcements. Otherwise, it'd be a pretty bloody battle to get out of here. It would help, too, if I knew where I was telling him to go."

Tasiya didn't hesitate for a moment. "Devil's Fork Island. It takes the ferry two hours from the North Carolina coast to get here. Does that help?"

His beautiful eyes narrowed. "What are you doin', Tasiya?"

She could feel the heat of his body through the barrier between them, almost as if there was an invisible link channeling his energy into hers. She curled her fingers around his where they hugged the bars and was rewarded when he shifted his grip to link their hands together. "Tomorrow night I will bring you my keys. I will help you and your friends escape."

Chapter Nine

"Why is Boone Fowler demanding more money?"

Tasiya listened to Dimitri Mostek's accusatory voice and wondered why she didn't fear it so much anymore. "He says training new militia soldiers is expensive."

"He's not pocketing any of that money himself?"

Thrusting her fingers through the hair at her temple, Tasiya resumed her pacing. "How would I know what he does with your superior's money? He makes me clean his toilet and burn his garbage. He does not show me his bank account."

"Are you taking a tone with me, Anastasiya? I will not tolerate disrespect from a woman."

She stopped at the blanket that was her door and bit down on her retort. Another marvel of American life she'd learned was that she could lose her temper; she could have a different opinion and not be punished for it the way she would back home. At least, Bryce Martin had accepted her in all her moods—from fear to anger to an awakening passion he did not believe she could feel for him. After tasting such a gift, it was difficult to remember the subservient mandate for women in Lukinburg society.

She lowered her voice and moved the phone closer to her mouth. "No. Of course, not. I meant no disrespect. Things have been very stressful here today, that is all."

Seemingly appeased by her quieter tone, Dimitri returned to the business of spying. "What things?"

Tasiya fingered the nearly completed basket on her bed, anxious to take it on her rounds tonight and get started on her dubious role as a double agent. She wanted to collect more grass to braid ropes and build the sides of the basket even higher, but with a handle and large, shallow base already, it would fulfill her need for a silent means to carry goods to and from the prisoners.

"Today Mr. Fowler began videotaping the soldiers he captured." She closed her eyes, but could not forget the terrible images she'd seen from the breezeway. "He marches them into the courtyard in chains and forces them to read letters he has written for them. Behind the camera there are men with guns aimed at the prisoners."

"It is an effective means of propaganda."

It was a cruel and dangerous practice. To the soldiers' credit, none of them had read their letters with any conviction. Nor did any of them make an effort to hide the injuries they'd received during their capture and imprisonment. If Boone Fowler thought the tapes would convince anyone that his ideas had merit, he was mistaken. But it had still twisted her stomach to see those strong, proud men denouncing the UN's planned invasion of Lukinburg, saying it would harm her people instead of help them. And then they read that their own lives would be forfeit if the militia's demands were not met.

Thankfully, Mother Nature had been their ally. "The salt air apparently is not good for the equipment," she explained. "Everything is damp here. There were some technical problems. A man was sent to the mainland for new batteries and cables. They will resume filming tomorrow. I overheard Mr. Fowler telling his security chief that they will send the tapes to the media the day after that."

"Good. I am tired of Boone Fowler dragging his feet. My superior is beginning to question his loyalty." Tonight she found Dimitri's lecherous laugh more annoying than intimidating. "And it keeps you away from my bed that much longer."

Tasiya pulled the keys from the pocket of her skirt and slipped them onto her wrist. She wanted to tell Dimitri that Boone Fowler was loyal to no one but himself, and that the hundreds of thousands of dollars he'd claimed to have spent on the Montana Militia for a Free America wasn't a sound investment.

She also wanted to tell him that she would never

willingly go to his bed. But somehow she didn't think willingness made any difference to Dimitri.

Swallowing her distaste for the man, she made her usual nightly request. "May I speak to my father?"

"Keep it short," Dimitri warned. "As you are always reminding me, you cannot neglect your duties for too long, or Fowler's men will become suspicious."

Tasiya didn't respond until she heard Anton's voice. "Tasiya?"

"Papa." An instant warmth swept through her like one of her father's bear hugs. "How are Mostek's men treating you?"

"I am fine, daughter. Well fed, but hungry for the sound of your voice. Are you well?"

"Papa." Tasiya peeked through the blanket at her door to make sure no one could overhear. Then she ducked her head and spoke with an unmistakable urgency. "Can you speak freely?"

There was a short pause. "For the moment. What is wrong?"

"Do not be afraid for me. I have met a man here. No matter what Dimitri preaches about American infidels, I intend to help him however I can."

"You are helping the militia?" His shocked concern only reinforced her resolve.

"No. They are no different than Mostek and his bullies. I am speaking of one of the prisoners. Bryce Martin is his name."

"Is this Bryce Martin a good man?" He sounded

less disappointed, though still cautious, with a touch of fatherly concern thrown in.

Tasiya smiled. Her voice softened as she sank onto the bed. "Yes, Papa. He is a very good man."

"He is special to you?"

More than she was ready to admit. She simply answered the truth. "He is my friend."

His long, weary sigh tore through her heart. "Then you must help him. Do not turn a blind eye to your captors the way our country has turned a blind eye for far too long to the king and his regime."

She'd never heard her father make any kind of political statement before. His words both worried and inspired her. "I will be as careful as I can, Papa. I do not want my actions here to harm you."

"I am a sixty-five-year-old man, daughter of mine. I have lived a full life. From the day your mother died in childbirth, I knew you would always be a special gift to me. Nothing you do could ever—" His startled catch of breath made her think Mostek or his guards had returned to eavesdrop. But Anton continued. "I raised you to be a good person. I have always been proud of you, and I will always love you with all my heart. No matter what happens, know that."

That sounded ominous. "Papa? What are you saying?"

He waited a deliberate moment. Long enough for her to hear Dimitri in the background. "You've talked long enough, Belov. Say goodbye to your daughter."

"I am not finished."

"What?" Dimitri snapped.

He was talking back? Tasiya shot to her feet. "Papa, no. Give him the phone. We will talk again tomorrow."

She heard the clicking rasp of metal against metal, and the distinctive sound of a bullet sliding into the firing chamber of a gun. "Now, Belov."

"Papa!" She'd screamed the word too loudly. Tasiya slapped her fingers over her mouth. Someone had surely heard her. She needed to disconnect the line now, and hide the phone before someone came to investigate. But she was so afraid it would be the last time she heard her father's beloved voice that she couldn't let go. "Papa, please," she begged on a ragged whisper. "Do as he says. I love you."

"I love you, too, daughter." Tears leaked through her tightly closed eyes. She prayed his defiance wouldn't cost him his life. "My highest regards to your friend."

The line went dead. Tasiya's breath rushed out on a painful gasp. "Papa?"

Had there been a gunshot after the disconnect?

Out of habit, she stashed the phone in its hiding place inside her pillow. But Tasiya could barely think, much less move. She was numb from the heart out. How much more of this could she take?

She laid her head in her hands and let the tears fall. But for only a minute. There was little allowance for tears in this place. She wiped her eyes with the back of her hand and sniffed through her stuffy sinuses.

"What did you mean, Papa? My highest regards to your friend."

He didn't know Bryce Martin. He'd been trying to tell her something. That he approved of her having feelings for a man he'd never met? Or was it code for something else? Was his rebellion against Dimitri an echo of her defiance against Boone Fowler? Maybe it was his way of giving her his blessing to side with the prisoners instead of the captors she'd been spying on.

"Be safe, Papa," she prayed. She slipped the basket handle over her arm, calmed her outward appearance with a steadying breath and forced one foot in front of the other.

She just hoped that hadn't been another man she cared about trying to say goodbye.

"IF I HIT YOU, I get to kiss the pretty lady."

Bryce perched on the edge of his cot and aimed the crumb of stale bread at his mouse buddy snuffling around in the corner.

He'd created his own version of Bull, the damn dumbest game ever, devised by his former platoon mate and buddy at Big Sky, Jacob Powell. Powell knew a lot about bull, to Bryce's way of thinking. But the guy's mouthy sense of humor grew on a fella after a while. His chatter filled a lot of the silences Bryce was known for. Powell's daredevil ways had caused Bryce more than one headache over the years, but he had to give the guy his props. He knew how to make even the dreariest of nights pass by a little quicker.

And this one was goin' way too slow.

Tasiya was running late tonight. Or maybe he was just more anxious than usual to see her.

With the steady, chilling rain falling outside, blotting out the moon and stars and muffling the sounds of sentry movement, it was impossible to keep track of the time. He'd had all day to think about what crazy notion she'd get into her head after her vow to help him escape. As much as he appreciated her promise, as much as he could use her help, it had been tearin' him up inside, worrying that she'd gotten caught where she shouldn't be. Maybe tossed into a cell herself. *Interrogated* by Marcus Smith.

Or something unspeakably worse.

"C'mon, mousie." He had to get rid of those waking morbid thoughts that haunted him every bit as much as his nightmares. "Ready, aim..." He closed one eye and chucked the bread.

Normally the game involved a dart board, a stupid dare and a lot of macho bravado. Hit the bull's-eye and everything was cool—miss and you had to pay up.

"Damn." He was payin' up tonight.

Now he had no excuse, lame or otherwise, to put his hands on Tasiya. It was tough to swallow, though he knew it was for the best. The sparks flyin' between them were definitely more than comradeship. But it wasn't a romance. It wasn't goin' nowhere—relationships with him never did. This was some gratitude-turned-attraction thing that had gotten out of hand because of these crazy circumstances. Shared danger, close quarters, lonely nights—they could play with a person's mind and make him or her think things were real that weren't.

In the real world a woman as kind and gorgeous and resourceful as Tasiya would be beatin' handsome, sociable—normal—men off with a stick. Away from all this, she'd see him for the scarred slow-talkin' hick he was, and move on to somethin' better.

Nah, it was just as well that he'd lost the bull game. It was harder to concentrate on business when Tasiya was around. And the hard truth of it was that, outside these bars, business was all he was good at. He was just askin' for trouble if he couldn't remember that. Better to distance himself now, so that soft spot inside him wouldn't be payin' an even heavier price later.

At least his mouse buddy would get some dinner. The mouse stuffed the crumb into his twitching cheek, climbed up the wall and disappeared through the window to dine al fresco in the rain. Bryce and his roommate were gettin' to be regular pals now. Maybe he could tie a note around the mouse's neck and teach it to swim. He hadn't come up with any other brainstorms yet on how he could contact Colonel Murphy at Big Sky to put together a rescue.

"Bryce Martin."

Bryce jumped inside his skin at the hushed call of Tasiya's voice. How the hell…? When was the last time anybody had gotten the drop on him? Just went to prove how his useless feelings for her were messin' with his head. But, showing no outward sign of being startled, Bryce set aside the little do-it-yourself project he'd been tinkering with and rose to meet her.

"Evenin'." This little exercise in control was good for him. It'd help keep him centered and focused on the job instead of the woman. He turned toward the ribbons of light and shadow in the passageway and saw why she'd been able to sneak up on him without a peep. "Where's your cart?"

Though she'd visited him late at night without the clanking metal monstrosity, she'd always used it to deliver dinner rations to the prisoners. Bryce squeezed the chain between his wrists in uneasy fists. That wasn't the only thing different tonight.

There was a jerky awkwardness to her normally capable hands as she unlocked the cage, without prepping his bread and water first. "Too noisy. I make basket."

Her broken English was another clue that something was wrong. His gaze slid to the woven grass basket on the floor, then back up to her red-rimmed eyes. An unwise need to make whatever was wrong right for her again simmered in his veins. "Tasiya?"

She knelt in front of him to unhook his leg irons, and he jerked the chain between his wrists, battling the urge to pull her back to her feet. "Honey, talk to me."

Dammit. No *honeys*. No touching. He could keep her safer, do her more good, if he focused on the job, not her. But she was pressin' her lips together so hard, Bryce worried she might bite through them. "What happened?"

She had difficulty getting the key to fit his wrist manacles. But before he could help, she'd yanked them off and dropped them where she stood. Then she fisted her hands in the front of his shirt and tugged him forward, burying her nose in the open collar at his neck. "Hold me, please. Just...hold me."

Jeez, Louise. Her cheek was cold as an ice cube against his chest. And if that stuttery hesitation was a sob, he was in real trouble. "Tasiya?"

And then he felt the heated moisture singeing his collarbone. Hell. She was cryin.'

So much for keepin' his distance.

Bryce closed his arms around her and gathered her as close as he dared without crushing her. He dipped his nose into the silky crown of her hair and rocked her back and forth, soothing her the best way he knew how.

"Hush, honey," he whispered, absorbing her distress through every fiber in his body. "Nothin's this bad, is it?"

Her hands slipped beneath his shirt, headed around his waist. His skin caught fire at the frantic touches, and he didn't think he'd even mind if she accidentally grasped the welts on his back. But with something like a curse in her throat, she pulled her hands back between their bodies and snuggled impossibly closer.

Damn. Boone Fowler had pulled another gun on her. Marcus Smith had put his hands on her. Bryce rubbed big, frictional circles up and down her spine, as much for his own comfort as hers, as his imagination took off and pictured a dozen ugly things that could have gone wrong in this place.

"Don't stop talkin' now. Did somebody hurt you? You gotta tell me what happened."

"My father. I think…" Her noisy sniffle was followed by a quiet sob that vibrated through her entire body and made mush of any effort at emotional detachment. "He might be dead."

His hands stilled their massage. "You never mentioned your daddy before."

"I heard a gun on the phone. He was trying to tell me something." Gun? Phone? Father? This nuthouse had just added a new dimension of craziness.

"There is a chance he is all right. But I have no way of knowing until tomorrow night."

He went with the flow of conversation, still not quite sure of the problem. "What's tomorrow night?"

Instead of answering, she crushed his collar in her fingers and turned her nose into the crook between his neck and shoulder. He had a feelin' if he wasn't so beat up, she'd be huggin' him good and tight. He reckoned her consideration of his injuries was a good sign. That meant she was thinkin' clearly. Or it could just mean she was thinkin' about pullin' away.

Bryce wasn't ready for that yet.

He backed up until his thighs hit the edge of the cot. Then he sat down and pulled her between his legs into his lap. "C'mon, honey. Tell me what this is all about." He smoothed aside the curls that stuck to her damp skin and palmed her cheek, letting his fingers massage her nape, holding her as close as she was willin' to be. "You know you want to. I've never met a woman who enjoyed talkin' as much as you do."

She made a sound that was half sniffle, half laugh, and the music of it eased Bryce's worry a fraction. She pushed herself up in his lap and threw her arms around his neck. *Now* she was holdin' on. "How can you have such a big heart after everything that has been done to you? I do not think I can be so strong."

He was less aware of the pinches of pain on his

upper back than of the supple hip wedged squarely against his groin. Who was he kiddin'? With Tasiya in his arms, sayin' sweet things and squeezin' up against him like she didn't want to be anywhere else, Bryce finally admitted he'd made the supreme tactical error.

He'd let his guard down. He'd started to care.

He would put his life on the line for this woman. He'd give her whatever she needed or wanted from him.

Anything.

Despite the fact his heart was gonna get ripped up one way or another, he couldn't help the way he felt about her.

She might give him a couple of weeks out of gratitude, like Maria had back in San Ysidro. But then she'd go home to Lukinburg and forget all about the beast who'd befriended her. More likely, she'd reject him once she got a good, hard look at him in the outside world. Or she'd die in this damn hole. No. Hell, no. That option he wouldn't allow.

Leaning back enough to put some space between them, Bryce studied the cautious faith shining in her eyes and then captured her mouth in a quick, sweet kiss. He wasn't sure if that was for her benefit or his own. But it startled some healthy color back into her cheeks and sealed his silent vow to keep her safe.

"We're as strong as we need to be, Tasiya. My

grandpa used to tell me that when I was growin' up. You'll find whatever you need inside you."

"That's how I got through losin' my folks when I was a kid." He shoved up his left sleeve. "A lot of these scars come from that. My colonel reminded me of my strength and helped me get through months in the hospital, after a minefield exploded on me."

"The rest of the scars?"

He nodded.

"You found the strength to stand up to the beatings here, too," she whispered.

"Yep."

That answer earned the glimmer of a smile. "And you think I have such a spirit inside me?"

"I know you do." He picked her up off his lap and set her on the cot beside him. Then he reached for her keys. "May I?"

She quickly pulled them from her wrist and handed them over in an extraordinary gesture of trust he didn't intend to betray again. "Where are you going?"

"Not far." Bryce checked the passageway, then unlocked the door and picked up her basket. He poured a cup of water, dabbed the corner of a napkin in it and sat beside her to wipe away the crystallized tears that had dried on her cheeks. "Now, tell me about your daddy."

He pushed the cup into her hands and watched her

take a drink before answering. She stared down into the water, and Bryce wondered if she was searching for words or doin' the I'm-not-good-enough-to-look-you-in-the-eye routine again. "You will think less of me."

He nudged her gaze back up to eye level. "Try me."

She handed him the cup and insisted he drink and eat first. He knew it was a stall, but he gave her the time she needed. He was licking the crumbs from his fingers before she spoke again. "Several nights ago you asked me why I was here. In America."

"You said you were workin' off a debt."

"It is not *my* debt."

He picked up the crude radio he'd been working on and started to tinker with it. He was pretty much to the point where all he needed was a power source to activate it, but his hands needed the distraction to keep from reachin' for her again. "I know you're not here voluntarily. What does Fowler have on you?"

Tasiya hesitated, watching him wire a battery port behind the walkie-talkie transceiver that would hopefully allow him to send and receive messages, at least over a short distance. He could see her curiosity about his work, but she didn't ask. "*I* am the payment. From a man in my country. I am the militia's reward for capturing you."

Bryce nearly snapped the plastic housing in two. "Reward?"

No wonder Smith couldn't keep his grubby paws

off her. The security chief thought she was some kind of toy who'd been sent for him to play with. But Fowler preached ethnic and nationalistic purity. He wouldn't allow Tasiya to prostitute herself with his men. But then, he had the marks on his back to prove that Smith didn't always follow orders.

Oh, man, he was practically shaking with anger and self-loathing. "You mean you're only here because we were too damn careless and got ourselves captured?"

He jumped when her fingers brushed across the back of his tight, white knuckles. But like he'd told her, she was stronger than she gave herself credit for. When he would have pulled away, she laced their fingers together. Needing the tender reassurance more than he could have imagined, he turned his hand, holding hers, palm to palm.

"The only reason my father is alive—" her whisper was muted by the dulling heaviness of the rain "—is that you are here. If men like you were not fighting for your beliefs about freedom, he would have been shot dead in the street in front of our house."

Bryce's guilt over her being used abated as she revealed the unfortunate kindred spirit they shared. Like him, she was no stranger to tragedy.

Sensing his newfound calm, Tasiya continued. "This man—his name is Dimitri Mostek."

"I know that name."

"He is our minister of finance. He is in the news sometimes." He'd more likely read the name in a few intel reports. Suspected terrorist? Foreign crime syndicate? Tasiya spelled it out. "Dimitri is holding my father prisoner. My father is an accountant. He took some money from Dimitri—we were so poor." She shrugged it off as if the poverty didn't matter. But her devotion to her father was clear. "To spare my father's life, I agreed to work for Boone Fowler. I have been spying for Dimitri and the man he works for, telling him everything Fowler and his men say or do. I have a special phone to call every night and make a report."

"Why would someone in Lukinburg—"

"They are funding the militia."

Bryce turned and saw the truth shining in her coffee-colored eyes. "Terrorists in your country are paying Boone Fowler to commit acts of terror here in the U.S.?"

"They are hoping Mr. Fowler can keep UN troops out of Lukinburg. Dimitri and his people are very powerful and very rich. They would like to keep it that way."

Snatching the napkin in her lap and wadding it up, Bryce rose and put away the cup and pitcher in the sturdy basket she'd brought, waiting on her the way she'd taken care of him for so many nights. "And they stuck you in the middle of all this?"

"I volunteered."

"You were coerced."

The frown between her eyes told him she didn't get the word. "They didn't give you any choice," he explained.

"I could have let Dimitri kill my father. He wants me to become his mistress, and would have let Papa go if I had agreed to that. When I return to Lukinburg, that will be the condition for Papa's freedom."

"This just gets better and better."

"It is not a good—"

He put up a hand to stop her confusion. "Sarcasm. I mean it doesn't sound like it could get much worse."

But it could. Ah, hell. He could read it in her tightly pressed lips. "There is someone else more powerful, a man even Dimitri fears. *He* is the one who ordered me to spy here."

Bryce squeezed his fist around the basket's handle as he set it on the cot beside her. Was she talking about The Puppet Master? The ultimate terrorist who'd masterminded prison escapes, sabotaged trains, organized kidnappings and murders? The man whose unknown identity kept him more than one step ahead of military authorities and a team of bounty hunters who wanted him behind bars? "Who does Mostek report to?"

"I do not know his name. It is only an angry voice I have overheard on the phone. He speaks our native language. King Aleksandr, perhaps?"

It wouldn't be the first time Big Sky had suspected the king of being The Puppet Master.

But there wasn't a hell of a lot he could do with this information from here. Bryce had to get back to thoughts of escape and the reason Tasiya had started this confession in the first place. Moving the basket to his lap, he sat beside her again. "So what happened during your phone call tonight?"

She took a deep breath and matched his gaze. "I was telling my father I intended to help you and the other prisoners. He gave me his blessing, I believe—Dimitri does not know what we were discussing," she reassured him, "Papa was speaking in code.

"Dimitri wanted Papa to hang up. But he wouldn't and…" Her eyes squeezed shut, and Bryce almost reached for her before the tears started again. But she forced them open and he stayed put. "I heard the sound of a gun—the clicking, not an actual shot."

"He loaded a bullet into the firing chamber."

She nodded. How sad that she recognized that lethal sound. "And then we were disconnected. I do not know if he shot Papa."

Bryce breathed a little easier now that he understood what had upset her. He couldn't tell her everything would be okay, but he did know a thing or two about the criminal mind and how thugs like Dimitri Mostek worked.

"I'm guessin' your daddy's in one piece. If

Mostek still needs intel from you, he's gotta give you a reason to call him. You're too far away for him to control you in any other way besides your love for your daddy."

"Do you really believe that Papa is all right?" She turned her whole body to face him, and her hopeful energy did silly things to his testosterone level. Yep, he was the big man. He'd made the lady feel better.

And there he was, reachin' for her again. With the tip of a finger, he smoothed aside a tendril that had fallen across her forehead. "He's just tryin' to scare you, honey."

She raised one eyebrow. "He succeeded."

Was that a sad stab at humor? Yep, she was gonna be okay. She was still too close to make it easy to keep his hormones in check, but he pulled his hand back to the basket, where he traced his fingers around the rim. "So your daddy said to go for it, hmm?"

"If that means go to work for you, yes. I am ready." She pulled a big clip from her pocket and twisted all that hair up into a loose bun she secured at the back of her head. "What do we need to do tonight?"

He liked that, too. A woman who knew how to get down to business. "I need a battery or some electricity to power the radio I pieced together."

She picked up the mesh of gerry-rigged parts he'd been working on, seeming to admire his handiwork. "What about the wires that connect the lights in the passageway?"

"They'd blink." He'd already considered that option himself. "I need someplace a little more private to tap into, or an independent power source, so I don't alert anyone."

"What else?"

"Some recon would be nice." He didn't wait for her to question the unfamiliar word. "I need to find out where they store their ammunition. Get my hands on some explosives. I've got parts to build a bomb, but not the main ingredient."

"What would you blow up?"

"The generator. Whatever powers the perimeter alarms."

"I can look for these things, too." She handed him the radio in exchange for the basket. "I can carry things in here without being detected. If you need something like this for your work, too, I can make more."

Bryce held on to his side of the basket as a glimmer of familiarity tried to turn itself into inspiration. "You made this?"

She nodded. "The grass grows like weeds on this island. I think it is the only thing that can stand up to the wind and salt air. I braid it into rope and then weave—"

"Cord grass." He snapped to his feet, startling her. Yes sir, a good soldier's training always made the difference when a man's back was against the wall. "That's what it's called. Cord grass." He picked up Tasiya in his arms and spun her around like he'd just earned shore leave. "Hallelujah, woman, you just gave me the idea of how to let Big Sky know where we are." He planted a kiss on her before letting her slide down to her feet. "We're gonna do this thing."

She clutched at his shoulders, blushing at his excitement, sharing it. "You are like a little boy. The grass is good?"

"The grass is everything. I recognize it from my army training days. You said we were close to North Carolina. That's Ft. Bragg and Camp Lejeune Marine Base. We used to use these abandoned islands off the coast to practice blowin' things up."

He let her go and paced to the window. He needed a little of that cool rain to splash in on him after feelin' Tasiya's body pressed so close to his—their thighs tangled together, her breasts rubbing against him, her soft lips answering beneath his. Just like that, he was primed to celebrate their first real possibility of success in the most elemental way a man and woman could. *That* was hardly what he needed to be thinkin' about right now.

"I wonder if anyone else would remember it."

"If you could show the grass on your videotape—"

"Exactly." He swiped his hand over his scarred, scruffy jaw and turned to face her. Hell. Even with the distance between them, and the reminder of what he must look like to her, his body was still on fire for her. Didn't matter. "You think you can convince Marcus Smith to tie me up in some of your rope instead of usin' the chains when he puts me on camera?"

"I will try. I could make the excuse of your injuries. Tomorrow at breakfast, I will speak to him. If he does not agree, I can trade—"

"Whoa, whoa, whoa. Don't give him anything."

Major reality check. Bryce didn't want her to be makin' deals with any man. He sure as hell didn't want her to be beholden to Marcus Smith. Another reason why he should never have let his feelings for Tasiya get personal.

"Do you think he will listen to *you?*" she challenged. She was right. And she knew it. "There is no other way, and we are running out of time. I will get you your rope, and I will take care of Marcus Smith. Tonight we will do your recon."

Her calm sense of acceptance as she hid her things beneath the cot and slid the keys onto her wrist put him to shame. Tasiya Belov knew as much about duty as any soldier he'd served with. He cared about her and he owed her.

If she got out of this alive, he wouldn't ask for anything more. He'd do his duty by her. That was all she really needed from him.

"Where's this Mostek holdin' your daddy?"

That quizzical frown reappeared. "There are hidden apartments in the Ministry of Finance Building in St. Feodor. Dimitri showed me."

"Do you wanna be his mistress? I mean—" this was killin' him "—you have any feelings for this guy?"

"Hatred. I used to fear him but..." A sigh of understanding replaced the frown. "I will do anything for my father. Even strike a bargain with Marcus Smith. Papa is all I have."

Bryce crossed the cell and framed her face in his hands. "He's not all you have." Damn it, he was gonna say it. "When we escape from this place, I want you to come with us."

"But my father—"

"I will find him. I will take him from Mostek and bring him home, back to you, wherever you two wanna be. Findin' people and puttin' 'em where they belong is what I do."

Her eyes searched his. Maybe she questioned his offer, maybe she simply didn't believe it. "You would do that for me?"

He'd go to hell and back for this woman. But all he answered was, "Yep."

Apparently, it was enough. She nodded. "Then I will come with you."

Marrying to a Mercenary

Chapter Ten

The communication center was crowded with more types of equipment than Tasiya could identify, much less operate. But Bryce seemed right at home, turning machines on and off, monitoring transmissions, taking things apart. Meanwhile, she'd been assigned lookout duty while he read diagrams and borrowed the necessary items to complete his short-range radio and construct something he called a jamming device.

Tasiya hovered by the iron door, keeping one eye on the passageway through the crack they'd left open and one eye on the big man at the console in the center of the room. On first meeting Bryce, with his shocking appearance and muscular physique, one would think this soldier-turned-bounty-hunter's specialty would be anything involving brute force. But Tasiya had learned that patience and observation, dexterous hands and a vast knowledge of all things technical were the tools of his trade. Bryce

Martin was as at home with his gadgets and machinery as she was in her kitchen.

She'd also learned that his brutishness was only skin deep. Beneath the scars lay kindness, compassion and the biggest heart she'd ever known a man to possess. A woman could do far worse than to have Bryce Martin care for her.

"Son of a bitch." Bryce's muttered curse pulled Tasiya out of her thoughts.

She was learning to recognize that grim look that hardened his handsome eyes. "What is it?"

He put up his hand to wave off her concern. "Stay put."

But she had already slipped across the room to look over his shoulder at the video camera's tiny view screen. Tasiya gasped, pressing her fingers to her lips to mute her shock at the cruel pictures. "Oh, my God."

"Honey, don't look." He reached for her hand.

Tasiya held on to his long, strong fingers like they were an anchor. Even when she turned her head, the voice speaking over the picture—Boone Fowler's voice—couldn't erase the image of a young soldier kneeling on the ground and being shot in the back of the head. "I will kill one man every day—until our demands are met. Americans should stay in America. Our government should put America first."

"How horrible." Bryce rubbed his thumb back and

forth across her knuckles, instilling warmth when she felt none. "That is how I imagined my father—"

"No." He turned off the picture, hit Rewind and turned to capture her hand between both of his. "If Mostek's the kind of man I think he is, he wouldn't have the guts to pull the trigger himself. Your daddy's fine. I can feel it in my bones he's okay."

Tasiya smiled at the utter seriousness on Bryce's upturned face. She rested her palm against his disfigured jaw and brushed her thumb across his lips, coaxing a smile. "What do your bones know about a simple old man who eats too much cake and dozes off every evening before he finishes his newspaper?"

The smile was slow in coming, but it was there. "You make a mean cake, do you?"

There was nothing mean about her cooking. "My cakes are very sweet."

That unexpected glimpse of boyish joy she'd seen earlier that night reappeared. "I imagine anything you touch is mighty sweet."

The look in Bryce's eyes filled her with a curious heat. She'd picked up on many colloquialisms the past few weeks, but with English, there always seemed to be more to learn. But Bryce was smiling, and her fear for her father was once again under control, so she…

Bryce stopped smiling.

"What—"

"Hush." He put a finger to his lips and stood.

Every cell in her body went on rigid alert, matching his wary posture. Pulling her along behind him, he hurried to the door, peeked outside, then pushed her flat against the wall beside him. "We got company."

Over the pounding of her pulse in her ears, Tasiya could hear the footsteps now, matched by the off-key singing in the passageway. Marcus Smith.

What was he doing here in the middle of the night?

"He must have pulled graveyard duty after pissin' off Fowler." Bryce answered her unspoken question. He hadn't expected an extra patrol tonight, either. Taking a deep, calming breath, he reached into his pocket and pulled out a steel bar. Like the ones in his cell. What did he intend to do with that? "Don't move."

He gave her hand a quick squeeze, then inched toward the door.

Tasiya held her breath. *Walk on by.* She willed the command through a telepathic wish. *Walk on by.*

She could hear Marcus grumbling now, mimicking Boone Fowler from the sound of it. "You've delayed the entire operation with your temper. If the man can't stand up, we can't broadcast. Bring him in. Let me look at him." He was coming for Bryce! Heading down the twisting path to Bryce's cell! "You've got sixteen other prisoners—who's gonna miss one who doesn't talk, anyway?"

He wouldn't find them in the communication room. But when he discovered Bryce's cell was empty, he'd set off every alarm in the camp to track him down. "What are we going to do?"

Bryce held the bar up like a weapon now. Attacking Marcus would surely wake the other guards. And a steel bar stood little chance against the pistol and hunting knife she knew Marcus wore on his belt. Tasiya clutched at Bryce's shoulder. "You must get back to your cell."

"Just how do you suggest I do that?"

Marcus paused, and she heard a stinging splat of sound. Tobacco juice. The nasty habit soured her stomach. How she'd love to clean up… Her gaze fell on the napkins and pitcher in her basket. Could she do that? Did she dare?

Marcus was singing again. Tasiya grabbed her basket.

"'Roll me o-ver, in the clo-ver.'"

"Tash—" She was out the door before Bryce could stop her. She felt rather than heard his curse and ignored it. He couldn't help her with this.

"'Roll me over, lay me down…' Hey, sugar."

Tasiya propped the iron door open, blocking Marcus's view into the communications room but forcing Bryce back into the shadows to stay hidden. It wasn't hard to act flustered when the stinky ox practically drooled at the sight of her. "Mr. Smith."

She strolled on past him, and he had to turn his back to the door to keep her in sight. "Whatchya doing over here this late at night, sugar?"

With a steadying breath and a silent prayer that she could pull this off, Tasiya faced him. "I finished delivering the bread to the prisoners. Some of them are very chatty," she added as an excuse. None of them were, but Marcus didn't know that.

She retreated another couple of steps, drawing the black-haired giant farther from the door. If she could get him to follow her around the corner, Bryce could slip out into the passageway undetected and return to his cell before he was discovered missing.

"I heard a noise." She remembered her deferring ways the militiamen liked so much, and ducked her head to focus on the tobacco stain at the center of Marcus's chest. "I unlocked the room to check. Should I not have done so?"

Marcus took the bait and drifted closer. "And here I thought you were lookin' for me, sugar. Now I find you're just trying to take over my job."

"No." He reached for a tendril of her hair and turned the corner with her when she backed away. "Please do not touch."

Run, Bryce.

"Fowler's not here to make us mind our manners." Tasiya clasped the basket to her chest, keeping it between her and Marcus. He braced his hands on the wall on either side of her head and leaned in until the basket pushed into her stomach. "You know, I nearly lost my job over you and the big guy. But if Martin says everything he's supposed to in the morning, Fowler will see that my methods work. Some men need a harder hand."

No man needed to be tortured so cruelly. But her time with Dimitri Mostek had taught her how to mask her emotions. She feigned ignorance. "The big guy?"

"Yeah, the ugly dude we beat the crap out of. Fowler says I can't have any more fun with him. But who the hell's gonna notice if that face is more beat up than usual, eh?"

Tasiya nearly choked on her anger at his crude laugh at Bryce's expense. She hoped Bryce couldn't hear any of this. Her palms were sweating at what she must do, but ironically, Marcus's callous comments infused her with a protective strength that made it easy to turn off both her nerves and her gag reflex. "I have an idea about the big guy that might help you regain favor with Mr. Fowler."

His tongue circled his lips in the middle of his bushy black beard. "I'm listening."

Tasiya unwound one of the cord grass braids from the basket's handle. "When you film him for the camera, so he does not appear to be more abused than he is, you should tie him up with this rope instead of so many chains. You will appear more humane."

Marcus pushed away from the wall. "He's too big a risk."

Had he figured out she was a diversion? When he turned back toward Bryce's position, Tasiya did the first thing she could think of. Reaching for Marcus's belt, she pulled out his knife and cut a swath of rope off her basket.

"What are you—"

"The rope is very strong." He spun around, snatching at the sheath on his belt as if she'd attacked him. Tasiya dropped the knife into the basket and set it on the floor. She held the rope up, taut between her hands. "I will show you."

"You want to tie me up?" His burst of temper turned into an amused grin. He twirled his finger through the rope and tugged her a step closer. "I didn't know you were into S&M, sugar."

Though she didn't understand the term, anything Marcus Smith seemed so intrigued with would no doubt disgust her. She released the rope he now held and backed away. "You can tie my hands, then."

"Now this is gettin' interesting."

Please be gone, Bryce Martin. Please be safe.

Tasiya held out her hands, and with no urging, Marcus looped the rope around her wrists. He pinched her skin in the knots he made, and pulled the grass tight.

"You see?" She strained at her bonds, pretending the panic that quivered across her lips wasn't real. "Very strong."

"God, you're a stupid woman," he laughed as he pushed her back against the wall and nuzzled the side of her neck. Nausea bloomed in her stomach. "But you're too damn pretty to resist."

"Mr. Smith." She inhaled a frightened breath and his gaze went straight to the heave of her bosom. "You are not supposed to touch me."

"Get real, sugar." He palmed the side of her waist, squeezed her breast.

Tasiya shoved her bound hands against his chest. "No!"

"You're waiting for me in a private corner? You ask me to tie you up?"

"I wanted to show you the rope." *Bryce? Bryce!*

Marcus's foul breath washed over her face just before he took her mouth in a bitter-tasting kiss. Tasiya's stomach churned.

"Smith!" Boone Fowler's voice crackled over the walkie-talkie strapped to Marcus's belt. "Get your butt back to my office now."

Marcus stopped grinding his mouth over hers and he cursed. "Go to the prison. Back to my office. I wish he'd make up his mind."

"Smith. Get on the walkie-talkie and answer me. Ike says the new camera isn't working. Bring the old one from the comm room. We'll switch out batteries and make sure it works before we release one of the prisoners."

Retrieve the camera from the communications room? No!

Marcus shoved her into the wall as he pushed away. He held up a warning finger as he pulled out his walkie-talkie. "Not one peep out of you when I press this button. I don't want him to know we've been together."

Together had such a horrible connotation when he said it. "Will you use the ropes in the video?"

"Smith!"

"All right. We'll tie his hands. But the leg irons stay."

Tasiya discovered she could smile without feeling anything. "My lips are sealed."

Marcus pushed a button on the walkie-talkie and answered. "I'm coming, Mr. Fowler. I'll bring the camera."

Smith strode around the corner to the communications room. Tasiya faded into the shadows, praying she'd given Bryce enough time to get back to his cell. When she heard the key twist in the lock of the iron door, she didn't know if he'd been sealed in or if he was in the clear.

But as soon as she heard Marcus Smith treading back toward the breezeway, she picked up her basket and hurried toward Bryce's cell. *Please be there. Please.*

"Bryce Martin?" She ran up to the bars and exhaled such a relieved sigh it left her light-headed. "Thank God. Thank God you are safe."

He stood inside, putting on his chains. As soon as he saw the grass rope on her wrists, he reached through the bars. "What the hell?"

His chains scraped against the bars as he untied

her, and Tasiya tried to hush him. "Someone will hear you."

But there was no stopping Bryce. "What did he do to you? Are you hurt?"

There was a desperation in his fingertips as he touched her cheek, cupped her neck, smoothed her hair. She wiped the taste of Marcus Smith from her mouth with the back of her hand, and Bryce's thumb was instantly there, brushing across her lips, stamping his care and concern there. Finally Tasiya latched on to his hands to stop his frantic inspection. "I am all right. I have been very successful. Marcus will use the ropes on you tomorrow."

He shook his head. "I hated what you were doing. Every minute of it. But you're a damn smart woman."

With that he palmed the nape of her neck and pulled her in for his kiss. It was wild and frantic, their bodies pressed against the bars, their faces meeting in between. Tasiya linked her hand behind his neck and parted her lips to drink in the deliciously potent taste of him. It was an assurance of lives spared, a prayer for future cautions, a joining of two souls who'd learned more about trust and survival in the past few weeks than they'd known their entire lives.

When Bryce pulled away, they both clung to the bars to catch their breaths. A wry smile softened the harsh lines of his face. "You'll never go down without a fight, will you?"

The admiration in his eyes filled her with pride. "I have a very good teacher."

His wry grin quickly faded. "You better get back to your room before someone misses you."

Tasiya picked up her basket and tucked the rope inside. "Good night, Bryce Martin."

"Watch your back."

She glanced over her shoulder. "I cannot see my—"

"Stay safe." That, she understood.

"I forgot." She handed him Marcus Smith's knife from her basket. "You, too."

Bryce took the knife and reached out for one last touch of her hair. "Damn smart woman."

BRYCE TOOK HIS TIME tying up the boots Boone Fowler had returned to him while Bristoe and Hodges stood watch outside his cell. Sure, stooping over to work around his leg irons pulled at the scabs just starting to form on his back and put pressure on his cracked rib. But he was more interested in stalling for time.

He didn't want to appear too eager to become a movie star.

The morning had dawned, red and overcast, with the biting threat of more rain on the wind. Everything inside Bryce's cell was damp, including the mattress ticking and the green camo jacket he'd buttoned over the khaki shirt that didn't quite fit. He knew these little amenities had nothing to do with a sudden attack of conscience over a prisoner freezin' his nuts off in a cell with an open window. They wanted to hide the marks of his abuse. Pretty him up for the camera.

Ha! There wasn't nothin' pretty about Bryce Martin and what he was planning to do to the militia.

"Move it, Martin." Hodges seemed a little out of his element, without his brass knuckles or permission to use Bryce as a punching bag. He paced back and forth in the passageway, checking his watch. "Mr. Fowler wants to get you on tape before the storm hits."

Bristoe had his rifle looped over his shoulder and looked as if he was taxing every brain cell tying and testing knots in the cord grass rope Tasiya had given Marcus Smith. "You're sure this'll hold the big guy?"

Hodges snatched it out of the kid's hands and shook it loose. "If Smith says to use it, we use it." He gestured through the bars. "You ready, Martin?"

Bryce nodded, still refraining from striking up any kind of conversation with his tormentors. They didn't seem to expect it, and he wasn't about to offer. Hodges ordered him to the back wall of the cell as he unlocked the door, and Bristoe held him at gunpoint while the older man bound Bryce's wrists. Once he was secured, Hodges pulled out a folded piece of stationery and his pistol.

He poked the gun into Bryce's gut, grinning at the

grunt of pain that was impossible to hide. "You give me any trouble, big man, and I'll shoot you where you stand. Got that?"

Bryce nodded.

"Good." He pushed the paper into Bryce's hands and shoved him into the passageway. Bryce gritted his teeth around his curse and breathed in deeply to control the waves of pain undulating across his back. "Now you be a good boy and read what Mr. Fowler wrote for you, exactly the way he said it, and we'll let you come back to your room for some more beauty sleep."

"Beauty sleep?" Bristoe laughed, pulling the door shut behind them. "That's a good one."

Hodges and Bristoe laughed, and Bryce began the long walk outside.

They passed through the familiar twists and turns, past the interrogation room and the communications center, past the blank corridors that led to other prison cells, past the room that housed the generators. Bristoe slipped aside a dead bolt and pushed open a solid iron door that led onto an open, porch-like walkway paved in stone.

Bryce squinted as he saw direct outdoor light for the first time in three weeks. Even with the clouds hanging overhead, the muted sun seemed harsh to eyes that had grown accustomed to functioning in shadows and darkness. This must be the breezeway Tasiya had mentioned—and that screen door at the opposite end would lead into the kitchen, mess hall and militia quarters.

"Wait here." Hodges tapped him in the gut with the pistol again, and Bryce winced, caught off guard because he'd been too busy searching for Tasiya on the other side of that screen door.

With Bristoe's gun fixed on Bryce, Hodges hopped down the two steps that led into the courtyard and hurried over to exchange words with Boone Fowler and the short, squatty man behind the camera. Beyond the crumbling stone wall at the far edge of the yard, Bryce could see the golden cord grass whipping back and forth in the wind blown ahead by the coming storm. Somebody at Big Sky had to remember the hours they'd spent cartin' heavy equipment across these rocky, sand-soaked islands, then clearin' it all away so they could use 'em for target practice.

Making a cut sign across his neck, Fowler dismissed the hostage being filmed ahead of Bryce. Jacob Powell, of the crazy games and annoying charm, strode into view. Flanked by two militiamen, Powell was doing his own version of creating chaos and making life difficult for the militia. He was talkin'.

Bryce studied the ground and battled the urge to grin.

"I don't know, I think I got the whole Tom Cruise thing workin'. You know, with the teeth and the hair." Despite a hoarse voice, Powell was speaking in code as he walked up the steps and passed by, and Bryce was paying attention. "I got it all over Craig O'Riley. He doesn't have the profile for camera work like I do." Riley had a broken nose? "And he's not pullin' off that Lex Luthor look at all." Shaved head? "You know, what one gal thinks is sexy—"

"Shut up."

So, with Bryce temporarily sidelined, Riley Watson had become the guinea pig du jour for torture and neglect. Powell had indicated that he was healthy enough to put up a good fight, but Riley was hurtin'. Bryce would have to keep that in mind if he got a chance—correction, make that *when* he got the chance to make their rescue happen.

While Powell jabbered on, Bryce communicated the best way *he* knew how. He lifted his hands and rubbed at his wrists to let Powell know he was onto somethin' with the cord grass. Then he looked him straight in those clever green eyes and prayed his buddy could still read his silences.

"I'm ready for my close-up, Mr. DeMille." Powell winked, telling Bryce he understood that somethin' was goin' down. "Oh, yeah, I'm ready for that."

"I said shut up."

"Shutting up now."

One of the guards poked Powell between the shoulder blades with his rifle, and the three of them disappeared behind the iron door.

Showtime.

At Hodges's nod, Fowler looked across the un-even paving stones and inspected Bryce. The mili-tia leader scanned him from head to toe, no doubt checking to see if he could play the part of a meek convert to Fowler's ideology.

But Bryce's effort to maintain a blank, downcast expression got sidetracked by the sound of Tasiya's voice. "I must return to the kitchen to wash up the breakfast dishes. Enjoy your coffee."

A door had opened up in the hall just on the other side of the screen. Bryce could see her back-ing into the hallway. She'd gone back to her jeans, which did as fine a job showing off her long, lean legs as any other damn thing she wore. A familiar longing tripped through his veins, suffusing him with the need to move, to go to her and wrap him-self around her and shield her from the hellish games of this place.

She spared Bryce a quick glance through the screen, just enough to let him know she knew he was there, but not long enough for anyone else to pick up the connection. She made a motion with her hand down at her side—signin' somethin' maybe—but Bryce didn't catch it. And then she had com-pany and there was no chance to repeat the message.

"I only wanted to see that you kept your word," she said through the open door. "Thank you."

"Anything for you, sugar." Marcus Smith materialized in the doorway, holding a mug of coffee. He stared down at the top of Tasiya's cowed head with a sick smile that heated Bryce's blood from the tender need to protect to the surprisingly violent desire to put that leering bastard out of commission.

"I must go."

Smith picked up a strand of Tasiya's hair and rubbed it between his fingers, holdin' on tight enough that she had to turn her head to keep it from pullin' at her scalp when she tried to leave. "Don't run off on my account, sugar. I think you and I have more to discuss."

"Later. I promise. I have to go." By the time she pried her hair loose and tried to move away, Bryce's toes were curlin' inside his boots, anxious to get to her and run interference.

That son of a bitch. Though Tasiya politely excused herself, Smith moved out right behind her. Bryce's hands fisted around Fowler's letter. A vein pounded in his jaw. *Why the hell didn't somebody stop him?*

With an all-important message to send on videotape, Bryce couldn't risk taking down Bristoe and the two guards who stood between him and the door. But his fists weren't the only weapon he possessed. "Should he be doin' that?"

The fact that he'd spoken startled Bristoe into answerin'. "What?"

Bryce nodded toward the screen door. "Him and that girl."

The kid wasn't slick enough to let it go. "Who? Smith?"

He said the name loud enough that Marcus stopped and turned. Thankfully, Tasiya trotted straight on out of sight, into the kitchen where she could grab a meat cleaver to keep Smith's hands off her. He hoped.

But Marcus wasn't near the fool Steve Bristoe was. His icy blue eyes met Bryce's through the screen. A silent message was exchanged between them. Boundaries were challenged. Paybacks were set.

Smith took a drink of coffee, then wiped his mouth with the back of his hand. "Sweet on the little lady, are ya, big guy?"

Bryce didn't answer the taunt. His attention had been drawn to something more worth his time. That's what Tasiya had tried to tell him with her hand signals. A C and a 4. He'd taught her a list of items to look for in their nightly searches. And his gutsy lady had delivered.

Inside Smith's quarters were rows upon rows of boxes, all marked with distinct military signage. The security chief bunked in the munitions room, complete with shells, ammo clips, rifles—and two neatly marked boxes of C-4. Plastique explosive.

As if sensing the open door was an invitation for Bryce to challenge him, Smith pushed it shut and locked it with a key. Then he walked right up to the screen and dangled the key like a golden apple in front of Bryce. "Don't get any ideas, hick. About anything. Or anybody."

Then he stuffed the key into his pocket and turned to follow Tasiya. Bryce's need to stomp Smith's sorry hide poured adrenaline into his muscles and deepened his breathing. He strained against the rope at his wrists. But he had to bide his time. He didn't have the upper hand. Yet. He'd only make things worse for Tasiya if he tried to help her now and got incapacitated or killed. If he was gone, she'd have no one. No hope of escape. No future.

In the end, he could do nothing but pray that Tasiya knew how to use that meat cleaver.

"Your turn, big man." Hodges motioned him down the stairs and Bryce fell into step in front of Bristoe's gun.

This had better work. For Tasiya's sake as much as anyone else's on the team.

After a few preliminary instructions from Fowler, Bryce faced the camera. He ignored the two guns pointed at him, positioned his hands on the paper and started to read. "The Montana Militia for a Free America has never forgotten the beliefs set down in the Declaration of Independence. But our government has…"

Ponderosa, Montana

"WHAT DO THE THREE FINGERS mean? Is he pointing to something?"

"The other hostages all wore chains. Why is Sarge different?"

"Has he ever said that many words all at once?"

"He's telling us something." Trevor Blackhaw hit the pause button and stared at the image recorded from that afternoon's special news report.

Bryce Martin, an immovable rock of a man, with a deceptive package of brains inside all that brawn, stared back from the plasma-screen TV suspended from the ceiling. He looked a little more battered than usual—from the swollen cut on his cheek to the distinct ligature marks beneath the crude rope that bound his wrists.

Every available member of Big Sky Bounty Hunters had gathered in the command center secretly located beneath the ranch lodge that served as their headquarters building. Their boss, Cameron Murphy, sat at the head of the conference table, with the portable oxygen tank that he still carried to appease his wife's concerns but rarely used anymore, on the floor beside him. "What do we know, people?" he demanded, expecting some answers.

Anthony Lombardi leaned back in his chair, drumming his fingers against the table. "I can't get a fix on any landmarks besides the stone wall behind him. There's no topography to look at. With the sun covered up like that, it's hard to get a fix on the time of day. Pretty windy there, though."

Owen Cook had his laptop open, clicking through information the average computer hacker could never gain access to. "I plotted the cloud movement over the six minutes he's on camera. They're moving at storm speed. According to U.S. Navy weather reports, the only storms of that size in the past week have been over the eastern seaboard. That fits in with the general area of their capture."

"Assuming this video was made in the last week," Murphy noted.

"It's recent." Interrogation was Trevor's area of expertise. "They've been missing three weeks. It takes a while to coerce a hostage, especially a hardhead like Sarge, into saying what you want him to. Fowler needed time to either force him to submit or find the bargaining chip that would make the hostage turn."

Michael Clark looked up from the observations he'd jotted on his notepad. "Sergeant Martin doesn't believe a word he's saying. You can see it in his eyes, and that succinct articulation doesn't come naturally to him. The three fingers are definitely a clue. Looks like a trident to me. Could be the number three. Third? Triple?"

"So we can place him somewhere on the eastern seaboard," Murphy summarized. Timing was critical. According to the first few minutes of the hostage video, a prisoner would be killed every day that the United Nations didn't withdraw its plans to invade Lukinburg and overthrow King Aleksandr's corrupt rule. They had fewer than twelve hours until day two and the next murder. "That narrows it down to a couple thousand square miles. Please tell me we can do better than that."

Trevor nodded. "You'd think of any of the prisoners, they'd have Sarge locked down tight. That rope has to mean something. Can you blow up that part of the picture?"

Cook typed and clicked on his computer, magnifying the braided rope around Bryce's wrists. "Coming up…now."

To a man they groaned and cursed and shook their heads.

"I recognize that from basic training."

"Cord grass."

"Devil's Fork Island."

Bingo.

Murphy braced his hands at the edge of the table and stood. "Get that FBI botanist on the horn and verify the species of grass and its exact location. There are several islands in that area. Call Major Hayes with Special Forces at Ft. Bragg and get us some backup. He owes me one. Take whatever you need and get yourselves booked on a flight out of here tonight. I want Boone Fowler back in a Montana prison."

As he snapped orders, his men went to work.

He stopped Trevor with a hand on his arm. "I'm not in any condition to travel yet." It was evident how much he hated to say it, but, "I'd only slow us down. I want you to take lead on this."

"Yes, sir."

"And Trev?"

"Yes?"

"Bring my men home."

Chapter Eleven

Trevor Blackhaw's voice crackled over the home-made radio in Bryce's cell. "I knew you'd have something rigged up, Sarge. Sorry it took us so long to find you."

Blackhaw and the rest of Big Sky, except for the colonel, were fewer than twenty miles away, camped out on the mainland and waiting to make their move. "I'm just glad this is finally gonna happen."

"We'll have the chemical agent on hand in twenty-four hours. You take out the perimeter alarm and we'll be there tomorrow night with the gas masks. The storms should subside by then, so we'll be able to get on the island undetected. If we can pull this off, we'll keep casualties to a minimum. We are not going to lose another man."

"Amen to that."

The rescue plan was far from simple, but Bryce had faith that his friends could pull it off. As long as he could get his part accomplished as their point man on the inside. At midnight tomorrow, Trevor Blackhaw and a group of bounty hunters would sneak onto the island and deliver gas masks for all the hostages. After a signal flare warned the prisoners to suit up, a Special Forces unit would drop a chemical agent that would knock out every living thing that breathed the nontoxic gas. With Fowler and his men sleepin' like babies, Big Sky and company could come in and round up the militia with far less danger of confrontation and a far better chance of getting everyone out alive.

"You'll get word to the others?"

"Will do." Bryce reached across the cot to take Tasiya's hand. She'd been listening to the hushed conversation as carefully as he had. And though he suspected she hadn't understood all the military jargon, he had no doubt she was ready to do her part. "I've found a pretty good friend here who can help us."

"Someone you trust?"

Tasiya's eyes widened in expectation of Bryce's answer.

"Yes." With that one all-encompassing word, she smiled, lighting up the gloomy cell and Bryce's lonely world. "Blackhaw, I've got another request."

"Name it."

"That friend—we need to take her with us when we go."

"Her?" He'd expected that kind of curiosity from

Powell, Blackhaw and the gang. The teasing inflection, the hint-hint, tell-me-more tone.

But Bryce couldn't brag about what wasn't his, and he didn't want anything to come between him and Tasiya during this precious time they did have together. So he overlooked the I've-met-someone-amazing speech, and stuck to business. "She works as a servant here. But she's basically a hostage herself. I want her to be safe."

It wasn't every day that Bryce Martin talked about a woman, but Blackhaw took the hint. "No problem. We'll get her a mask, too."

Tasiya tugged on Bryce's hand and whispered. "Remember, the militia cannot know I helped you, or that I have left with you. Even in prison, they will have contacts. If word gets back to Dimitri that I have betrayed him, then Papa…"

She didn't have to explain how her father's life would be forfeit. Bryce moved the radio to his lap and pulled her to his side, wrapping his arm around her strong, slender shoulders and pressing a kiss to her hair. "You hear that, Blackhaw? We have to make it look like she's been killed so there won't be any repercussions on her family back in Lukinburg."

"We've done some witness-protection-program work. We could pull off something like that." He paused in that unflappable, Native American way of his, and considered their options. "There are some herbs I know—a recipe from my grandfather—that can slow down the breathing and heart rate enough to fake death, unless you've got some medical equipment there to detect a trace pulse."

"The only thing high-tech around here is the security grid." He hugged Tasiya tighter. "Is it safe to take?"

"My ancestors used it on vision quests. Your friend might have some funky dreams, but she should come out of it okay. I'll have a vial for her when she picks up the masks."

"Understood. And Blackhaw?"

"Yeah, Sarge?"

"Thanks."

"Are you kidding? Of course *you* had to do it the hard way, but you've given us the means to finally bring in Fowler and his men. If I never bring in another bounty, knowing we put that bastard away will be worth it."

"Amen. Martin out."

As Bryce dismantled the radio and hid the parts alongside his chains beneath the mattress again, he noticed that Tasiya seemed unusually quiet. She still put up her hair and cleaned up any trace of her visit the way she had each night before their recon missions. But quiet wasn't Tasiya's way—not with him.

"You all right?"

He barely touched her shoulder and she flinched away. She loaded her basket, unlocked the cell door and carried her things out into the passageway. For a minute he thought she wasn't going to answer him. And when she turned to face him, her eyes were so big, so sad, that he made a promise he wasn't a hundred percent sure he could keep.

"We're gonna get out of here. You're gonna be safe."

"Tonight, we get the C-4. Yes?"

"Yeah. I'll need it to knock out the generators tomorrow night so Blackhaw can get inside the perimeter and deliver the gas masks." Was that what she was worried about? "An explosion will create enough of a diversion that you should be able to slip out and meet him and get back without anybody missin' you. There should be plenty of time before things die down for you to take those herbs and fake your death."

"So the explosives are imperative to your mission."

"*Our* mission." He slipped the stolen knife into his boot and followed her to the door. "You ready to play lookout?"

Without any guards in the locked-down prison wing at night, Bryce had discovered he could pretty much have the run of the place. But getting into the militia's wing through the open breezeway was gonna be damn tricky, with sentries patrolling the grounds and Marcus Smith sleeping in the very room where Bryce needed to be.

"I will get it from Marcus Smith's room," she announced.

That's what she was stewin' about? Absolutely not. No way. "I'll go. It's too risky."

"It is my freedom, too." She was choosin' now to be stubborn?

"What if he puts his hands on you again?"

"Then he will put his hands on me. It must be done."

Hell. That's what she was worried about. *His* reaction. She knew he didn't want her in that kind of danger. Knew he'd fight her on this.

She pressed her palm squarely in the middle of his chest and shut him up when he opened his mouth to argue. "Do not think for one moment that his stinking breath and his foul fingers and bullying strength mean anything to me. Dimitri Mostek smells better, but he is no different beneath his skin." Her fingers curled into the front of his jacket. "Sometimes I think my beauty is a curse, that no man will ever look inside me to see who I am, what I dream about, what I need."

That sort of prejudice sounded achingly familiar. Maybe better than anybody he understood what she was sayin'. "Yeah. Sometimes it's hard to get past what a person looks like on the outside."

She slipped her hand up to cup the scarred side of his jaw. "*You* see inside me, Bryce Martin. For that I will always be grateful."

Yep. Just what he wanted, gratitude from the woman. Sucker. He pulled her hand down and tried to break away from any connection to pity or gratitude. "Yeah, well, we'd better get started if we're gonna do this. And just for the record, I hate it."

But she twisted her hand and latched on to his wrist. He'd wanted her to talk, right? She wasn't done speakin' her piece. "I see inside you, too."

What the hell did that mean? What sort of dreams and wants and needs did she think she knew about him?

Maybe the most private secret of all. The one he'd never be able to share with her. How pathetic. If she'd sensed everything he felt about her...

Tasiya dropped her basket to the floor and reached for him. She framed his face between her hands and rose up on tiptoe to kiss him. His body lurched in an instantaneous, hungry response, and his hands automatically went to her waist. His pride was a little slower to catch up and deepen the sweet kiss.

But when her arms wound around his neck, her hands skimmed and clutched against his hair, and she moaned that needy whimper in her throat, Bryce snaked his arms around her and lifted her clear off the floor. He palmed her butt and grabbed a fistful of her sweater. He swept his tongue into her hot, honey-sweet mouth and took everything she offered. His blood caught fire and his heart pounded in his chest. If he could have consumed her on the spot he would have.

This was some friggin' goodbye, and he wasn't ready for it. He didn't want to let her go. He didn't want to lose her. Ever. Not to Marcus Smith, not to

Dimitri Mostek, not even to the promise of the freedom she so richly deserved.

But when she pulled away, when she brushed her shaky fingertips across his sensitized lips and smiled that serene smile of gratitude, he let her go.

He set her back on her feet and looked away from her eyes only long enough to see the keys she pressed into his hand. "Give me fifteen or twenty minutes. Then come find me. I will be able to get in, but—"

"I'll make sure you get out."

If that was the only promise she wanted from him, he'd keep it. Or die trying.

Bryce watched her walk away. He held on to her hand, her fingertips, her gaze, for as along as he could. And then she was gone.

This plan stunk. Life stunk. Love stunk.

But, damn it all, it was the only way.

EVERY TIME THE THUNDER smacked against the sky, Tasiya jumped inside her skin. The storm outside was a blessing of sorts: the clouds blotted out any natural light; the rain and wind and angry waves muffled any suspicious sounds and kept the sentries huddled at their posts with their chins tucked in.

But she couldn't help making a fatalistic analogy about nature's fury and the retribution that would be unleashed if their escape plan failed. If *she* failed Bryce Martin.

Lightning flashed outside, spotlighting for one eerie moment the walls lined with deadly weapons and ammunition that surrounded her. Knives, guns, bullets, explosives. But the most dangerous thing in the room stood at the table beside his cot, pouring her a shot of whiskey she didn't want.

Tasiya gripped the edge of the shelf behind her as the answering thunder echoed down around her ears. She wished she could think of a convincing reason for Marcus to open the door again, so she'd feel a little less like a helpless mouse caught in a trap, waiting for the slavering cat to spring upon her. But the wind off the breezeway had blown it shut, and the puddle of water already staining the doorway gave her no argument against Marcus's claim that it would continue to rain in through the screen door until the storm subsided.

"Here you go, sugar." He crossed the room through a path between stacked crates and handed her a dingy glass half-full of a potent amber liquid. She had to hold it in both hands to keep herself from shoving him out of her personal space. He clinked their glasses together, showing his yellow teeth in a suggestive grin. "Bottoms up."

Unlike her conversations with Bryce, where he patiently answered every question she had about the peculiarities of the English language, Tasiya didn't care that she didn't understand the significance of Marcus's words. He tipped his head back and emptied his glass in a single gulp. Then he wiped his lips and licked the residue off his fingers.

"Good stuff. Now, when you talk about *repaying* me for helping out your ugly friend, what exactly am I lookin' forward to?" He frowned, nodding toward her untouched glass. "Drink up."

She'd hoped to spot a potted plant she could pour hers into, but the militiamen had no such amenities. With Marcus standing close enough to smell the liquor on his breath and showing no signs of moving until she did as he asked, Tasiya had no choice but to raise the glass to her lips. Her eyes watered as the bitter liquid burned all the way down her throat.

"Oh, my." She hoped that light-headed feeling was due to the huge gasp of air she'd taken and not the immediate effects of the alcohol.

"Smooth stuff, huh?"

Not exactly the description she would have used. But the horrid taste gave her an idea. She held up her glass. "Perhaps it gets better the more I drink. May I have another?"

"Happy to oblige." He took her glass and returned to the table. With his back turned, Tasiya quickly went to work. "My old man used to work at a distillery down in Tennessee. Best thing he ever did for me was introduce me to the fine taste of whiskey. I went into the family business, too. But then I discovered I had a higher calling—one that paid better, too."

Tasiya had positioned herself next to the boxes of C-4. She'd already managed to unhook the latch on the top box while Marcus had dug through his duffel bag for the whiskey and glasses. Now that he was consumed with his favorite topic and pouring her another drink, she could reach inside and move the paper-wrapped explosives into her basket. One brick would suffice, Bryce had said. Done. Two would be even better.

But Marcus was turning around. The second brick would have to wait. Tasiya covered the C-4 in her basket with a dish towel and pretended an interest in the guns on the shelf above her. "Do you know how to use all of these weapons?"

"Of course I do." He walked up right behind her, making no effort to hide his arousal as he pressed against her bottom, trapping her between the shelf and his body. Tasiya closed her eyes and cringed, wishing she could walk through walls. "I'm an expert on firing things. That's why Fowler recruited me."

Tasiya didn't have to grasp the language to understand the lecherous undertones in Marcus's words. She should have told Bryce five minutes. She might not last fifteen minutes with this man.

She shuddered with the next clap of thunder and pushed away from the shelves, hating Marcus's groan of satisfaction as she couldn't avoid rubbing against him. "But there are so many different kinds." She circled to the opposite side of the room, hoping to turn his attention away from the explosives and the basket. He set down their drinks and followed her. "What about this one?" She picked up a black steel rifle that was surprisingly heavy. The metal felt unnaturally cold, the weight of it, lethal. "What do you use one like this for?"

"Sometimes a man needs a big gun to make him stronger than his opponent." He reached over her shoulder and plucked the rifle from her grasp. This time, she wisely scooted aside as he replaced it on the shelf. But she didn't get far enough, fast enough. He snatched her wrist and pulled her back beside him. His overgrown beard tangled with her hair. "Sugar, are you here to talk or to give me some action? 'Cause I guarantee you, talking isn't the payoff I had in mind."

He nuzzled her ear. Tasiya's breath lodged in her throat. "I thought I would bake you something special. Do you like cake? Pie? Cookies?"

He laughed and licked his way down her neck. "You're the sugar I want."

Tasiya tried to slide away but his hands locked around her hips. She wedged her arms between them and pushed. "What about Mr. Fowler?"

His mouth hovered over hers as he unhooked the snap of her jeans. "He's asleep. I won't tell if you won't."

Lightning flashed, giving her a frightening glimpse of his stained teeth and lustful intent.

"No." She couldn't take his groping hands and foul scent any longer. "No!"

Tasiya stomped down on the instep of his foot and shoved with every bit of strength in her. Marcus stumbled back a step and knocked over a crate. Tasiya didn't waste any time dashing across the room to grab her basket and run for the door. "I am your cook! Not your prostitute!"

Marcus knocked over another crate as he pushed himself upright and propelled himself after her. "Uh-uh, sugar. *No* is not an option once you get me goin' like this. *You* came to me. You will be whatever the hell I tell you to be."

He grabbed her arm, jerked it in its socket as he swung her around. Thunder shook through the walls as Tasiya screamed. She slammed into a stack of crates and sent them flying before toppling into the midst of them. Ignoring the bruising jolt to her bones, she scrambled to her feet. She'd lost the basket! But as she knocked her shin on a crate, stumbling to retrieve it, she knew it was already too late.

She froze. The basket and its scattered contents were strewn on the floor between them, with the brick of C-4 sitting like a traitorous alarm beacon right on top.

"You thieving bitch."

Marcus's fist hit her square in the cheek, knocking her to the floor and swirling the room around inside her head. Waves of agony radiated through her jaw and skull. She was too dizzy to even steady herself on her hands and knees.

Marcus grabbed a handful of hair and yanked her upright. The zillion pinpricks of pain erupting across her scalp cleared her vision long enough to see the pistol he pulled from his belt and jammed to the center of her forehead.

"Don't touch you, huh? I will touch you any damn way I want!"

Thunder crashed through the room. The door sailed open. The rain poured in.

But it wasn't the storm.

"Tasiya!" A monster charged in from the darkness and plowed into Marcus.

Tasiya collapsed and crawled out of the way as Bryce knocked Marcus Smith clear across the room. They smashed into the shelves and hit the floor as an avalanche of heavy crates and weapons cascaded over their heads.

"Bryce!" Her screams were drowned out by the beating of the wind and the rain.

She learned that a fist hitting muscle made a terrible sound. A fist hitting bone sounded even worse. Boxes broke. Marcus cursed.

The rain through the screen door soaked her sweater and weighted her hair. But the hug of cold water clinging to her skin reminded her of the world outside this room. Though she wavered on her feet, Tasiya mustered the sense to close the door. With the cacophony of the storm, the fight might not be heard, but a man walking by might see.

"Bryce," she whispered, desperate to help but not knowing how. "Please. Please."

Like two leviathans, the men rose through the flood of knives and guns and splintered wood. Marcus had his hands on Bryce's throat now. His pistol had disappeared. Tasiya wanted to retrieve it, but in a sea of weapons, which was his? Which was loaded?

Marcus found his footing first and rammed Bryce against the broken wall. Tasiya flinched at the momentary grimace that contorted Bryce's face. His back! The wounds on his back!

But Bryce pounded on Marcus's arms, loosening his stranglehold. He pounded again, driving Marcus to his knees.

"Run, Tasiya!" Bryce growled.

Marcus clipped him around the ankles and dragged him to the floor. With a sickening sense of déjà vu, Tasiya was suddenly back in that interrogation room. Bryce was putting his life on the line. Again. For her.

This time she would listen.

She grabbed the basket, along with the C-4, and stumbled toward the door. But one last look at her hero stopped her cold.

"Bryce!"

Marcus had found his gun. He was on his knees over

the man she loved. Blood spewed from his ugly mouth as he squeezed the trigger. "Die, you big bastard."

"You first."

Marcus jerked. His eyes widened like saucers. Bryce shoved his hand into Marcus's gut, and Tasiya realized he'd stabbed him. With a twist of Marcus's own hunting knife, Bryce finished the job.

The gun fell from Marcus's grip. His oversize body went limp. Bryce pushed him aside as the big ox fell dead.

"Bryce?"

He was shaking as he climbed to his feet and Tasiya ran to him. She wrapped her arms around his waist and braced him with her strength as he pressed his lips into her hair and hugged her close. "I had to bust the damn lock open. You didn't have a key that fit. I heard you scream."

She could feel the sticky warmth of blood soaking through the back of his cold, wet jacket and knew that his wounds had been reopened in the fight. She'd been just as frightened for him as he'd been for her. "It is all right now. I am safe."

With a steadfast determination, he pushed her away. His ragged breathing warned her that the fight had sapped most of his strength. "We're not safe. Somebody might have heard."

"But the storm—"

"I won't risk it. Back-up's not comin' till midnight tomorrow. We're still on our own." He turned her toward the door. "Go back to my cell. I need to clean up this mess and hide the body. Go. Now."

She planted her feet. "I will help. It will go faster if we work together. Then we can both leave."

For once his overblown sense of chivalry took a backseat to practicality. He reached out and brushed his gentle fingers across her cheek. Tasiya winced at the swelling there. Regret colored his voice. "I was too late, wasn't I?"

"I am alive, Bryce Martin," she whispered. "I believe you were right on time."

Chapter Twelve

For the second time in his life, Bryce awoke to find a beautiful woman gently tending his wounds.

This time he wasn't whacked out of his head with pain and anguish. He knew where he was and, thanks to the spicy, wholesome smell that wafted beside him on the cot, he knew who was with him.

He rolled onto his side and looked up into Tasiya's dark, exotic eyes. "Evenin.'"

It was about ten o'clock, he guessed, judging by the first stars dotting the sky outside his window. Melancholy and anticipation battled to dictate his mood. In just a few hours he'd be on his way to freedom—but his time with Tasiya would be over.

With her typical devotion to practicality, Tasiya urged him back onto his stomach to finish doctoring his shoulder. "Some of your cuts look infected. I wish I had an antibiotic to give you."

What, no 'Good evening, Bryce Martin'? He was growing used to the trills and musical articulation of his first and last name together. Her soft accent made it sound as meaningful a declaration of trust and caring as any words he'd heard from a woman.

She was probably nervous or preoccupied about her tasks tonight. Or still fearful that someone would discover Marcus Smith's body in the unused prison cell where he'd stashed him.

Deciding she was done taking care of him, Bryce pushed aside her protests and sat up next to her on the edge of the cot. He took the cloth and ointment from her hands and set them on the floor beside the food she'd brought.

"The medics can pump me full of antibiotics once we get off this island tonight," he reassured her. He hiked up his jeans and turned to prop one knee on the cot so he could face her and take her hands in his. "From the sound of things, I'm more worried about Craig O'Riley's injuries."

"When I gave him your message to be ready at midnight, he said he would be strong. He will be greatly motivated to 'kick butt,' he says." Bryce grinned at her endearing recitation of words that didn't fit a literal translation. "Your friend, Jacob Powell and Mr. Campbell, said they would be there to help him."

Tasiya looked down to where her smaller hands joined his in his lap. Her fair skin glistened in the dim shadows against his darker fingers. The differences in color and size created an evocative contrast of male and female, yesterday and tomorrow, despair and hope—and just how intrinsically linked and delicately balanced they each could be.

Bryce turned her hands so he could stroke the racing beat of her pulse at her wrists. Somethin' was eatin' her up from the inside out. "You worried about your daddy?"

She shook her head, stirring the long fall of hair that only partially hid the swollen purple bruise on her cheek. "No more than usual," she admitted.

"You afraid of what's gonna happen tonight? I promise you, Blackhaw's a stickler for details. Nobody's gonna get hurt. I'll whisk you outta here before Boone Fowler knows what hit him. I'll see you all the way back to Montana or New York City or Lukinburg, if that's where you wanna go."

Tasiya stiffened. Her eyes darted up to his. "You think I want to go back to Dimitri?"

"When you're free, you have the right to choose wherever you want to be." Bryce swallowed hard. Maybe this was the part she was dreading. He knew he'd been avoiding the inevitable. "I know you're probably feelin' grateful for me helpin' you out, or listenin' to ya talk, or thinkin' we're a team or whatever. But don't feel like you have to choose me or Montana when we get out. You don't owe me a thing. I don't want you to think you're tradin' one kind of blackmail for another. I wouldn't be any better than Fowler or Smith, then. I promised you freedom. And I'm a man of my word."

Even in the semidarkness, he could see the color flooding her cheeks. She pulled her hands away and stood, pacing clear to the steel bars before she turned and fired away. "I swear to God, Bryce Martin, if you were not injured, I would slap your face."

Huh! Maybe his looks weren't the only reason he'd never had a decent relationship with a woman. He threw up his hands. "Then what the hell's buggin' ya, honey?"

She twisted her lips together, struggling to contain somethin' that was too much for her to bear. "I have learned more about freedom inside this prison cell than I ever knew existed in my own country. You've taught me that I have value in this world. That I can make choices."

"Yep."

Her breath emptied out in a hushed sigh. "I choose you, Bryce Martin."

He squashed down the surge of boyish joy and lifelong hope that licked its way through his veins. "Honey, I'm just one man. You'll meet others on the outside. Better-lookin' ones. Ones who know what to say to a lady." He rose and paced to the window, scrubbing his hand over his bristly jaw and starin' up into the sky. He couldn't look her in the eye and say this, couldn't see her sweet face and send her to another man. "You're a beautiful woman, with a kind heart and a stubborn streak a mile wide. You're smart. Gutsy. There'll be plenty of other men for you to choose from."

"Like Marcus Smith?"

"No." Bryce fisted his hands around the bars at the window. "I'm talkin' about good men. Ones who'll treat ya with respect. You can choose any one of 'em. Or no one, if that's what you want."

He flinched when he felt her cool hands on his shoulders. "I choose you."

Bryce turned around. He lost his resolve to keep his distance in the sirenlike call of her innocent smile. He brushed aside the hair at her temple and gently cupped her jaw, smoothing his thumb across her velvety cheek. "I might look pretty good to you right now, honey, but that's just 'cause I'm the only man here."

She leaned her cheek into his fingers and kissed the palm of his hand. "The first night I met you, you frightened me. I thought you were a monster."

Yep, he got a lot of that.

But she took away the sting of reality with her next words. "Since that night I have seen into your beautiful eyes. I have seen into your heart." She spread her fingers across the left side of his chest. "There is no monster in you. I do not believe there are better men than you out there."

Bryce covered her hand with his own, holding her gentle acceptance against his beating heart. "That's sweet of **you to say**, honey, but—"

"Make love to me, Bryce Martin. I may not live through this night. I may be forced to return to Lukinburg and give myself to Dimitri Mostek in order to save my father."

Make love? His body lurched in shameless response at the mere suggestion. The blood seemed to rush from his extremities and pool behind his groin.

But he listened to everything she said and shook his head. "I won't let anything happen to you."

"You cannot promise that. As well as you mean, you cannot know that something will not go wrong." She dug her fingertips into his skin, pleading by her touch as well as her voice. "I want one night with a man whose hands do not make me feel dirty. Whose words inspire me with hope instead of fear. I want to know what it is like to be loved by a man who cares about the woman I am inside. If this is to be my last night in America, or on this earth, I want my memories to be of you."

He was already on fire for her. But to ask this, to give him this… "You don't know what you're sayin' to me, honey."

"You told me that, in America, a woman may ask for what she wants. I want you to make love to me. I want…you."

"I want you, too, honey. More than my next breath. It hurts sometimes to think how much you mean to me."

"Then it is settled." Ever practical and efficient,

Tasiya's hands went to the hem of her sweater and she pulled it up. "I will try not to hurt you."

Damn. All that creamy skin and a plain lace bra that clung to pert, ripe breasts. He wanted to laugh at the irony of her promise, but his breath seemed to catch in his throat. "I should be sayin' that to you."

He tried to be a gentleman. He tried to look away. But he was a man. And he loved her. And his hands were drawn to that skin like a magnet. He skimmed her flanks, caught the weight of her breasts in his palms, moaned along with her, then joined her hands on the sweater, pulling it off over her head and tossing it aside.

Her hair cascaded down and she shook it loose, filling the air with her scents and covering her shoulders and breasts in a cloud of ebony silk. "If I do something wrong, you will tell me?"

Screw being a gentleman. This might be *his* last night on the planet. His last night with Tasiya. He wasn't a strong enough man to walk away from somethin' they both wanted.

"You're beautiful." His voice came out as a husky growl and she blushed. Bryce gathered her into his arms, binding them together skin to skin. Her curves fit snugly against his harder planes, and the twin buds that pearled at the tips of her breasts branded him with a searing heat.

She was supple and cool to the touch, yet he thought he might burn up with need for her. This was no slow fuse, no time-released detonation. He'd been primed to make love to this woman from the first moment she'd shown him tenderness, that first night they'd touched through the bars of his cage and an electric current had sparked between them.

Her hands rested on his biceps while her gaze darted back and forth across his chest. Seein' his scars? Havin' second thoughts?

"I do not know where to begin."

"You put your hands on me wherever you want. Ask for whatever you want. Tell me no if you've had enough or I scare you in any way." He nudged her beneath the chin. "And you look me in the eye."

She skidded her hands across his shoulders and clasped them together behind his neck. "I am not afraid of you, Bryce Martin. I was only admiring how strong you are. How very—" the frown appeared between her brows "—not like a woman you are."

Bryce laughed and kissed her frown away. "Honey, you're gonna discover there's not much like a woman about me anywhere."

And then he was kissing her, drinking in the generous gift she offered, giving her everything there was in him. He skimmed his hands along her spine down to her bottom and lifted her up into his rising heat. He swept his hands into her hair, scooted the straps off her shoulders as he came back down. He pressed his lips to the delicate point of her collarbone, supped at the straining swell of her breast. He swirled his tongue around one distended nipple, wetting it through the lace.

Tasiya gasped. "I... You..."

Speechless. Bryce grinned.

Her fingers latched on to his head and took his mouth to the other breast. He toyed with it, teasing it through the lace, making her hips squirm against his. And when he didn't think *he* could take any more of those whimpers of pleasure that hummed in her throat, he unhooked her bra and let it join the sweater. A shiver of goose bumps pricked across her wet skin and Bryce eased the shock by taking her into his mouth. She was delicate and sweet and more responsive than he could have imagined.

This was a crappy place to make love to a beautiful woman, but when she threw her head back and arched into his mouth, Bryce thought he was in paradise.

"I want you, Tasiya," he whispered against her breast. "Any way you want." He kissed the thrumming pulse at her throat. "Now." He suckled her bottom lip, caught her stuttered breath in a kiss. "Tell me now if you want me to stop."

"No." She planed her hands across his chest, flicked across a flat male nipple, and he groaned. "You like that, too?"

"Yes. Oh, yes."

A quick study, she kissed the spot, then ran her tongue around it. Bryce's arms convulsed around her at the sweet agony of her innocent touches. "Honey, I won't last much longer if you keep doin' that."

She raised her mouth for a kiss and her fingers dropped to the snap of his jeans. "I do not want to wait. Now, Bryce Martin. Please."

Bryce needed no further encouragement. With the frenzy of last chances and moments stolen out of time, they stripped off their remaining clothes. Bryce laid them over the cot to make a relatively clean bed for them. Then he reached for Tasiya's bottom and picked her up, stretching her warm, moist heat against him. He sat down with her straddling his lap and the evidence of his desire butting against her thigh.

For one precious moment, she tore her mouth from his and looked down with a little bit of awe and worry in her eyes. "You are so…big."

Bryce caught her face between his hands and laughed. It was a tender, intimate sound shared in the darkness. "You know, ninety-nine men out of a hundred would take that as a compliment. But I don't want you to worry. Nature has a way of making things…fit…the way they should." He kissed her then, deeply, reverently, stirring things inside him that had nothing to do with sex. "But if I hurt you or scare you in any way, I will never forgive myself. I can still stop."

"I said I was not afraid of you, Bryce Martin. Not of your scars, not of this."

Bryce forgot to breathe when Tasiya wrapped her hand around him.

Unable to help himself, he thrust into her curious grip. He leaned his forehead against hers and willed enough patience into his system to wait until he knew she was ready.

But Tasiya Belov had had a taste of freedom. She knew how to ask for what she wanted "Oh, Bryce. Please be inside me…now…"

With no answer but a kiss, Bryce lifted her. She held her breath as he sheathed himself inside her. She gasped against his neck and dug her fingers into his shoulders when he pushed through her barrier, and then he felt her relax. She sank down around him, took him deeper and deeper. She hugged him tight and he hugged her tighter. Mouth to mouth, chest to chest, sex to sex.

Her glorious hair was their only cloak as they rocked together and fell into a rhythm that transcended any differences in language or culture. Tasiya gave him her body and trust. Bryce gave her his heart.

Their joined mouths muffled their cries of passion and pleasure, and in the deepest corner of a solitary prison cell on a forgotten island, their lonely spirits finally soared free. Tasiya whispered his name as the tremors of her release broke through her and around him. "Bryce Martin. Bryce Martin. Thank you. Thank you."

He poured himself into her, stunned by the humbling power of his release. Then he gathered her into his arms and lay down beside her on the cot, keeping her warm with the blanket of his body until she drifted off to sleep.

Bryce Martin had been to hell and back more than once in his life. But tonight was the first time he'd been to heaven.

EVEN WITH HER ears covered, the explosion was deafening.

But Tasiya didn't wait for her nerves to settle or her courage to falter. Bryce and his friends were counting on her. And she had no intention of letting them down.

She darted through the shadows, unseen in the sudden darkness illuminated only by hastily drawn flashlights and the flames from the generator room where Bryce had set the charges. Her footsteps were silent beneath the shouts of men and the slap of the ocean against the shore. She clambered over the stone wall at the edge of the courtyard, then took off at a dead run through the sea of cord grass and sand.

Her body was still tingly and replete from making love with Bryce, her mind on a euphoric high. The parts of her that were slightly tender from the newly discovered intimacy had nothing to complain about. He'd given her everything she wanted and more.

And it hadn't been a fluke, a one-time gift that

would nurture and sustain her if her life turned dark again. Bryce's frenzied need and gentle touch had set a bar by which all men would be forever judged in her life. He'd awakened her later in the night and, without a word, he'd rolled her onto her back and made love to her all over again, communicating all she needed to know with every loving touch of his hands, mouth and body.

Bryce had been patient when she'd needed him to be; he'd been eager when she'd needed that, too. He'd been tender and thorough and demanding enough to make her heart sing with the worth and power of the woman she'd become in Bryce's arms.

That confidence gave her strength now as she slowed her pace and picked her way closer to the rocky drop-off where she'd discovered the dead soldier's body. Gruesome as it was, it was the only landmark she was sure she could find in the middle of the night that would be far enough away from the docks to avoid detection.

Trevor Blackhaw found her first, shushing her startled gasp with a finger to his lips before pulling her down to a crouch beside him in the sand. "Tasiya Belov?"

She nodded. Bryce's description of his bounty hunter friend had left out the intense blue color of his eyes. But she recognized the straight black hair and angular features that clearly reflected his Cherokee heritage.

"You are Bryce Martin's friend?"

"Trevor Blackhaw."

She should have breathed easier at the two rafts and twenty or so soldiers and bounty hunters hiding on the beach. But the weapons they carried and the funny, green-lensed telescopes they wore on their heads—night-vision goggles, Trevor explained—made Tasiya feel as if she was caught up in the middle of an invasion.

An army of prisoners inside, an army of rescuers outside. A frantic militia caught in the middle, dashing about the compound like ants scattering from a crushed ant hill. One lone woman, caught in the middle of it all didn't seem to stand a chance of surviving.

Oh, how she longed to be back at Bryce's side, in Bryce's arms. A single word in his gruff, loving voice would have bolstered her flagging courage.

But the clock was ticking. Once Bryce took out the generators that powered the perimeter alarm and security lights, he'd told her she'd have about twenty minutes, tops, to retrieve the gas masks and get them to the prisoners before returning to her room and drinking the herb mixture that would fake her death.

Trevor Blackhaw's instructions were as clear and concise as Bryce's had been. He looped the duffel bag with the masks over her shoulder and pushed a small vial into her hands. "We shoot the flare in fifteen. You'll have about a minute more after that before the gas hits. Give it another ten minutes for the wind to disperse it before you drink that."

"Fifteen. One. Ten," she repeated.

"You'll be out for several hours. But from what I hear, the sarge plans to take good care of you." Trevor smiled. "Is Sergeant Martin hangin' tough?"

Tasiya frowned at the question. Didn't he know? "Bryce Martin is very tough, though he is very gentle with me. He will get us all safely home."

Trevor's grin widened as he sensed something amusing that she didn't get. "Yes, ma'am. That sounds like the sarge to me."

Several minutes later Tasiya was panting for breath as she handed Bryce his gas mask through the bars of his cell. It was impossible to keep her gaze from drifting over to the cot where they'd made love, or to keep the blush of heat from staining her cheeks.

Bryce reached through the bars and touched her cheek. Those wintry gray eyes looked deeply into hers. "I know. Tonight will always be special to me, too."

On impulse, Tasiya pulled herself up on tiptoe and kissed him, square on the mouth, telling him in a few short heartbeats how much he meant to her. "Thank you for everything, Bryce Martin. Be safe."

And then she had to go.

"I'll be there when you wake up, Tasiya," he promised. "I will always be there for you."

"WE ARE UNDER ATTACK," Tasiya shouted into the phone, playing her part just the way Bryce had told her. She'd already said goodbye to her father, promised him that she would be all right. No matter what he heard, she asked him to have faith in her American friend. She paced back and forth in her tiny room off the kitchen. She only had a minute or so until midnight, a minute or so to convince Dimitri Mostek that she was about to be killed. "There are many soldiers on the island. Americans. There was an explosion. Everyone is running. There are guns."

"The Americans have attacked the island? That is not supposed to happen. Where is Boone Fowler? When did it begin?"

"I do not know. I only know I am afraid." She picked up her gas mask off her bed and glanced at the clock—11:59 p.m. A minute away from starting a whole new life. "Tell Papa that my friend sends him a hug and his highest regards, as well." She paused for a bit of dramatic emphasis. "If I do not see you again, give Papa my love."

"What friend are you talking about? I said you were not to be touched! You must come home. You belong to me. To me!"

Stick it to yourself, Dimitri, she wanted to say.

"Tell Papa I love him. Give him my message." Hopefully, Anton would remember their secret code. He might not understand the details, but it should clue him in enough to know she was up to something, and not to believe everything he heard—like the news that his daughter had been killed in a raid against the militia compound on Devil's Fork Island. "I must go."

"Anastasiya!" Dimitri shouted. "Anastasiya!"

The sky turned red outside her window and Tasiya hung up the phone.

Tasiya's lungs filled with a breath of air that felt free and unfettered. The chaos outside her window was merely background noise to the song of hope dancing in her heart. Soon it would all be over and she would be free. Then she could find out if Bryce Martin had been telling her the truth—that he could rescue her father from Lukinburg—and that she could choose any man she wanted in America.

She hoped she could find the right way to tell him that she'd chosen him.

As the clock flipped over to midnight, Tasiya pulled the gas mask on over her face. She patted the jeans pocket where she'd slipped the vial of the knock-out draught Trevor Blackhaw had given her and sat on the edge of her bed to wait.

But her satisfaction over finally beating Dimitri at the intimidation game and her enervating hopes for the future had distracted her a moment too long to warn her of the voice in the kitchen.

"Smith! Smith! Where the hell are you?" She shot to her feet at the bellow of Boone Fowler's voice. She ran to the window, but the bars blocked any escape. She spun around, but her sparse room offered her no place to hide. It was hot inside the mask, hard to see and hear, but there was no mistaking the approach of footsteps or the angry, hateful, damning voice of retribution. "I swear to God, Smith, if you are with that foreigner…"

A fisted hand ripped the blanket off her door frame. Tasiya backed into a corner. Found. Trapped. Denied her chance at freedom.

Boone Fowler's calculating black eyes drilled her across the tiny room. He held a gun in his hand, but it was the fanatical gleam in those eyes that scared her more. His absolute hatred for all things foreign seeped into her skin and turned her blood to ice. He made her want to shrivel up. Automatically she bowed her head.

"What the hell is going on here?"

She made a futile lunge for the door, but Fowler ignored the no-touch rule. With a surprisingly agile move for a man his size, he shoved her onto the bed and ripped the mask off her head, plucking several strands of hair with it.

He shook the mask in her face. "What have you done to me? You turned Marcus against me, and now this?"

A vinegary scent stung Tasiya's nose. She felt light-headed. "Marcus Smith is dead." She tried to protest, tried to hurt Fowler in any way she could. But she was powerless. Just like she'd always been.

Before Devil's Fork Island. Before Bryce Martin. "Smith attacked me. We killed him."

"We? Who's in this with you? Who's helping you?" Her lungs felt heavy; she couldn't catch her breath. Boone Fowler's pock-marked face swirled in front of her. "What's this?" He picked up something on the bed beside her. The phone. The chain that bound her to Dimitri. He grabbed her by the collar of her sweater and shook her, but it only spun her vision out of focus. "Who have you been calling? What have you done to me, you damn foreigner?"

Tasiya sagged. Fowler's grip was the only thing holding her upright.

"What's wrong with you?" Fowler coughed.

He tossed her onto the bed and ran to the window to look outside. "They're all dying. That's what I smelled. Some kind of gas." Fowler pounded on the bars at the window. "No. No!" He slipped her mask on over his head and took a deep breath. "You won't take me out like this, Murphy. Nobody does this to me!"

The last words she heard were Fowler's. "That's right, foreigner. You die. It'll be the most useful thing you've ever done for me."

The last thoughts she had were of Bryce. He would come for her. He'd promised. She would be safe.

Chapter Thirteen

"Tasiya!"

Where the hell was she?

Bryce flipped over the mattress in her room in an impossible attempt to find her underneath. He stormed back into the kitchen and tossed open drawers. He smashed his foot through the locked pantry door and searched for her there. The refrigerator, the mess hall, Fowler's office. He'd covered every inch of this compound from prison cell to latrine. She was gone.

How the hell could Tasiya be gone?

"Damn it!" Bryce rammed his fist through a cabinet door, heedless of the pain.

"We just have to get the bad guys, Sarge. We don't have to kill their furniture." Jacob Powell had stopped by the kitchen door, leading a handcuffed Steve Bristoe toward the courtyard where Big Sky and the Special Forces unit were rounding up the militiamen once they'd regained consciousness. They all had a one-way ticket to prison in Montana.

"Not funny, Powell. She's missing."

"Well, have you looked—"

"I've looked everywhere. She's supposed to be unconscious in her room, waiting for me to pick her up. She's gone."

"Let me get rid of this scumbag and I'll help you look. Have you checked the docks?"

"Just once."

Powell nodded. "I'll check again."

Trevor Blackhaw walked in as Powell and Bristoe left. "We've got another problem, Sarge."

His Native American friend wore the responsibility of leadership well, and Bryce had to admire how Blackhaw and the rest of the Big Sky team had homed in on Bryce's clues. They tracked them down, put together a flawless plan and recaptured the militia.

But as far as Bryce was concerned, there was no other problem besides the fact that the woman he loved and had sworn to protect was missing. "Can't somebody else deal with it?"

"You're our man on the inside, Sarge. You know this place better than anybody." Apparently, not well enough if he could lose track of a willowy brunette hell-bent on obtaining her freedom. Blackhaw thumbed over his shoulder toward the breezeway. "We've rounded up enough supplies and weaponry to man a small invasion. I've accounted for the thirty militia members you reported, including the body of Marcus Smith."

Bryce couldn't concentrate on what he was saying. "So you came for thirty men, you got thirty men."

"Thirty men plus their leader." Every muscle in Bryce's body clenched with dread. "I've got no sign of Boone Fowler anywhere. And one of the speedboats is missing."

No Tasiya. No Fowler.

"That son of a bitch." A desperate sort of helpless anger squeezed his heart. "He took her."

"That's what I figured. Fowler's got the girl and he's using her as a hostage to escape."

Bryce's heart was bleedin' out. "We have to find her. And fast."

Because from everything Tasiya had said, according to Boone Fowler, the only good foreigner was a dead one.

"I CAN'T. I CAN'T DO THIS." Tasiya refused to cry in front of Boone Fowler, but she was sobbing inside.

After recovering from the nontoxic sleeping gas, she'd awakened into a real nightmare. Those weren't Bryce's loving arms that had held her when she came to, but the vicious bond of Boone Fowler's controlling grip.

He'd spirited her away on a boat to a hidden cove in the middle of the night. He'd taken her phone line to Dimitri Mostek and called him, telling him the traitorous Trojan Horse he'd sent to his camp had been discovered. In the crudest of terms, he told Dimitri that his foreign tramp had seduced his chief of security and several prisoners, as well. Enraged, Dimitri had threatened to kill her father—he had no use for a defiled woman. But Tasiya had pleaded with Fowler to take her life instead.

And that's when she'd seen the true depth of Boone Fowler's madness. He'd caressed her bruised cheek with the barrel of his gun and answered, "Done."

But she was denied the quick execution she'd prayed for.

She became a tool again. Dehumanized. Expendable.

He'd driven her all the way to Montana. She'd finally gotten to see the mountains. But there was no beauty for her in their snow-capped granite peaks—only the visual reminder, everywhere, of Bryce Martin's beautiful gray eyes; his craggy, eloquent, wonderful face; his unflinching, immeasurate strength.

Boone Fowler had brought her here to destroy all that.

For her father's life, she had to walk into Big Sky headquarters and kill them all.

"Get out of the truck." Fowler pointed the pistol at her head and Tasiya climbed out into the snow. The bite of the wind was less sharp here than it had been on Devil's Fork Island, but the air itself was colder. Tasiya could barely feel it through the layers of rage and despair and guilt she wore. "The building's less than a mile over that rise. I can watch the fireworks from here. Start walking." He caught the door when she would have closed it. "And remember, fail me and your father dies."

The fireworks. Right. A sick, deadly version of the American Independence Day lights and colors and concussive sounds Bryce had once told her about.

The fireworks that would go off the instant she released her thumb from the arming trigger attached to the bomb Fowler had strapped around her waist.

A BLEARY-EYED BRYCE opened the door to the most beautiful sight in the entire world. "Tasiya!"

Relief and love and a joy so profound it made him giddy shook through him as he ran to pick her up and never let her go again. "I was so worried about you. We've been lookin' all across the country for you. Anybody Fowler knows, anywhere he's been. Did he hurt you? How'd you get away?"

"No."

A blip of static tempered his joy at seeing her after nearly three days of constant searching and fearing he'd never see her again. "No, what?"

She braced her hand against his chest and stared at it. Downcast eyes, tightly compressed lips and skin beyond pale stopped him in his tracks. Ah, hell. "Please do not touch me."

For the briefest of moments, Bryce thought maybe she'd come all this way to tell him they couldn't be together, that, as he'd predicted, she'd found another man. She'd chosen someone better. Or she was goin' home. Goin' back to that place that kept her beautiful spirit under its thumb.

But just as quickly, he nixed those thoughts. Somethin' wasn't right. Despite the quivering protest of her lips, he slipped a finger beneath her chin and nudged her gaze up to his. "You promised you were always gonna look me in the eye."

Crap. The fear was back. And somethin' more. What was she tryin' to say?

"I...it is good to see you Bryce Martin."

Cameron Murphy limped up to the doorway on his cane and introduced himself. "So you're the pretty lady who's got Sarge tied up in knots. Invite her in and get her out of the cold." His voice sounded like an order, but he was smiling. "I appreciate all your help in getting my men home safely. Welcome to Montana."

Then Trevor Blackhaw was behind him. Jacob Powell and the others all gathered round. But every friendly welcome, every thank-you, every invitation to join them only seemed to make that lip quiver more.

Finally the words burst from her lips. "I cannot do this." Tears flooded her eyes and spilled down her pale cheeks. "I love you too much, Bryce Martin. My father and I will die, but I cannot kill you."

I love you too much?

But she gave him no opportunity to question whether he'd understood her right. He would have swept her into his arms and kissed her right there in front of God and the colonel, but Tasiya shook her head, urging him back with a single look.

She unbuttoned the front of her coat and pulled it open.

"That lousy son of a bitch."

Bricks of C-4, wired to detonate, were strapped around Tasiya's middle. She wore enough of them to bring down the entire two-story building and collapse the secret rooms underneath.

"Boone Fowler did this to you."

Tasiya nodded. "He has sent me here to kill you all."

BRYCE PACED the command center like a caged tiger while Owen Cook read the intelligence report that said UN forces had launched a covert strike into Lukinburg. Political hostages were being freed, corrupt officials were being taken into custody, and an all-points search for King Aleksandr Petrov—the man believed to be behind the American terrorist attacks, the kidnapping attempt of his own daughter and the funding of Fowler's militia—was underway.

Murphy's wife, Mia, had taken Tasiya aside to help her freshen up or whatever it was that women did when they went off together for a quiet talk. Mia had been a well-trained bounty hunter long before becoming Cameron Murphy's wife and partner, so she had a working knowledge of explosives and dealing with hostage victims. Tasiya was in good hands, but she wasn't safe.

In the meantime, Colonel Murphy had summoned the bounty hunters together to discuss their options. As far as Bryce was concerned, there were no options. "Just let me take the damn thing off her."

Trevor Blackhaw was a steadier presence at the moment. "You sure you can disarm it without killing her or yourself?"

"Do you see anyone else around here who can?"

"Nobody's questioning your skills, Sarge. But there's a little objectivity missing here."

Screw objectivity. Bryce wanted Tasiya to be safe. He wanted her in his arms. He wanted to tell her how much he loved her and that he would move heaven and earth to make things right for her in this world. They'd find her father. They'd get Boone Fowler. He'd teach her everything he knew about loving her, and then, together, they'd learn some more.

Colonel Murphy tapped his cane against the table to get their attention. "We can use this as an opportunity to put Fowler right where we want him."

"Nobody's using Tasiya," Bryce insisted. "Ever again."

Theoretically, the plan Murphy outlined made

sense. Fowler's hot button was Cameron Murphy and Big Sky. They could use that to their advantage to get Fowler to make a mistake. "He wants us dead? Let's oblige him. We all have safe houses across the country. We could evacuate Big Sky, then blow the place to smithereens. If he thinks we're all gone, he'll make a move."

Riley Watson, also known as Craig O'Riley and a dozen other aliases, leaned forward. His body was still recovering from the injuries he'd received while incarcerated, but there wasn't a thing wrong with that crackerjack mind of his. "When Fowler took us prisoner, he told me he had no use for hippies and shaved my head, he's seen me with a lot of hair and none at all. I believe I can alter my appearance enough that I could stay in the area without him recognizing me. As far as Fowler's concerned I'll be presumed dead like the rest of you."

Murphy nodded. "You could infiltrate the militia itself. Since we just put twenty-nine of his men back into prison, he'll be looking for new recruits."

"We'll bring him down from the inside."

Bryce scraped his hand across his jaw. "I want Boone Fowler dead or in prison as much as any man here. But I will not let you use Tasiya to do it."

A hushed sigh turned his attention to the two women who'd just joined them. Tasiya wore the same game smile she'd used when they'd been plotting their escape from Devil's Fork Island.

"What if I volunteer?"

"TALK TO ME, Bryce Martin."

Tasiya looked down to the top of Bryce's well-shaped head as he knelt in front of her, diligently working to remove the armed vest she wore without setting off the bomb. She sat in a chair in the middle of a secluded room with reinforced walls.

Everyone else she'd met today, the good men of Big Sky, were bustling around, packing things, carrying them into a secret tunnel that led into the mountains. From there they would go their separate ways, undetected, and hide out until Riley Watson contacted them. Once the vest was removed, she hoped she and Bryce would escape through that tunnel together.

She stroked her fingers through Bryce's short, crisp hair, urging him to look at her. She thought she'd be more frightened than this, sitting with her numb thumb taped to the trigger of a bomb. But Bryce was with her. His agile fingers seemed to know exactly what to do. His quiet strength provided an emotional rock to latch on to.

But she needed to hear his voice. Like those quiet nights inside his cell. His voice had given her hope. He'd instilled her with pride. He'd allowed her to dream and he'd made her feel safe. But most of all he'd made her feel special. She mattered to Bryce Martin. Until Bryce, she'd never believed she would matter to any man except her father.

His big shoulders shrugged, apparently healing now since the movement didn't seem to cause him undue pain. "Whaddya wanna talk about?"

"Anything. If it will not distract you from your work."

"Nah, honey." He lifted his wintry eyes to hers. "You're easy to talk to."

Tasiya smiled at the compliment. "Tell me more about your Ozarks."

He resumed his work. "The fishin's great there. The lakes and rivers are full of bass and catfish." He picked up the trigger and pulled the tape off her thumb, his nod telling her it was now safe to release it. He paused a moment to rub the circulation back into her hand. "You know how to cook a catfish? Breaded? Deep-fried? Or smoked on the grill?"

"I can cook fish. Why is it called a cat fish?"

He touched his callused fingertip to either side of her mouth. "'Cause it's got whiskers."

He reached for a pair of surgical-looking scissors and began to cut through the vest's webbed material. "I inherited my grandpa's cabin in the hills near Table Rock Lake. It's built of logs, but it's not really a cabin. It's got three bedrooms and a basement, and a porch that goes clear across the front that has a view of nothin' but trees and water."

"It sounds beautiful."

"You should come see it sometime. You could sleep in a real bed. I'd love to make love to you on a set of clean sheets and see what you could whip up in the kitchen." Tasiya caught her breath. She dug her fingers into his shoulder. Was that an invitation?

"No whipping. Please." She hesitated to hope, in case she'd misunderstood. "You want me to come to your home in Missouri?"

"I'll teach ya how to fish. Your daddy, too."

"Papa?" What did Bryce know about Anton?

Bryce clipped through the bottom of the vest, then set aside the scissors. He took her hands and pulled her to her feet. "We've gotten word that the troops have taken over the Ministry of Finance Building in St. Feodor. Apparently, your daddy wasn't the only hostage being held there. There are several of Lukinburg citizens in military custody now, en route to a base in Germany. I asked Powell to get us some names."

"Papa is coming to America?" Tasiya jumped onto her tiptoes and reached for Bryce.

"Whoa, whoa." He caught her by the wrists and urged her to remain still until he had the vest removed. But she danced inside her boots, waiting impatiently for him to explain. "If that's what he wants. I've got a spare room in Missouri he could bunk in."

Tasiya curled her fingers into the front of Bryce's shirt and pretended she was strong enough to shake him. "Bryce Martin, you must speak in English. What are you saying to me?"

In answer, he smiled. Then he palmed the back of her head and kissed her. It was a quick, hot, soul-stealing kiss that left her shaking. "You understand that, honey?"

And then he left her. He took the vest and his tools and left her.

Before her knees gave way, Tasiya sank into the chair. Understand what? She needed a dictionary. Fast.

TASIYA FLINCHED against Bryce as he counted down. "Four, three, two, one." The explosion's report jarred the air around them. Even at this distance, hidden more than a mile away in the abandoned miner's shack Bryce had used as a lookout point, he could see the satisfying evidence of his handiwork. The vehicles they'd left in the garage had caught fire, and splinters were still rainin' down and kickin' up a cloud of snow and debris that engulfed the air where the Big Sky building used to be.

"Like clockwork." Bryce turned off the cell phone he'd used to remote-trigger the explosion and slipped it into his pocket. "We are all now unofficially dead."

"I'm not going to miss that building as much as

I thought." Colonel Murphy lowered his binoculars and shook Bryce's hand. "Nice job, Sarge." He nodded to Tasiya. "Miss Belov. Couldn't have done it without you."

Tasiya seemed surprised to be included in the congratulations. "You are welcome, Mr. Murphy. Good luck with your plan."

"Thanks." He snugged his arm around his wife and headed for the shack's door. "Men? Watch your backs. Lie low. I'll see you later."

With a friendly cacophony of handshakes and back slaps and goodbyes, the others left, taking off in different directions, each heading for his own safe house. Riley Watson was headed back to Ponderosa to assume a new cover, while Trevor Blackhaw was headed for Idaho. Soon Jacob Powell was the only man left, and he was sharing an animated conversation on his cell phone.

"You're sure about that? I'll pass along the good news. Oh, yeah, babe. That's right. You'll be the first thing on my list tonight."

He was grinnin' like the Cheshire Cat when he disconnected and pocketed his phone. He was waitin' for Bryce to ask. "What?"

"I just heard from Isabella." Powell's fiancée was a Secret Service agent with some definite D.C. connections. "She's accessed a list of freed Lukinburg hostage names. Does Anton Belov ring a bell?"

"Papa?" Tasiya's face lit up. Her smile brightened the entire dingy shack. "Papa is free?"

Powell grinned. "Yes, ma'am."

"Thank you. Thank you."

She looped her arms around Powell's neck, and for one unguarded moment, Bryce had the urge to punch his buddy in the nose. But the stab of jealousy quickly vanished. Hell, if he could get his grandparents or his parents back, he'd be huggin' on Powell, too.

Besides, Tasiya shared the love. She released Powell and walked right into Bryce's arms, wrapping her arms around his waist and hugging him. Tight. He hugged her right back.

"Oh, Bryce, that is such wonderful news."

"Yep, honey. Nobody's holdin' anything over you now." He pressed a kiss to her temple. "You are finally and officially a free woman."

She leaned back against the circle of his arms and lifted those beautiful, star-kissed eyes to his. A shimmer of tears glistened against their dark color, and Bryce's thumb was there to wipe away the first one when it spilled over. "*You* have made me free, Bryce Martin. Not just from blackmail and evil men. But in my heart and in my dreams."

"Tasiya—"

She pressed a finger against his lips to silence him. "Earlier this afternoon you said something to me.

Sometimes, because of my language, I miss something. I want to be sure I completely understand."

"Just talk to me. I'll answer."

Tasiya smiled. "I love you. And I think that you love me, too. But when you invited me to your home—"

"I meant for forever."

"Forever?"

"If that's what you want." He framed her face between his big hands and tunneled his fingers into her hair. "It's what I want. I love you, Tasiya Belov."

Damn. He'd said it. Out loud.

And it felt right. It didn't hurt.

Not when she smiled at him like that.

Not when she wrapped her arms around his neck and kissed him. Like he was a man. Not a monster. Like she loved him. Like she'd love him forever.

Bryce buried his hands in her hair. "Will you marry me, Tasiya? Will you come see the Ozarks with me?"

"I will go to the Ozarks, or stay in the mountains, or even go back to that horrible prison—as long as I can be with you, Bryce Martin."

"So is that a yes?"

She grinned and articulated her lips around one sweet word. "Yep."

Bryce scooped her up in his arms and twirled her around.

Powell cleared his throat. "Well, um, yes. I'll just

be going. I have a fiancèe at home who needs kissing."

"Good idea." Bryce opened the door.

"I could stay, though, big guy, if you need me for backup?"

"Go away, Powell." Without releasing Tasiya, Bryce shoved his friend's face out the door and shut it behind him. "I've got my own woman to kiss."

He pulled her up into his arms and covered her lips with his own.

No matter how tough—or easy—the job was, Bryce Martin was the man to get it done.

* * * * *

Next month Harlequin Intrigue brings you the exciting conclusion of
BIG SKY BOUNTY HUNTERS
when good and evil go head-to-head in bestselling author Rebecca York's
RILEY'S RETRIBUTION!